DUKE OF RENOWN

Dukes of Distinction
Book 1

Alexa Aston

ARE YOU SIGNED UP FOR DRAGONBLADE'S BLOG?

You'll get the latest news and information on exclusive giveaways, exclusive excerpts, coming releases, sales, free books, cover reveals and more.

Check out our complete list of authors, too!

No spam, no junk. That's a promise!

Sign Up Here

www.dragonbladepublishing.com

Dearest Reader;

Thank you for your support of a small press. At Dragonblade Publishing, we strive to bring you the highest quality Historical Romance from the some of the best authors in the business. Without your support, there is no 'us', so we sincerely hope you adore these stories and find some new favorite authors along the way.

Happy Reading!

[signature]

CEO, Dragonblade Publishing

Additional Dragonblade books by Author Alexa Aston

Dukes of Distinction Series
Duke of Renown

Medieval Runaway Wives
Song of the Heart
A Promise of Tomorrow
Destined for Love

King's Cousins Series
The Pawn
The Heir
The Bastard

Knights of Honor Series
Word of Honor
Marked by Honor
Code of Honor
Journey to Honor
Heart of Honor
Bold in Honor
Love and Honor
Gift of Honor
Path to Honor
Return to Honor

CHAPTER ONE

London—March 1812

P HOEBE'S EYES FLEW open as she was jolted out of sleep. Nausea caused her stomach to roil. She tossed the bedclothes away and raced to the chamber pot, barely reaching it in time as she dropped to her knees before it. She rose unsteadily and went to the basin, where she rinsed the sour taste from her mouth and then washed her face for good measure. Padding back to her bed, she climbed into it, sinking into the pillows.

She was with child again.

Joy filled her as she finally admitted to herself the obvious. It had been over three months since her courses had come. She had waited years for this to happen.

She had conceived Nathan on her wedding night. Nine months to the day of her marriage to

Edmund Smythe, Earl of Borwick, she had given birth to a healthy boy. Nathan had become the light of her life and made these past five years the happiest she'd ever known.

She had thought more children would quickly follow since she was obviously fertile but none made an appearance. After she birthed their son, Borwick rarely came to her bed. He was two decades older than Phoebe and she'd heard women talk of how men aged and had trouble performing the marital act. His infrequent visits to her bed troubled her but she had no say in the matter.

Until last Christmas.

Borwick had indulged in more wassail than he should have—and Phoebe used that to her advantage. She crept into his bed that night, sliding under the bedclothes, something she'd never done and would probably never have the courage to do again. Her husband had always come to her bedchamber. Their couplings were short and took place in the dark. She did what she could to tease his cock to life as he drunkenly slurred a series of words together that made no sense to her.

Her efforts were now rewarded. She couldn't wait to tell her husband the news. He would probably want another boy but she would like a girl this time. One to dress in pretty clothes. She'd put ribbons in her daughter's hair and buy her dolls. They would be as close as sisters and Phoebe would take care in helping the girl choose her wardrobe when her Season arrived.

And she would never, ever make her wed a man if she didn't love him.

Her own father had done that to Phoebe. He scoffed at the notion of love, taking matters into his own hands and arranging her marriage to Borwick. The earl was a widower almost twenty years her senior, childless, and as practical a man as Phoebe had ever met. Love hadn't come but at least they got on well enough, though she preferred their country estate in Devon, while he enjoyed the social aspects of London.

They'd arrived in the great city last night. Borwick was happy to be back at their townhouse so he could meet up with his friends in the House of Lords and at his various social clubs. Though shy, Phoebe would have been happy to attend a few events of the Season with her husband. Now, though, her gowns would grow too small for her. Relief filled her, her increasing being an excuse to forego all the social events.

Of course, she would have to attend the ball at the end of the first week of the Season since it was being given by her sister, the new Viscountess Burton. Letty had wed at Season's end last year, her first, and was eager to host her first large social gathering. That would be held three weeks from now. Phoebe would work with her modiste on designing a gown that would hide her condition and still be fashionable. After that, it would give her more time to spend with Nathan.

She closed her eyes, feeling tired, knowing her maid would appear soon with her morning breakfast tray. Moments later, a knock at the door sounded. Not only did her meal arrive, but Nathan came with it, barreling in gleefully and jumping into bed with her, snuggling close. These were the times that meant the world to Phoebe. While her husband remained distant, her son was always happy to give her a hug and a kiss.

"Good morning, Mama."

"Hello, my beautiful boy." She kissed his brow.

Frowning, he said, "Girls are beautiful, Mama. I'm a boy."

"Well, then. Good morning to my handsome boy," she declared. "Is that better?" she asked, tousling his hair.

"Papa says we're going to see the dinosaurs today," he said excitedly.

"At the British Museum?"

Nathan shrugged, obviously not knowing the location of these dinosaurs.

"You'll need to be on your very best behavior, Nathan. You may see one of Papa's friends while you are out. Remember your manners."

"I will," he promised and kissed her. "I need

to eat breakfast with Nanny."

He clambered from the bed as his nursery governess appeared at the door.

"There you are, Viscount. You've got a nice porridge waiting for you in the schoolroom."

Nathan ran across the room and took the servant's hand. Looking over his shoulder, he called, "Goodbye, Mama."

"He's a whirlwind," her maid declared.

Phoebe smiled. "I wouldn't have him any other way."

She ate her toast and drank her hot chocolate, happy not only about the new baby but also glad that Borwick was taking Nathan on an outing. He'd told her he knew nothing about babies when Nathan was born and had never once held his son. Her husband had kept his distance while Nathan learned to crawl and then walk and talk. It was only within the last six months that Borwick had anything at all to do with the boy. Phoebe hoped today's trip to the British Museum would be the start of a new relationship between father and son.

Setting the tray aside, she dressed for the day with the servant's help. She wanted to speak to Borwick before he and Nathan left the house.

Going downstairs, she spied their butler. "Do you know where Lord Borwick is?"

"Still in the breakfast room, my lady."

"Thank you."

Phoebe headed there and stopped just outside the door. It wouldn't do to share her good news in front of the footmen stationed about the room. She entered and went to her husband, who pored over the morning newspapers as he sipped his tea.

Kissing the top of his head, she said, "I hear you are taking our son to see dinosaurs today, my lord."

He looked up in surprise since they were never demonstrative toward one another.

"Why, yes. There is a new exhibit of bones that have been reconstructed. It's a something Rex and is supposed to stand thirteen meters high. The bones, that is. I gather they've tried to restore what they've found on some archaeological dig."

"Nathan is terribly excited. As much to see these dinosaur bones as to spend time with his father." She paused. "Would you come see me in my salon before you leave the house, my lord?"

He frowned. "I'll be another half-hour or so."

"Very well. I will see you then."

Phoebe left and went to her salon. She dashed off a brief note to Letty, asking her and Burton to come to tea this afternoon so that she could share her news with them and rang for a servant.

"This is to be delivered to my sister at once," she instructed.

After that, she worked on menus for the coming week, which she hadn't done yet because of their late arrival Monday night. All yesterday had been spent supervising the unpacking and seeing to things in the household as they opened the place for the next several months.

Just as she completed her task, her husband entered. Phoebe rose and met him.

"What do you need?" he asked brusquely, sounding inconvenienced to have been asked to stop by and visit with her briefly.

She tried not to be hurt at his tone. They rarely spent time together, which she'd discovered was actually a good thing. They lived under one roof but led separate lives.

"I know I rarely ask you to come here, Borwick, but I have some very good news." She beamed at him. "We're going to have another child. Next autumn."

His usually solemn face lit with pleasure. "You are certain?"

"As much as I can be. It should be in late September."

Borwick took her by the shoulders and kissed her cheek, surprising her. "This is most excellent news, my lady. You will need to see the doctor, of course, and confirm things with him."

"Yes, I can arrange that," she replied.

"I don't want you doing anything strenuous."

She smiled at his sudden thoughtfulness. "I

won't."

He frowned. "I had wanted us to host a dinner next week."

Chuckling, she said, "I am having a baby, Borwick. Months from now. I can plan a dinner with ease."

"It's just that it has been so long. I know we have Nathan but . . ." His voice trailed off.

"I understand. I will be careful. I doubt I'll go to many events this Season, though. Most likely, just Letty's ball."

"No dancing," he told her firmly.

Though she loved to dance, Phoebe merely nodded in agreement and added, "Who is it you wish to have for this dinner? And should I plan entertainment for afterward?"

"I'll give you a list of guests to be invited. It will include a few men who might invest in one of my mines. You could think about having—"

"There you are, Papa!"

Nathan flew into the room and stopped short, seeing the stern look on his father's face at being interrupted.

"Decorum, young man," Borwick chided.

Phoebe wanted to protest. Nathan was only five years old. He was a boisterous child, full of good cheer. But what Borwick said was law in their home. When her son looked to her, she shook her head.

Contritely, he said, "I'm sorry, Papa. I'll be

good today."

"Of course you'll be good, my boy. You are the future Earl of Borwick."

Her husband looked back to her. "Thank you for sharing the news with me. We'll discuss the matter at further length once the boy and I return from our outing." He touched his son's shoulder. "Now, kiss your mother goodbye and we'll be off."

Phoebe bent and hugged her little boy tightly and then kissed him once. If Borwick hadn't been present, she would have smothered Nathan's face in kisses. Her husband didn't approve of overt physical affection, though, saying it would make their son weak.

She walked them to the front door and said, "I do hope you will return by teatime. Letty and Burton are coming."

"We should return long before that," her husband promised.

She watched them head toward the waiting carriage. Nathan looked so happy as he accompanied his father to the vehicle and climbed inside with the help of a footman. Pride filled her, knowing how special her little boy was. Then she held her hands to her belly, thrilled at the new life growing within her and feeling doubly blessed.

Phoebe called at her seamstress' shop later that morning, explaining to the modiste that she was with child and would need to change the previous order that she'd placed by mail. Fortunately, Madame Toufours hadn't started on much, wanting Phoebe to pick out several of the materials. They settled on a half-dozen gowns now and she would return as her waistline expanded and new dresses would be created for her.

She returned home and found Letty had replied to her note, assuring her that she and Burton would come for tea today and to catch up, since it had been several months since they had seen one another. Phoebe smiled, thinking how Letty had been her first child. Their mother had died when Phoebe was ten and Letty three and it had fallen to the older sister to mother her younger one.

Retreating to her bedchamber because she was exhausted by the outing, she took a nap. Upon awakening, she completed what she believed would be a suitable menu for her husband's investors when they came to dine and discuss business. She would share the dinner party menu with Borwick when he returned and they could talk over ideas regarding the evening's entertainment. She was fond of the pianoforte and hoped they might book a pianist.

By now, it was almost time for tea and she went downstairs to await her sister and brother-in-law in the drawing room. They arrived and it was obvious the couple had grown close since their marriage last August. Both greeted her warmly and she had them sit as the teacart arrived.

"Will Lord Borwick be joining us?" asked Burton.

"I told him you were expected before he left this morning. He took Nathan to see the new dinosaur exhibit at the British Museum. I would have thought they would have returned by now," she replied, recalling that Borwick had said they should arrive home in plenty of time for him to take tea.

"How is my darling nephew?" Letty asked. "Growing straight and strong?"

Phoebe laughed. "You will be surprised when you see him. He's grown so tall in just a matter of weeks."

"Nathan will be going away to school before you know it," Burton proclaimed.

The thought saddened her and she determined to make the most of the next few years before her boy left home to continue his education.

Letty swatted her husband. "No mother likes to think of her darling boy leaving her."

Grinning, Phoebe confided, "There may be another boy in the family. Or perhaps, a girl. We also are expecting a child in late September."

"What?" Letty gasped. "How wonderful!"

The sisters hugged again and Phoebe poured

out for them. They all chose sandwiches for their plates and various sweets. She only hoped she would be able to keep the food down.

Burton found the spice cake to his liking and said, "Your cook must give ours this recipe."

As teatime ended, Phoebe grew concerned that Borwick and Nathan hadn't yet returned. She hid her anxiety as she walked her guests to the door.

"Thank you for coming."

She and Letty embraced and the butler opened the door. It took her aback to see a man standing there, his fist raised to knock on the door.

"My lady? Lady Borwick?" he asked anxiously.

"Yes, I am Lady Borwick," she replied warily.

"Might I come in?" he asked. "I am Dr. Morris."

"Did my husband send you?"

This man wasn't their usual physician. She had told Borwick she would take care of arranging to see a doctor.

"In a way," he replied vaguely.

"Come in," she invited, confused by what he'd said.

Letty slipped her hand around Phoebe's and said, "I am Lady Burton. This is my husband, Lord Burton. I am Lady Borwick's sister."

"Very good," the doctor said, looking slightly

relieved. He turned to Phoebe. "My lady, I'm afraid I am the bearer of bad news. And there is no easy way to tell you."

Her heart quickened. "Just say it then."

"Lord Borwick and your son were in a carriage accident."

She tightened her grip on Letty's hand. "Where are they? I must go to them at once."

"That is not possible, Lady Borwick." Sadness blanketed the doctor's face. "I'm afraid your husband and son did not survive."

Her entire body went numb, cold seeping in as if it were a blustery winter day. "What?"

"Your son died instantly. Lord Borwick lingered a bit. I was passing by and saw the accident occur. I rendered aid as best I could." Morris shook his head. "My condolences."

"No," Phoebe moaned, dropping to her knees. "No."

Burton and the butler rushed to her, grasping her elbows and trying to bring her to her feet. She grew lightheaded, dizzy, and then queasiness filled her. Then an awful cramping clawed within her. She groaned.

"My baby!" she cried. "No, no, no . . ."

Something warm spilled from between her legs, dribbling down them. She felt herself being lifted and carried up the stairs as everything went black. Then someone was shaking her. A cup was held to her lips.

"This will calm you, Lady Borwick," the awful man said. The one who'd told her about Nathan and Borwick.

The doctor forced her to drink it. Shadows huddled around her as the cramps grew stronger. She was losing her unborn child and couldn't stop it. Bitter tears spilled down her cheeks.

Then darkness crept over her and dragged her under.

CHAPTER TWO

Spain—August 1812

A NOTHER DAY IN hell.

Captain Andrew Graham urged his men on, their third assault of the day. Weariness filled him, yet as a British officer and leader, he encouraged the soldiers to push onward. The sounds of war assaulted his senses. Swords clanging. Cannons firing at regular intervals. Cries from the injured—and dying. He ignored it all, continuing to swing his sword, cutting down men both left and right. Sweat dripped into his eyes, stinging them. He blinked rapidly, not able to take the time to wipe a sleeve across his face, else a blow of steel might be the last of him.

From a distance, he heard the sound of retreat being called by the enemy. Relief swept through him, knowing he wouldn't lose any more of his men today. The opponent that rushed toward him froze in his tracks, having reached Andrew.

"Go!" he shouted at the man.

The soldier hesitated a moment and then lowered his sword. As scores of men turned to flee, Andrew saw something in this man's eyes, however.

"Don't," he warned as the man tried to thrust his sword a final time.

To stop him, Andrew sank his own blade into his enemy's belly. His action halted his opponent. Confusion—then pain—filled the man's face.

"I told you to go," he said quietly, bitterness filling him as he placed his boot flat against the injured man's hip and pushed hard. The solider fell to the ground that already ran red with blood as Andrew claimed his sabre again.

"I told you to go," he repeated, anguish in every word.

This soldier would have lived to fight another day. He might have survived this interminable war. Gone home to his sweetheart. Or wife and children. Instead, his greed at wanting to take one more life cost him his own.

Turning, he surveyed the battlefield as men retreated both to the north and south. His eyes swept across the still forms as far as the eye could see. He should be hardened to war by now after five years. It might be another five—even longer—until the threat of Bonaparte was put down and Andrew could return to the green fields of his beloved England.

With a heavy sigh, he made his way back to give his third and final report of the day to Colonel Symmons, his commanding officer. He passed men bearing wounded soldiers on stretchers, their agonizing cries adding to his heartache.

"Andrew!" a voice called.

He turned and saw the Marquess of Marbury headed his way. Sebastian was an old chum of his from their university days. Together with Jon, another Cambridge friend, and George and Weston, whom he'd attended both Eton and Cambridge with, the five had spent years together studying, laughing, and talking incessantly about the fairer sex. Only he and Sebastian had entered the army after university. The other three men, now all dukes, had remained in England. In this moment, Andrew longed for those simple days of sitting for examination and celebrating afterward at the local alehouse with his comrades.

"It's good to see you survived today's skirmishes," he said, shaking his friend's hand. Then he noticed the change in his Sebastian's uniform. "You're a major now! Congratulations."

Sebastian shrugged. "I think enough of the officers ahead of me have been killed in action. With their ranks thinning, I'm just at the right place in the right moment."

"You've always been much too humble," Andrew chided. "If there is a break in the action, we should celebrate your promotion, Major."

"I'd like to catch up," Sebastian said. "I have much to tell you. I've been appointed to Wellington's staff."

Andrew beamed. "Then we have even more to celebrate. I must go and make my final report of the day to my commanding officer. I'll look for you later, all right?"

The two men parted. Before he reported to Symmons, Andrew made a detour toward the surgical tents. After their second charge, Andrew had witnessed the fall of Thomas Bagwell. The young private had earned a special place in Andrew's heart and he'd thought to ask Bagwell to be his batman since his was retiring at the end of next month. Having seen Bagwell's leg injury, he didn't know if the young man had survived or not.

He entered the first of the two tents where operations occurred. The tinny smell of blood assaulted him. Making his way to the surgeon operating, he asked, "Did Private Bagwell come through here?"

The weary man looked up. "What injury? I don't know names anymore. They come and go too fast, Captain."

"His leg. The right one. Bagwell has carrot

orange hair."

The surgeon nodded toward his right. Andrew saw a huge mountain of severed limbs, the legs still wearing their boots. He pitied the poor souls who would be required to strip the boots and bury the limbs.

"I amputated his leg. He'll be that way if he made it," the surgeon added, indicating the exit to the tent. "Try one more over. The hospital."

"Thank you."

Andrew quit the tent and went to the hospital, walking rows of cots as men moaned. Then he spied Bagwell's familiar mop of hair and knelt next to him.

"It's Captain Graham, Thomas." He took the private's hand. "How are you?"

With a crooked grin, Bagwell said, "I'm right well, Captain. Missing a leg and all, but I'll get by."

He knew Bagwell came from a dairy farm near Hertfordshire and wondered how easy it would be to milk a cow sitting on a stool with only one leg for balance.

"Chin up, Bagwell. I'll come to see you tomorrow."

The young man grimaced and then said, "Thank you, Captain."

Andrew left and made no other stops as he headed to Colonel Symmons' tent. He fell in line, no one joining him after he arrived, so he was the last to enter the officer's tent. He gave his report, estimating the number of casualties in his unit and citing two individuals for exceptional bravery during action.

"Thank you, Captain Graham," said the older man. He paused and studied Andrew for a moment and then said, "I have a letter for you, Captain."

The colonel picked it up from a pile of papers before him. Handing it over, he said, "Read it here—then we will speak."

Curiosity filled him as he looked at the letter, the handwriting unfamiliar. Why would he need to read it and then discuss the contents with Symmons? Andrew broke the seal and his eyes fell to the signature, seeking a clue as to the sender's identity.

Lord Raymond Barrington.

The nobleman worked in London's War Office. He was also the oldest friend of the Duke of Windham, Andrew's father. Trepidation filled him.

Captain Graham –

I am sorry to be writing to you under such circumstances. I have not seen you for many years but your father has kept me apprised of your endeavors for king and country. Know that your service is much appreciated by the citizens of England.

Having said that, I regret to inform you of two grievous events, both related, and both affecting you and your future.

Your brother, Ward, was involved in a tragic accident in his phaeton and was buried at Windowmere this morning. When news of this first reached your father, Windham suffered a heart attack. According to the doctors, he is on his deathbed in London.

That leaves you, dear boy, as the new marquess and heir apparent. Even if your father survives, he will be in no state to see to the many affairs being the Duke of Windham entails and if the doctors are to be believed, you will become the new duke sooner rather than later.

I have taken the liberty of writing your commanding officer, informing him of the situation. You'll need to sell your commission and return home immediately. Send word to me once you reach London in order to inform me of your father's health. I will do all I can to help you make this transition.

Yours sincerely,
Lord Raymond Barrington

Shock filled Andrew. Then anger set in. Ward had always lived on the edge, taking unnecessary risks. The so-called phaeton accident was undoubtedly a race gone awry. Knowing his older brother, Ward had pushed the horse and vehicle beyond their limits. His careless actions had caused his death. It shouldn't surprise anyone. Ward had lived in luck for too many years. His recklessness had finally caught up to him.

It was his father's health which concerned him now. The duke had always been physically and emotionally strong. He'd outlived two wives, both of whom died in childbirth, the first when she birthed Andrew and the second delivering his half-brother, Francis. Windham had always been larger than life. To see how Ward's death had affected his father pained Andrew.

What Lord Barrington left unsaid was that Andrew better not get himself killed, else Francis would inherit the dukedom. His half-brother was immature, irresponsible, and none too bright. He'd been tossed out of Cambridge. At least that's was what their father had shared in a letter to Andrew. He suspected things were far worse, but the duke had always turned a blind eye to his youngest, allowing Francis free rein to do whatever he pleased.

Colonel Symmons cleared his throat. "I see you've finished. Lord Barrington also wrote to me and I understand you are to resign your commission immediately and return to England. I can help arrange your transport." He paused. "I am sorry for your loss, Graham. I lost my own brother and it's never easy. I hope His Grace will recover quickly. But if not, you have the fine makings to be a duke."

"Thank you, sir," Andrew replied with a sinking feeling. He only hoped to arrive at their London townhome to see his father one more time.

It took Andrew a week to reach London. Colonel Symmons had helped him to arrange transport on a vessel bound for southern England. He had arrived with the clothes on his back, a spare shirt, and his razor. His commanding officer had even given him pocket money to help him reach London. He now disembarked at the docks and walked off the ship with nothing but a small satchel, all he had to show for five years at war against Bonaparte. He'd left England with a light heart, prone to teasing others. He returned now at twenty-seven, feeling twice his age, no spark of fun left within him. He'd witnessed too many deaths to ever think to smile again.

London's streets teemed with others as he made his way from the docks. Before long, he spied a hansom cab and flagged it down.

"Returning from the war, Captain?" the driver asked with a friendly smile.

"Yes," he replied curtly.

Once upon a time, he would have carried on a conversation with this man. Today, he was too weary to engage in small talk. Andrew boarded the vehicle and gave his father's London address. The cabbie merely nodded and climbed into the driver's seat and they were off. As they made their way through the streets, he thought how civilized things seemed. Well-dressed people going about their business. Carriages making their orderly way down the streets. Stalls open, people shopping for wares. He closed his eyes and rubbed them, still seeing bloodshed and hearing cannon fire in his head. He shook off the thoughts. He was home now. Where he'd longed to be for so long.

But not under these circumstances.

I need to prepare myself, he thought. Especially since from Lord Barrington's description, he should expect the worst.

Arriving at Belgravia, he emptied his pocket and handed over the last of his coins.

"No need, sir," the driver said, refusing to take the money offered. "You've been at war. Fighting for the rest of us."

"I insist," Andrew said. "You need to make a living." Then he noticed the cabbie was missing a hand and understanding flooded him.

"The war?" he asked.

The man nodded. Glancing down at his missing hand, he said quietly, "I've learned to live without it. I care for my horse and all the equipment. When it gives me a bit o' trouble, I just think about all the men in my squadron who weren't as lucky to come home as I was."

"Do you have a family?"

"I had my parents but they both died while I was on the Continent. No wife or children. And now?" He shrugged. "Who'd have me?"

Andrew made an instant decision. "I would. What's your name, Soldier?"

"Robbie Jones, Captain," the driver replied, his posture indicating he was unsure of what Andrew wanted.

"Do you like driving, Robbie Jones?"

"I do, Captain. As I said, I've learned to adjust."

"My father is the Duke of Windham. I'm sure he could use an additional driver. I'd be happy to extend an offer of employment to you. Unless, of course, you enjoy what you do now, working independently."

Robbie broke out in a huge grin. "I'd love to come work for the duke. I rent this buggy and horse and most of what I earn goes toward that."

"Well, then return your horse and vehicle at day's end and report to this house tomorrow morning. Ask for me. I can't guarantee you'll always stay in London. We have several estates throughout England and you might be sent to one of them."

"Fine by me, Captain." Robbie grew serious. "I can't thank you enough, Sir. Life is hard, being as I am and on my own. To have a meal each day and a roof over my head means the world to me."

Andrew offered his hand and they shook. "Then I'll see you tomorrow, Robbie. I'll know more about your duties by then."

Tears misted the former soldier's eyes. "Thank you, Captain. God bless you."

He watched the driver depart and felt good that it was within his power to change at least one veteran's life for the better. He went to the front door and rapped. It opened and a smiling Whitby greeted him.

"My lord, it does my soul good to see you."

For a moment, Andrew froze. Then he realized he was no longer Captain Graham or even Mr. Graham. He was a marquess.

Destined to be a duke.

Thrusting out his hand, he shook the butler's offered hand. "It's been quite a while, Whitby."

"It has been that, my lord. Do come in. Let me take that for you." The butler's face showed a moment of astonishment at how light the satchel was.

"I didn't have much to bring home, Whitby," Andrew explained.

Only memories . . .

"If you'd like, I'll have the tailor come around tomorrow, my lord. Would you care to use the one your father or brother uses?"

Knowing Ward's taste ran to the fashionable and flamboyant and his father was always conservative yet elegantly dressed, he said, "I'll go with Father's man."

"Very good, my lord. I've had Mrs. Bates prepare your room for you. Would you like a bath first or would you rather see His Grace?"

"His Grace."

"Follow me."

Whitby handed off the satchel to a nearby footman and they ascended the stairs. Andrew found he approached his father's rooms with trepidation and prayed Windham would recover from this recent heart attack. It had been too many years since they'd seen one another. All he wanted was a bit of time to spend with the man he worshipped.

Arriving at the suite of rooms designated for the duke, Whitby opened the door. The butler's sympathetic look told Andrew all he needed to know.

"Thank you, Whitby. I'll take it from here."

With a deep breath, Andrew strode through the rooms and reached the bedchamber. Steeling himself, he turned the knob and entered the room.

CHAPTER THREE

Moreland Hall, Cornwall—August 1813

ANDREW STOOD. "GOOD morning, Aunt Helen."

He helped seat her. A footman quickly filled her cup with tea as another brought her usual poached egg and toast to the breakfast table.

"Are you packed for your return to Devon?" he asked, hoping to avoid the topic he knew was on her mind—and knowing he'd failed by the look of determination of her face.

"You know how I look upon you as a son, Windham," she began.

He cringed inwardly. His father had been in his grave almost a year now and Andrew still wasn't used to hearing everyone call him Windham or Your Grace. Even this dear maiden aunt, his father's sister, had abandoned use of his Christian name and always referred to him as

Windham, even in private.

"Yes, Aunt. I am most blessed that you have always been more a mother to me than my aunt."

She had indeed mothered both him and Ward when his own died giving birth to him. Aunt Helen had done the same with Francis, though she'd had less success in that endeavor. Francis was all about himself and what a person could do for him. Andrew dreaded the next time they met. He'd last seen his half-brother in London a month ago, as the Season had ended. Francis had begged him to pay a slew of debts.

Andrew had refused.

He'd discovered upon his return to England that Francis owed everyone in town and that their father had covered all markers on several previous occasions. When the duke died two weeks after Andrew's arrival from Spain, the two remaining brothers had sat for a heart-to-heart talk. Andrew told Francis he'd be given a quarterly allowance from now on and he gave him one property to manage in Somerset. A year later, Francis was already begging for more money and the steward in Somerset had resigned in frustration.

He turned his attention back to his aunt.

"You are twenty-eight, my dear boy, and not one to sow wild oats."

Like Ward.

"You need to take a wife," she said firmly.

"I participated in the past Season, Aunt," he said patiently, thinking back to the spring and early summer, grateful that he'd been able to reunite with George, Weston, and Jon. None of his friends were remotely interested in finding a wife, especially George and Weston, since their earlier brushes with engagements had ended in disaster. Jon said he'd learned from those two that marriage wasn't for him. As for George and Weston, they now cut a wide path through Polite Society, being known as the Duke of Charm and the Duke of Disrepute, both swearing never to wed.

"And you made absolutely no progress," she retorted. "You are the most eligible bachelor in Polite Society, Windham. Women flocked to you at every social event you attended."

He grimaced. "That's why I found no one who interested me," he said, his temper rising. "Aunt Helen, every woman in the *ton*— unmarried or even those who are wed—sidled up to me. No one wanted to know *me*. All they wanted was to become my duchess. Or at least say they'd slept with a duke."

He rose and paced anxiously around the room, a flick of his hand dismissing the ever-present footmen. If they were going to have this conversation, he wanted a small slice of privacy for it.

"Do you think any of those ladies would have

given me a second glance before I became Windham?" he asked angrily. "Beyond a few desperate wallflowers who might have considered marriage with an army officer who would never be home?"

Aunt Helen clucked her tongue. "You are too hard on yourself, Andrew."

Immediately, he noticed the change of name and grew wary.

"You are handsome. Educated. Accomplished. Of course, you would have had your pick of several young ladies. It's true, a lofty title has attracted more females to you but surely someone appealed to you?"

He stopped pacing. "Frankly? No. Most are girls. Barely out of the schoolroom. They either giggle incessantly while they blush profusely and can make no worthwhile conversation or they are married and have provided their heir and now look for amusement."

Andrew sighed. "Is it too much to ask for a nice woman of good character and family who can hold a decent conversation? A wife who would be faithful to me and not gallivant about later?"

"Do you mean you are seeking love?" Aunt Helen asked in quiet wonder.

"No," he said quickly. "Not a love match. I'd never consider the idea. I gave my heart and soul on the battlefield and lost too many men. I have nothing like that left to give. I merely want a good companion. Someone who wants to be a mother and would be devoted to our children."

He plopped into his chair again. "Sometimes, I wish it had been me who perished on the battlefield and not Ward in his phaeton."

She gasped. "*Never* say that, Andrew. You spent a good half a year or more after your father's death traveling about England, looking after all the estates. Much as I loved your brother, that is something Ward never would have considered doing."

"I wanted to become familiar with all my properties and how each estate was being managed. Father rarely took us anywhere except the ancestral home in Devon and our townhouse in London. It was good to see the other places."

"What about this small property in Cornwall? Why are you here now?"

"Because it is far away from London. From people. From people who want something from me," he admitted. "I love the sea. Walking on the cliffs or along the beach. I needed some time alone after all that's happened this past year."

"I understand." She patted his hand then rose. He followed suit.

"I will see you back in Devon at some point. That is, if you don't mind me still living at Windowmere with you."

He took her hand and kissed it. "It is *our*

home. I will always want you there. Even when I wed. You are the mother of my heart, Aunt Helen, and always will be."

She smiled. "Will you promise me you'll be open to marriage in the future? I could introduce you to a few eligible women in the neighborhood once you return to Windowmere. If none of these ladies catch your eye, might I draw up a list of young beauties for next Season? But you truly must wed by this time next year, Andrew."

He wanted neither a young nor especially beautiful woman as his duchess. Andrew thought somewhere among the *ton* must be a woman other men had overlooked. Not a diamond of the first water but a woman of substance.

"I will find a wife myself, Aunt," he promised. "I'm eager to start a family."

She smiled. "That is music to my ears. It has been too long since children freely roamed the grounds of Windowmere and brought laughter to the halls." She sighed. "I am packed already. I will see you soon?"

"Most likely. I need a little more time here on my own. I've correspondence now to deal with."

She offered her cheek and he kissed it.

"Safe travels, Aunt."

PHOEBE CLOSED THE window, where the gentle sea breeze from the south had called to her as she'd worked. She set aside her drawings and put on her bonnet, hoping it would keep some of the sun off her face. With her fair skin, she burned easily. Her mother had always taught her to carry a parasol when outdoors but she didn't want to bother with one now. She placed a basket over one arm and carried another in her other hand as she left Falmouth Cottage and headed the two miles into Falmouth.

Leasing Falmouth Cottage was the best decision she'd made in months. For the first year after Nathan's death, she'd been like a sleepwalker, moving from room to room, no emotion within her beyond a grief so deep she thought she might drown in it. For once, Letty took care of her instead of the other way around. Her sister had been a godsend, though nothing could quell Phoebe's sorrow. She'd lost her precious, perfect boy.

And the baby.

Oddly, she'd almost felt more grief at missing her unborn child than in losing Nathan. At least she'd had five wonderful years with her sweet boy. Phoebe grieved for a baby she'd never know. Never hold. She would never see its first smile or watch its first steps. Her body had recovered quickly from the loss but her mind and heart never would.

As for Borwick, she didn't miss him at all. Her husband was rarely home and when he was, she'd barely seen him. Though they had been wed for six years, she knew little more about him than she had on their wedding day. It hadn't troubled her when John Smythe, Borwick's first cousin, claimed the title of Earl of Borwick and the estate. After the funeral, he'd made a cursory offer by asking her to stay on. John had a young family, though, and she didn't think she could remain around them and keep her sanity. Her things had been sent for from both London and the country and taken to her brother-in-law's London townhouse.

Letty's husband had graciously insisted that she stay however long she liked, knowing how close the sisters had been since childhood. When their father passed a year after Phoebe's marriage, she'd claimed guardianship of her sister, bringing her to live with her and Borwick. Her husband hadn't cared at any rate and it had made for good company for Phoebe, having Letty with her. The pair had spent hours with Nathan and later enjoyed preparing for Letty's Season, where she'd wed Viscount Burton after the Season ended.

Phoebe hated her sorrow intruding on Letty and Burton's happiness, though. Finally, she'd gone to Burton first to let him know she was ready to move on. Fortunately, she had sufficient funds in order to do so and her brother-in-law had made all the arrangements for her.

Then she'd told Letty of her plans.

Her sister had been hurt at first, being left out of the initial decision making but she had come to understand why Phoebe wished to have some privacy. Especially when Letty shared that she was with child. Phoebe said she would return in time for the baby's birth in mid-January. After two months in isolated Cornwall, she knew that only the soft breezes from Spain would heal her in a way no one else would understand.

As she walked along the path to town, she thought of how close she felt to her son these days. Phoebe had always told Nathan bedtime stories and he'd always begged for more, claiming hers were much better than any she or Nanny read to him. In Cornwall these past few weeks, Phoebe had begun writing some of them down, remembering the ones Nathan had loved best and adding new ones. She had even begun several simple illustrations to go along with them. She enjoyed drawing as a child but once her mother passed away, she'd put aside the hobby to care for her sister.

Phoebe reached the small town, which rested nine miles south of Truro, a larger place where all the rich mine owners lived on Lemon Street. Her father had once brought her and Letty near here on holiday and when she'd needed to escape London, Cornwall had come to mind. Of course,

Letty was horrified that her sister was living in a small, two-room cottage with no help, doing her own cooking, cleaning, and laundry, but Phoebe didn't care. The simple, mundane tasks helped to pass the time and she thought of new stories to write down as she worked.

"Good morning, Mrs. Butler," she said as she entered the store.

"Why, hello, Mrs. Smith. Don't you look lovely today in your pretty bonnet?"

Phoebe had come to Falmouth under an assumed name. She knew being the Dowager Countess of Borwick would cause people to look at her differently and draw undue attention. She didn't want to tell her story over and over again and feel pity, the rich countess who'd lost three members of her family on the same day. Instead, she'd had Burton rent the cottage for her through a local agent. The agent was merely told that the viscount's distant cousin, Mrs. Smith, had been recently widowed. No mention was made of her stature in Polite Society. The people in Falmouth had accepted her, asking few questions.

"Here to do a little shopping?" asked the proprietor's wife.

"Yes. I need more writing paper and pencils and I'd like to see if you have any drawing paper."

"I have all of that," the older woman said. "Perhaps a sketchbook would do?"

"That would be lovely," Phoebe replied.

She'd had one as a girl and liked keeping all her work together.

"I have some charcoals. Pastels, too, if you'd like. Are you drawing the scenery around Falmouth Cottage?"

"Yes," Phoebe said, determined to keep her project under wraps.

She'd decided to send a few of her stories, accompanied by the illustrations, to an associate of Borwick's. She didn't know if they were worthy of publication but Nathan had enjoyed them and she hoped other children might, too. If they did see print, it would be a way for her boy to live on.

Mrs. Butler assembled the requested materials and placed them on the counter. "Anything else for you?"

Phoebe picked out several items since she was running low on supplies. Mrs. Butler promised that her husband would deliver them in a few hours.

"Thank you. I think I'll walk over to the fish market and pick up a few items there. Then I'll try and beat Mr. Butler back," she said.

"If you'd care to wait, he could take you in the wagon."

"I enjoy walking," she answered, enjoying the freedom and solitude of the habit.

Phoebe stopped at the bakery for bread and then went to the market. Already, several boats had returned from their early morning run and she selected a piece of cod, one of lemon sole, and a few scallops. Living by the sea whetted her appetite for fish. She would miss eating it when she returned inland to Oxfordshire, where Burton's country seat was located. Of course, knowing Letty and her love for London, she would prefer to give birth to her child in the city. A decision would need to be made soon since travel would become more difficult the more Letty increased.

Her two baskets full now, she reversed direction and returned to the cottage, putting her purchases away. By then, she heard Mr. Butler's vehicle outside and opened the door to greet him.

"Let me bring things in for you, Mrs. Smith," he said and carried in two crates, emptying them on the table and then asking, "Anything else I can do for you?"

"Not a thing, Mr. Butler. Thank you. I appreciate you delivering my goods."

"It's my pleasure, Mrs. Smith."

He tipped his cap and returned to the wagon, giving her a cheery wave before he departed. Phoebe returned it and then went back inside and put away the goods he'd brought. She sliced some bread and coated it with jam and devoured it, hungry after her trip to the growing village.

Then she took up her new sketchpad and lost herself in her drawings.

CHAPTER FOUR

ANDREW SPENT THE next two hours dealing with correspondence regarding his various properties. As Windham, he'd gained seven estates scattered throughout England, not including Windowmere, the country seat of the Duke of Windham in nearby Devon. He'd only visited some of these properties as a child and none as an adult, having left university to go straight into the army, thanks to the commission his father had purchased for him. Once Windham passed, Andrew made a point to go and see each place, becoming familiar with the house, grounds, and servants, as well as having each property's steward introduce him to his tenants.

It was then that he'd given Francis full authority to manage Monkford, the small estate in Somerset, hoping the responsibility of running the place would help him mature and settle down. Sadly, it looked as if his half-brother had run it into the ground. Andrew would need to reclaim control, hire a new steward—or rehire the old one—and see that no tenants were left wanting.

He finished going through and then answering all the various letters, surprised there hadn't been appeals from Francis for more money. He'd received two letters already and had ignored them both. He'd made it clear that he wouldn't raise Francis' quarterly allowance or advance him any monies. Andrew had thought by assigning Francis a property to manage that it would keep him away from London and all the bad habits he'd formed there, as well as allowing him time away from his questionable friends. Having to remain in Somerset on a regular basis should have kept the boy out of trouble. No, not a boy. Francis was a man. He needed to start acting like one.

A light knock sounded and he bid them to come. The butler inquired if he wanted any luncheon and Andrew decided the break would do him good. He dined on a roasted duck breast and hearty vegetables, enjoying the solitude. While he enjoyed his aunt's company immensely, being alone calmed him nowadays.

Deciding to go for a ride once he'd finished eating, he changed clothes. Since the day was warm and he'd see no one, he decided to forego wearing a coat and waistcoat and cast aside his cravat, as well. He dressed in an old shirt and pair of breeches which had seen better days. He also removed his gleaming Hessians and replaced them with a pair of old, worn boots that he wore when he traipsed about his various estates, aiding the tenants in their work by helping to repair fences or roofs.

Andrew hadn't brought a valet with him. Hadn't even hired one, which would have appalled most of Polite Society. Instead, he'd written to Private Thomas Bagwell that the job awaited him when he was well. Andrew knew it would take time for Bagwell to heal, having one leg amputated and been shot in the other foot. Knowing the young man would get lost in the army hospital and never gain the attention he needed, Andrew had arranged for Bagwell to return to England and seen he'd gotten the best medical care available in London. He'd taken the soldier to a doctor who used a design recently created by James Potts, which was an above-knee prosthetic with a calf and thigh socket made of wood. What Andrew had liked was the flexible foot that was attached with catgut to the steel knee joint and how it would give Bagwell better range of movement.

Afterward, he'd sent the former soldier to convalesce in a cottage on the grounds at Windowmere. After several months of country sunshine and air, Bagwell was now in London, staying at the Windham townhouse. He was taking well to the prosthetic and from his most recent letter this morning, he was ready for service. Andrew had written for him to return to Windowmere, where the new valet would take up his duties once Andrew left Cornwall and returned to Devon. It would be odd having someone wait on him after having spent the last year doing for himself. Still, it would make Thomas feel useful.

He saddled Mercury himself and then rode out toward the cliffs. Since coming to Cornwall, he'd spent many hours riding and often walked to the cliffs or down the steep path to the beach below. Andrew rode to them now and tied Mercury's reins to a low tree branch. He walked for half an hour and returned. Surprise filled him when he found a second horse standing next to his, its rider none other than Francis. His half-brother quickly dismounted.

"Francis, what are you doing here? You have an estate to run in Somerset."

Francis sneered. "It's small and doesn't produce much of anything. It's a waste of my time."

"I disagree. If you learn to manage it properly and turn a profit, I will gift it to you," he said, hoping that would change Francis' tune. "You'll need to give it some time, though. The Season has only been over a month. Once you've been there several months, I guarantee you'll see progress."

"Why the bloody hell would I want something in boring Somerset?" Francis asked, his face red with anger. "It's too far from London. There's nothing to do there. My friends refuse to come see me. They think Somerset is ready to drop off the edge of the world."

Telling himself to practice patience, Andrew said, "That's a good thing, Francis. You were running with a fast crowd that got you into trouble. Being in the country after the Season will do you a world of good."

"I'm bored, Windham," Francis complained.

He gave the younger man a withering glance. "There's plenty for you to do. Hard work builds character."

"Blast it all. You sound just like Father. I'm not like either of you. Ward and I had much in common. Now he was a man other men admired, not some stick-in-the-mud like you."

Andrew's anger had simmered until now. He asked, "What did you have in common with Ward? A love of gambling? Coupling with strumpets? Buying too many fashionable clothes?" He glowered. "It's time you grew up, Francis. You are twenty-two now. A man. You need to start acting like one. I've been generous with the allowance I've given you and I've provided an opportunity for you to learn estate management. If you can show me progress at

Monkford, I've said I will gift it to you outright," he reminded. "It will be a solid, reliable income and a place you can raise your family someday."

Francis cursed. "You say it as if that's something I want. I don't, Windham. I want London. I need to be with my friends. I want to box at Gentleman Jack's and race. Gamble from midnight until dawn. Sow my wild oats for a decade or more and then find me a woman with an enormous dowry."

"That will be hard, Francis. You've no title. In my experience, heiresses have papas who are looking to buy a title and position in the *ton*. You have neither," Andrew said coldly.

Francis spat. "You weren't even meant for the dukedom. You never wanted it. *I* did."

He shook his head. "You don't want to be Windham. It comes with too much responsibility. You want to be a wastrel and play your life away."

"What if you die?" challenged Francis. "Ward did. He drank until he couldn't remember his own name. Lost more money gambling in one night than some men earn in a lifetime. He had a zest for life you'll never have. You're dull and morose and all you think of are duty and obligations. What's the point of being rich and powerful if you don't enjoy it?"

Andrew was fed up with this conversation.

Coldly, he said, "You'll never know. The only

way for you to become wealthy is to marry money and I don't see that happening. You're lazy, Francis. Forget Monkford. I'll take it back. Return to London for all I care. I tried to help you mature."

"You've only tried to hold me down," Francis said petulantly. "Besides, I can't go back. Not until I can pay my debts." He paused. "I need money, Windham. You must help me out. We're family. Father would expect you to take care of me."

Disgust filled him, knowing he was related to this worthless man. "I'll do nothing of the sort. If you spent your quarterly allowance unwisely, you'll have to figure out what to do until the next installment is paid. And don't bring Father into this discussion. He would be appalled at what you have become."

Francis moved closer and, for a moment, Andrew felt threatened. He stood near the edge of the cliff. He saw desperation in his half-brother's eyes. It wouldn't surprise him if Francis attempted to push him over.

Andrew started to take a step forward and froze.

A pistol now sat in Francis' hand. He had visions of Francis killing himself and knew he must talk him out of it.

Calmly, he said, "Francis, I—"

"It's too late, Windham. I gave you a chance.

I pleaded with you to pay my debts. I have no other choice," he said bleakly.

The gun began to rise and all Andrew could think of was stopping Francis from committing suicide. He made to dive at Francis when a loud noise occurred and his shoulder caught fire. Andrew looked down and saw blood—and realized that Francis had shot him. The bloody idiot had never planned to kill himself.

He'd come to murder a duke—and claim the title and fortune for himself.

Andrew's hand went to his shoulder, pressing against the wound, hoping to stanch the bleeding. He was far from his house. Riding would only aggravate the wound. Walking home would also keep the blood flowing and take too long.

He had fought in how many battles, only to come home to this madness?

Rage filled him. He wanted to charge Francis but weakness overwhelmed him. His knees buckled and he dropped to them, his vision blurring as pain set in.

"You're a pompous ass," Francis said snidely. "I'll be a better Windham than you or Ward."

With that, his own flesh and blood kicked him in the chest. The thrust caused him to fall backward. Suddenly, he sensed open air about him. Wildly, he reached out and grabbed onto something. A branch growing from the cliff.

How long would it hold his weight? And how

long could he even hold on to it? Already, removing his hand from his wounded shoulder had caused more blood to rush from the hole. He grew dizzy and weak.

A shadow loomed over him. He looked up and saw his gloating half-brother hovering above him.

"Goodbye and good riddance. Windham is dead. Long live Windham."

With that, Francis kicked Andrew in the head. His hands were torn from the branch as pain rushed through him. Then he sailed through the air, falling into the sea, which swallowed him whole.

AFTER AN HOUR of sketching, Phoebe decided to take a walk along the beach. Her current tale was about a fish and she decided she needed some inspiration. She'd always found walking seemed to spark her creativity and so she set Caesar down from her lap. The cat merely jumped into it again.

"I need you down, my sweet friend," she told her furry companion. "But I suppose you'd like it to be your idea."

She stroked the cat a few times and then of his own accord, Caesar leaped to the floor and strolled out the open door. Once Phoebe had tied on her bonnet and stepped outdoors, she saw the cat sunning himself, a pleased expression on his face.

"I'll be back soon," she told the feline.

She'd never had pets of any sort as a girl. Her father couldn't abide either cats or dogs. Thinking she might get one after her marriage, she'd been saddened to learn Borwick was allergic. Even though Nathan had begged for a pet, promising to keep it outside and out of his father's sight, Borwick refused to waver.

When she'd leased the cottage, Caesar had simply appeared the day she'd moved in and taken up residence as if he owned the place. The cat had made for a good companion to her and she found herself carrying on conversations with him regularly.

Phoebe walked the short way to the beach, inhaling the strong smell of the sea. She'd already spent a fair share of her time these past few weeks walking the sandy shore, even sitting and watching the waves wash in and out. The constant movement soothed her like nothing else.

Two gulls flew overhead, brilliantly white against today's bright blue sky. Her eyes followed them as the sound of their calls drifted away. She paused, soaking in the warm breeze, knowing how this sojourn renewed her spirit. Perhaps she would return and spend time at Falmouth Cottage each year, drawing strength from the vast ocean.

If her husband allowed her to do so.

Phoebe had come to the conclusion that she would need another husband. Because she desperately wanted another child.

No boy or girl could ever replace Nathan in her heart but she knew she was made to be a mother. It was almost a shame that she would need to marry again in order to do so. Her first marriage had been a disappointment, Borwick remaining a stranger to her for the most part. Not that she was foolish enough to expect a love match but, this time, her husband would be one of her own choosing. Closer to her age. A man who valued family as much as she did.

That meant a return to Polite Society. Phoebe had resigned herself to that fact. When next spring came, she would be long past her mourning period and could participate in the Season. Though Letty would be a new mother and might even skip the Season altogether, Phoebe still had enough friends in London who would be kind enough to invite her to some events. She didn't care for a title or great wealth. Just a man who would be respectful and courteous, one who would focus on being a good father. Maybe a widower with a young child would make the most sense. A man who needed a woman of good breeding to act as mother to his child, one still young enough to consider providing a brother or sister to that child.

The thought pleased her immensely. A child—and man—who would need her.

She would not put any of this to paper. Instead of corresponding with her friends, she'd visit them once she returned to London for her niece or nephew's birth. It would be easy to make known that she was ready to consider taking a husband again. While she would be much older than the young misses in their first Season or two, she did have other things to offer. She'd run Borwick's household with efficiency and participated in charity work. She wouldn't expect a man to fawn over her. She had no need of love. Just another child or two in her life would suffice.

Phoebe walked down the beach and returned in the direction of her rented cottage, ready to begin work again on Freddie the Flounder and his friend, Walter the Whale. As she neared home, though, she spied something on the sand.

No. Someone.

Lifting her skirts, she raced along the beach, frustrated at how long it took her. When she reached the body, she feared the man was dead. He was so still. She thought he must have drowned. He lay face down, a head full of dark hair. She rolled him over with great effort. Though tall, he was slender. This man was over six feet, with broad shoulders and narrow hips. The wet clothes that clung to him left little to her imagination, his sleek muscles obvious. The tide was up around them, soaking her skirts, as she brushed the thick, wet hair from his face.

My, he was handsome, though very pale. She felt his cheek and thought he must be dead because it was so cold. Her fingers slipped to his throat and she felt the faint pulse.

Alive.

Phoebe needed to drag him from the water. Now. She moved to his head and thought to try and lift him under his shoulders. Her attempt failed miserably. The stranger was dead weight. She fought tears of frustration.

And then her eyes fell to his shirt—and the hole in it, blood trickling.

He'd been shot.

The cold water must have stopped the bleeding but now that he no longer was submerged in it, the wound had started bleeding again.

Fear rippled through her. Was he some smuggler who'd been in a dispute with a fellow pirate? Cornwall was full of coves and tales of smuggling. This man could be a criminal. But he was hurt and needed her help. She was all he had.

Phoebe shook him. "Wake up, whoever you are. Wake up!"

When that didn't work, she slapped him hard. She'd never resorted to any kind of violence and hadn't even spanked Nathan or allowed Nanny to do so. But she was desperate.

So, she slapped him again.

His eyelids fluttered. Progress. She clutched the abundant hair, lifting him toward her.

Practically shouting now, she cried out, "Wake up, you bloody fool! If I'm going to save you, I'll need your help."

Then he blinked several times and his eyes remained open. They were a warm, rich brown with flecks of deep amber. She could lose herself in them for days. She licked her lips nervously.

"You've been shot. You're half in the water. And you're far too large for me to get you out on my own. I'm afraid to leave you. You might bleed to death. The water was cold enough to contain the bleeding but it's already started up again. We must get you out, Sir. You could freeze to death if you don't.

"So, are you going to help me or not?" Phoebe demanded.

A smile crossed his face. She had thought him handsome before but his smile dazzled her. Her heart caught in her throat and, for a moment, she forgot to breathe.

"Then I suppose I need to do my part."

CHAPTER FIVE

FOR A MOMENT, Phoebe stilled. The rich timbre of his voice and the warm, brown eyes mesmerized her. She couldn't have him dying on her, though. She'd never get over the guilt. Even if he were some smuggler, probably shot in a dispute over who got the lion's share of the profits from bringing in French brandy to England.

As the waves lapped around them, making her own skirts heavy, she said, "You must stand. I'll help you the best I can."

Phoebe stood and bent over him. He gripped her elbows and she placed her hands on his waist. With all her might, she pulled back, trying to right herself and bring him along with her. Somehow, they both wound up on their feet. The stranger swayed, though, and she wrapped her arms tightly about his waist, knowing if he went down again, she would never get him up.

An odd sensation ran through her. She'd never held a man in this manner. Never been pressed against one, much less a man whose chest was a wall of hard muscle. She looked into his eyes and swallowed.

"Thank you," he managed to say and then asked, "what now?"

"I am not good at estimating distances but it's not far to my cottage," she told him.

"Hmm. *Not far* may be more than I can manage."

"Please, you must," she pleaded. "I cannot leave you on the beach. It's two miles to the nearest village and the doctor. By the time I returned with help, you . . ." Her voice trailed off.

"I might be dead?" he asked.

"Let's just get you to Falmouth Cottage," she insisted.

The stranger gave her a wry smile. "I suppose I shouldn't question an angel of mercy. Lead the way."

Phoebe turned slightly, still keeping her arms about his waist. For his part, he draped an arm about her shoulders. It hung heavily. His body pressed against hers as they began shuffling along. They had to pause several times. His breathing was labored.

"There! You see it? That's where we are going," she told him, relieved the cottage was now in sight. Caesar still sunned himself but stood and stretched lazily, coming toward them with interest.

It took several more minutes until they reached it. When they did, she propped him against the doorframe and opened the door.

"You left without locking it?" he asked.

"Yes."

"That isn't wise," he said wearily. "Too many smugglers along the coast."

He would know.

She latched on to him again and he clung to her as she maneuvered them inside, leaving the door open for now. Caesar strolled in and jumped onto the table, tucking his paws in front of him as she half-dragged the injured man across to the table and pulled out a chair. He collapsed onto it.

Phoebe saw the blood on his shirt now, the exertion causing it to flow more freely. Worry filled her. His eyes looked glassy and she figured he was going into shock.

"I need to look at your wound," she said, unbuttoning the three buttons and trying to push the shirt back enough to see.

"Take it off," he commanded.

She'd never seen a man without his shirt. When Borwick came to her, he always left his nightshirt on and doused the candle. He would climb atop her and hike her night rail past her hips and then make her take his flaccid cock in hand and rub it until it hardened. Then he jammed it into her and pumped away before it fell out.

Reaching for the hem with hesitation, she pulled it up. The stranger raised his hands, hissing in pain as she removed it and placed it on the remaining chair, avoiding looking at his bare chest and focusing on his face instead. His eyes had darkened with pain.

"Do you have any whiskey?" he demanded harshly.

"No," thinking he wanted to dull his pain. "I do have some brandy."

She'd discovered an unopened bottle of it in the cupboard when she'd moved in. Having never consumed strong spirits, she had left it where it was, thinking the next tenant who leased the cottage might appreciate it more.

"Fetch it."

Phoebe rose and retrieved the brandy, opening it for him since she knew the motion would cause him pain.

"Was it a through and through?"

"A what?" she asked, unfamiliar with the term.

"Did the bullet pierce my front and exit the back?"

She frowned. "I don't think so. I would have noticed the hole when I found you since you were face down."

Still, she leaned over his shoulder to check,

once again experiencing an odd tingling, being so close to him.

"No," she informed the man.

"I didn't think so." He grimaced. "That means the ball is still in me. You're going to have to remove it."

"What?" she gasped.

"I'll walk you through getting it out of me."

"You're familiar with bullet wounds?"

He nodded grimly. "I saw enough of them in the war."

So, he was a soldier. Or former soldier. Phoebe wondered why he'd left the army. Probably because of the miserable pay and rotten food. Smuggling would be much more profitable and wouldn't involve near the killing that war did.

"You'll need a few basins of water and clean cloths. Something made of cotton or linen to bind the wound."

Immediately, she began gathering the supplies. Fortunately, she still had some fresh water on hand and poured it into three separate bowls. She placed them and clean cloths on the table and then excused herself to go into her bedchamber, the only other room in the cottage. Taking one of her linen chemises, she brought it back and began tearing it into strips.

"I suppose I'll need to buy you another one." A roguish grin graced his face.

Her cheeks flooded with warmth. Embarrassment filled her at the thought of this man purchasing such an intimate item for her. She kept her eyes on the chemise and finished her task, placing the strips on the table as Caesar watched with interest.

He shuddered and she glanced down, taking in not the wound but the bare chest before her. Dear heaven, he was beautiful. As if sculpted from warmed marble. He was lean yet muscled in both his arms and chest. A dark matting of hair covered it, tapering down and disappearing beneath his snug breeches. An awareness rippled through her, a new and unfamiliar feeling. She shoved it aside and her eyes flicked to his wound, which rested just below his shoulder.

By now, he was looking down, prodding it with his fingers, gasping in pain.

"Stop that," she said, though she wished he could be the one to find the lead shot instead of her.

"The ball is still inside me. Thank God it didn't hit and shatter bone. I'm not at an angle to reach it, though. You'll have to remove it."

"Me?" she squeaked. "How?"

He gazed up at her, his eyes turning glassy. She noticed his breath had become rapid and shallow. Phoebe reached and touched his throat. His pulse was also rapid, his skin cool and clammy.

"You are going into shock," she said, drawing from a well of strength she wasn't sure she possessed. "Tell me quickly what to do."

He grabbed the bottle of brandy and took a long pull, his throat muscles working as he swallowed. He drank another sip and put it down.

"Wash the wound with water and then brandy. Dip your fingers into the brandy, too, to cleanse them." He grimaced. "You'll need to reach in the hole and feel around for the shot. Pull it out and any cloth with it. It's a death sentence to leave the cloth behind."

He paused. "Pour more brandy into the wound and then stitch the hole closed. Bind the wound with several layers of linen. Make sure it's tightly wound around my torso and shoulder. Pressure is good."

The man took another sip of the brandy. Phoebe hoped he would leave enough for her to accomplish her tasks.

"I'll fetch needle and thread," she said and returned to her bedchamber, claiming her sewing basket and coming back to the stranger.

He sat with his eyes tightly shut, a scowl on his face.

Touching his good shoulder, she said softly, "I am here."

He raised his eyes and met hers. Instinctively, wanting to comfort him, she smoothed his hair.

"Close your eyes," she ordered, not wanting him to see the look on her face. She was already squeamish, thinking about what she had to do and didn't want to frighten him.

With a bravery she didn't know she possessed, Phoebe began cleaning his wound as he'd instructed and coating her fingers in brandy. She pushed one into the gaping hole and he sucked in a quick breath.

"Keep on," he said through gritted teeth, his eyes remaining closed.

It took two fingers to locate the bullet. The stranger stiffened beneath her as she held his shoulder steady with one hand and hunted with her fingers with the other. Locating the ball, she captured it between them, praying she could hold on to it at she pulled it from him. He groaned low as it came out and opened his eyes wide. He caught her wrist and held it as he removed the ball from her fingers and studied it. Phoebe held her breath as he did, aware of his burning fingers wrapped around her bare flesh.

He released her and said, "Go back in. It looks intact but a sliver may have broken off. Feel also for any cloth from my shirt. It must be removed. For some reason, leaving it inside will kill a man as much as the bullet would."

She bit her lip and pushed a finger back into the hole. He sucked in a quick breath and held it.

"I don't feel anything sharp but I do think I've

found a bit of your shirt."

"Remove it."

The cloth proved harder to grasp and she had to drag it to the hole. His face scrunched in agony, a low moan coming from him as she brought the cloth out. He exhaled the breath. She was so close, she saw the sheen of sweat that had broken out along his brow and dipped a cloth into the water, smoothing it across his face to soothe him.

He leaned against the chair back and sighed. "Thank you. I know that was difficult."

"Almost as much as cleaning a boy's skinned knee," she murmured, thinking how Nathan thought the world would come to an end every time she had to do so.

"Exactly." He grinned but his eyes glazed again.

Phoebe knew she must act quickly, else he pass out and fall to the floor. She soaked a piece of cloth in water and rubbed it over the wound, then ran it lower to wipe up the blood. She tried to push all thought of how intimate her actions seemed and focused on cleaning him. Taking the bottle of brandy, she poured some over the gaping hole. He sucked in another quick breath and howled. Taking the bottle from her, he took a long swig from it before returning it to her. She placed it on the table.

"I'll need to sew the wound now."

"Dip the needle in the brandy," he suggested, his words slurring slightly.

She touched the back of his forehead with her hand. His skin was still cold and clammy but his eyes were now growing bright. Fever would soon strike.

He turned his head away as she bent to sew the hole closed after cleaning the needle with the spirit. It was awkward bending over and she blew out a breath of frustration.

"What's wrong?"

He looked up at her, the flecks of amber in his eyes more prominent than before.

"Standing is not the best angle for this work," she admitted. "And if I sit in a chair, I'm too low to see what I'm doing."

Without asking, his hands captured her waist and pulled her onto his lap. Her eyes widened.

"Sit here. I promise to be still. It should be the right height."

It was—but being so close to him made her nervous. Still, the more quickly she worked, the sooner she could stand.

Unless she didn't want to.

This was insane. A man whose name she hadn't even learned was causing her heart to race and a giddiness to rush through her. He was a criminal. For goodness' sake, someone had *shot* him. People didn't just go around shooting others for entertainment. Someone had meant to kill this man, wounding him and then most likely shoving him off a ship for good measure. It wasn't the done thing to be attracted to a criminal.

Even if he was the most sinfully handsome man she'd ever laid eyes upon.

Phoebe calmed herself and concentrated on the task at hand. He only flinched when the needle entered the first time. She grew queasy performing her task, having never sewed flesh in her life. Hoping she'd never have to do so again.

She finished and tied off the thread. Setting the needle aside, she stood. Now, she was between his muscular thighs, almost imprisoned, but this was the best place to be to accomplish the rest of her task. She leaned and picked up several strips, draping them over her shoulder. Taking a few of the handkerchiefs she'd brought along with the chemise, Phoebe placed them gently against the wound before removing a linen strip. She wrapped it tightly over and around the bandage as he'd suggested, adding more strips to fasten the bandage in place.

Finally, she used the last strip, securing it to the top of his shoulder by tying a bow. She retreated from between his legs, all too aware of his masculinity.

"You need to lie down. You're already flushed." She gently touched his brow again and felt the heat. "The fever will strike soon. I only hope that we've prevented infection from setting in."

"I should go," he murmured. "I've troubled you enough."

She chuckled. "You aren't going anywhere except into the other room so you may lie on the bed. I'll be right back. Don't fall over while I am gone," she teased.

She hurried to the bed and yanked the bed-clothes back and then returned to him. Grasping his elbow, she helped him rise from the chair. Knowing they were leaving, Caesar stood and jumped from the table, making his way into her bedchamber. Phoebe knew when they got there, the cat would be lying on the bed. He slept with her every night. She supposed Caesar thought his job was to be company for whomever rested in the bed.

Slowly, they made their way into the other room. They reached the bed and she wanted to lower him, but he stopped her.

"My breeches are wet. I can't lie in them."

"You want them *off*?"

Having never seen a bare-chested man had been adventurous enough. But for him to remove his breeches? Impossible. She didn't care how much like Adonis he looked. She'd lived twenty-six years without seeing a man totally naked and expected she'd go to her grave in that same state.

"I'll ruin the bedclothes."

"I don't care."

She gazed up at him and saw a smile playing about his sensual lips. The bloody sod was *enjoying* this!

"Lying in wet clothes could make me more ill, Madam," he said. "Surely, you want me gone from under your roof as soon as possible."

He had a point. Phoebe supposed if she closed her eyes, she might be able to get the pants off and him into bed without seeing anything.

"Remove my boots first," he told her.

She bent and he braced his hands on her shoulders to steady himself as she worked the boots off and placed them aside. Gathering her resolve, she worked on loosening his breeches. She closed her eyes and dragged them down his long legs. Oh, why did he have to be so tall?

Reaching his ankles, she gruffly said, "Sit."

He shuffled back and his legs brushed the bed. He sat. She kept looking at the garment bunched around his ankles. Then she worked the material until one leg was free and then the other. She nudged the breeches aside and, eyes still closed, stood.

"Lie down," she ordered.

She waited a moment and assumed he'd done as asked from the squeak the bed made.

"Pull your legs onto the bed and cover your-self."

She listened and didn't hear anything. She

should hear something. Frowning, she opened one eye and gasped.

He'd fallen back against the mattress, his legs still dangling off the bed. And he was naked. Gloriously, embarrassingly bare.

Phoebe leaned down and shook him before she realized he'd passed out.

"Blast!" she cursed.

She had to touch him. She couldn't leave him as he was. Gritting her teeth, she worked for several minutes, pushing and pulling and maneuvering him until he lay prone on the bed. She mopped her damp brow with her forearm, the exertion tiring her.

And then feasted her eyes upon him.

He was long and lean but muscular in his upper arms, chest, and in his thighs. His calves were so beautifully shaped that she almost wept. Her eyes roamed over him, taking in every detail. The scar along his ribs. Another along his right forearm. And his manhood, nestled in hair. She'd never seen anything like it. He was made so differently from her.

Her body heated as she studied him. Embarrassment flooded her. He might be a criminal and a stranger but she hadn't the right to take advantage of him as she had. Phoebe tucked his feet under the bedclothes and raised them to his waist. She didn't want them up to his neck because she didn't want him tangled in them and agitating his wound. At least that's what she told herself as she continued to admire the bare expanse of his chest.

She touched his forehead again and felt the heat beneath her fingers. It worried her how quickly the fever had set in. She didn't know how long the bullet had been inside him. Did it leak some kind of poison into him? Had that spread infection throughout his body? What if he died? How was she to explain harboring a naked, dead smuggler in her bed?

"Worry about that later, Phoebe," she told herself as Caesar jumped onto the bed and curled up at the man's side. "You've got a patient to nurse."

CHAPTER SIX

ANDREW FELT HIMSELF deep in darkness, as if he were buried underground. He struggled to push through and finally did, forcing his eyes open. The room was small and mostly dark, a single candle flickering somewhere nearby. He thought to turn his head but it felt so heavy. He left it resting against a pillow.

The first thing that hit him was the pain. He reached to touch his shoulder. It was wrapped in a swath of linen. Something vague tugged at his memory, hovering about the edge of his mind. He sensed himself falling and his heart quickened, racing until he thought it might explode within his chest.

It isn't real, he told himself, bearing down against the rising hysteria. He deliberately took long, even breaths, as deep as he could despite the throbbing ache in his shoulder.

A flash startled him, the memory of a gun

being fired. This was no pistol on the battlefield, though.

It had been fired by his half-brother. At him.

Rage boiled through Andrew as the shadowy memory took shape. He remembered Francis confronting him. Shooting him after they'd argued. His pulse pounded as hard as his shoulder now at he recalled everything with clarity. The pain. Francis kicking him. Sailing through the air. Crashing into the water.

Then everything was a blank.

Or was it?

Andrew tried calming breaths again, something else niggling in the back of his mind. It was the same as having something on the tip of his tongue, something he wanted to recall but it was just out of his reach.

A sigh sounded. He stilled. His eyes darted about the small bedchamber. He still didn't know where he was.

He needed to find out.

Though a blinding headache made him want to keep his head still, Andrew turned to his left. Nothing to see but a wall and window. The window was open and a slight breeze caused the curtains to flutter. No light penetrated the room so he knew it was night. Gritting his teeth, he swiveled his head slowly to his right.

Ah, this was interesting. A woman sat in the chair beside him. The candle was on this side of the bed so he could see her somewhat. A wave of memories flooded him. Her arm about him as he leaned against her. The struggle to walk. Sitting as she ministered to him. The ambivalence on her face changing to determination as she tended his wound. Andrew didn't know many men who could have dug the lead shot from his shoulder, much less sewed his wound closed. She was as brave as she was beautiful.

He remembered shivering from the fever. The dreadful cold that had settled into his pores. Waking once to the scent and feel of warm woman next to him. She must have climbed into bed with him and used her own body heat to quell his tremors because he could still smell a whiff of lavender wafting up from the pillowcase.

He studied the sleeping angel. Candlelight was always flattering to women but this female would be beautiful in light or dark. She was fair and had hair like he'd never seen before, shades of brown swirled with golden highlights. It reminded him of caramel. He recalled looking up at her on the beach. Her eyes had been azure, the blue of a summer sky, clear and deep and caring. She wore a simple gown of some dark color that he couldn't distinguish in this light. Small, perfectly round, high breasts. A tiny waist.

She sighed again, which had drawn his attention in the first place. She must have been dreaming. He wondered what of. Her lips twitched and he focused on them, suddenly wanted to kiss them. They were pink and luscious and calling out to him.

Tired, Andrew fought the heaviness of his eyelids. He wanted to keep looking at his angel but weariness blanketed him. He closed his eyes and could still smell lavender. Smiling, he let the dark curtain descend once again, knowing he was safe because she watched over him.

PHOEBE AWOKE, THANKS to Caesar rubbing against her legs. She reached down and lifted the tabby into her lap. He curled up as she stroked his silky fur.

"You haven't gotten much attention lately, have you, my boy?"

The cat purred loudly. She kissed his forehead and then lowered him to the ground, her thoughts now on her patient. She glanced at him. He was still asleep. Rising, she leaned over and placed her palm against his brow. Finally, it was cool. It had taken three days but his fever had broken.

Suddenly, fingers tightened about her wrist. Panic seized her. She was staring into those eyes of melted chocolate, the flecks of amber swirling about the edges. Nervously, she licked her lips as she gathered her thoughts. This man was weak. He couldn't hurt her. At least she told herself that. His grasp on her certainly seemed strong, though.

"Might you release me?" she asked quietly.

His eyes flicked over her. She bit her lower lip, worried that he wouldn't.

He let go, though. Phoebe sank into her chair.

"I don't know how much you remember," she began, "but you've been shot. Somewhere at sea. I found you three days ago. No, four now. You'd washed up on shore."

The stranger nodded slowly. "I think I remember that."

"What? Getting shot? Almost drowning? Or me finding you?"

He gazed at her, a crease forming along his brow as he thought.

"I recall you finding me," he said. "You somehow got me to my feet. We came here, wherever that is."

So, he didn't remember being shot. She pushed that thought aside for now, tamping now her anxiety at having a smuggler in her bed.

"Yes, I brought you to Falmouth Cottage and have been nursing you ever since. You had quite a fever. You were delirious for a time."

"Did I say anything?" he asked quickly.

"You talked quite a bit but I couldn't understand anything," she assured him, remembering how he railed against someone named Francis. It was the only word she'd been able to make out from his mumbled tirade. "Are you thirsty?"

"I am."

"Let me make you some weak tea. I also have broth."

He sighed. "I need sustenance. I'm as weak as a kitten. Bread would be nice if you have it. Meat, as well."

She shook her head. "We will start slowly. Your stomach won't tolerate heavy food at this point. It will take time to build up your strength. I'll be back."

She left the bedchamber and returned to the other room, busying herself making tea and heating broth. She changed her mind, thinking he could have some bread and sliced it. The bread was slightly stale but would have to do for now. It was time to make another trip into the nearby village. Now that her so-called guest was awake and his fever had broken, Phoebe would need to leave him for a short while to go for more supplies.

Returning with a tray, she noticed he now sat up, the pillows propped behind his back. The covers were pulled to his waist, still leaving a large amount of bare flesh on display. While she'd nursed him, she'd been able to divorce her feelings about seeing him naked. Now that he was awake, though, she was uncomfortable in the extreme. He was far too male, with his broad shoulders and ridges of muscle. This stranger had her thinking of doing things she'd never done before. She determined as soon as he was strong enough, she must ask him to leave.

Before her hands tried to roam over those muscles.

Caesar jumped on the bed and curled against his hip. He looked startled for a moment and then petted the cat as she rested the tray just above his lap.

"Have I been sharing my bed?" he asked, eyeing her with interest.

Phoebe felt the blush rise up her neck. She had, in fact, gotten into bed with this man whose name she still didn't know. At one point, chills racked his body, causing him to shudder violently. She'd brought the covers to his neck, trying to keep him warm but he continued to tremble. Finally, she'd climbed next to him, draping herself over him, snuggling close to his side, hoping her body heat would warm him. She'd fallen asleep that way and had awakened, feeling secure and satisfied until she realized where she was.

Did he remember that? If so, would he tell others? It would be just like a criminal to go sounding off about it. Her reputation would be ruined. Of course, it would be Mrs. Smith's reputation and not the Dowager Countess of Borwick. Still, it would keep her from ever returning to the area in the future.

"Why do you say that?" she asked cautiously.

His gaze met her own and pinned hers. Its intensity caused Phoebe to hold her breath.

Then he smiled, that wicked, radiant smile that had melted her when she'd discovered him. A pirate's smile.

"I seemed to remember something warm nestled against my side."

Her cheeks burned now. She would have to beg him to keep quiet.

He stroked the cat. "So, what is my bed partner's name?"

Phoebe swallowed—and then realized he had been talking about the cat all along.

"Caesar," she managed to say.

His fingers slid through the tabby's fur. "Well, hello, Caesar. I believe you've been quite the companion for me. Along with your mistress." His eyes turned to her. "Might I ask the name of my angel of mercy?"

"Mrs. Smith," she replied, wishing her cheeks would cool.

"Ah, Mrs. Smith," he repeated as he picked up the mug of tea from the tray and took a long drink from it. "Nice and sweet and oh, so hot. Just as I like it."

Now Phoebe's cheeks lit on fire as he gazed

at her. She knew he couldn't be talking about her. Or was he?

The man lifted the slice of bread to his lips and bit into it. He chewed thoughtfully.

"Never has a meal tasted so good to me," he praised.

She laughed. "Invalid food. Broth. Weak, sweet tea. Bread with jam. It's all you're getting for a good day, at least. I need to see how you tolerate it before I give you something more substantial."

He finished the bread, leaving a tiny bit of jam in the corner of his mouth. Without thinking, she took her thumb and brushed it away, much as she would have if Nathan had a bit left on his lips. This was different, though. Immediately, Phoebe saw heat in his eyes as he looked at her. She swallowed. No man had ever looked at her as this one did. She tore her gaze away and stood.

"I need to retrieve things to clean your wound. I haven't unwrapped it since I first cleaned and dressed the wound. It's time to look at the stitches and see how the swelling is."

As she stood, he caught her hand. A ripple of warmth ran through her.

"Pardon me, Mrs. Smith. I thought I should introduce myself to you."

"I'm not sure you should," she blurted out, trying to remove her hand from his and failing.

"Why not?" he asked, puzzled.

"Because I know you are a criminal."

The stranger frowned. "And how did you come to that conclusion, Madam?"

"We are in Cornwall, Sir. Home to smugglers too numerous to count. You've been shot. It had to be a dispute over whatever you brought back from France. Frankly, I don't want to know what goods you smuggled or who might want you dead. The fact that you are in my home is bad enough. If I don't know your name and learn nothing about you, then when you leave I won't be able to tell anyone in authority about you."

"You think whoever shot me will come looking for me?" he asked.

"That—or some of your compatriots. Or whoever shot you." She jerked hard and freed her hand. "I don't care. I'm a simple widow who was only trying to help a stranger in distress. I will do my best to see you healed and then I want you gone, Sir. Is that understood?"

He gave her a brilliant smile. "I see. Well, you're going to have to call me something while I'm here." The man thought a moment. "Why not . . . Andrew?"

She was appalled. "I cannot call you by your first name!"

The smuggler gave her a lazy smile. "Who said it was my first name?"

"Oh. Mr. Andrew. I'm sorry. I'm a bit flustered."

He grinned. "It must a little bit disconcerting, having a naked smuggler in your bed."

Phoebe's jaw dropped. So, he was a smuggler. Admitting it to her. She shook her head, trying to rein in her wild emotions.

"I shall be back, Mr. Andrew. Then I'll see to your shoulder."

She grabbed the tray and left the room, irritated at the chuckling she heard.

CHAPTER SEVEN

ANDREW FOUGHT TO keep from chuckling and quickly lost that battle. The chuckles became laughter, which he tried to muffle so as not to embarrass his hostess.

It amazed him that Mrs. Smith thought he was a criminal who brought illegal goods into England. Wouldn't his friends have a laugh at that? Andrew was the most law-abiding, straight arrow of the group. While George and Weston had always been the most adventurous of the five of them, both had now gone wild since their broken engagements, being known by their nicknames, the Dukes of Charm and Disrepute. Even Sebastian and Jon were more daring than Andrew ever thought to be.

He rather liked that his angel thought he was a callous smuggler.

Besides learning her name, he now knew she was a widow. Being experienced, she might be willing to share his bed now that he was awake. Something told him she wouldn't consider it, though. She seemed eager to have him out from under her roof. It was true if it became known he was here that it could damage her reputation immeasurably. But who would learn of it? If she had any visitors, she could entertain them in the front room, where she now was.

And entertain him in this bedchamber later.

No, she seemed much too strait-laced for those kinds of shenanigans. He supposed it was only widows of the *ton* who engaged in such reckless behavior. A widow in Polite Society could have all the affairs she wanted, as long as she was discreet. He supposed for someone of Mrs. Smith's station that was far from true.

He smiled, thinking of the hot blush that had stained her smooth cheeks, making her even more appealing than he'd thought possible. When she'd licked her lips, he'd found himself wanting to do the same to them. They were full and called out to him.

Idly, he petted the cat that seemed perfectly happy to be in bed with him. If only his angel would relax a bit and want to do the same.

She was right, though. He was weak and needed to build up his strength before he confronted that rat bastard half-brother of his. Andrew wondered what Francis had done after shooting him. Had he returned to Somerset and

ALEXA ASTON

waited for news to be sent to Monkford of
Andrew's disappearance? Or had he ridden to
Moreland Hall, pretending he'd just arrived for a
visit, and waiting for Andrew to come in from his
ride? A ride from which he was never supposed to
return.

Either way, four days had passed, from what
Mrs. Smith said. By now, his servants would have
scoured the countryside looking for him. Mercury
would have been found, tied to the bush. Would
they think he'd been accosted by highwaymen?
Kidnapped and held for ransom?

Andrew knew that it wouldn't matter. Francis would try to lay claim to the title once the
duke didn't return. Little did his ignorant half-
brother know that without a body, it would be
years before he could be named Duke of
Windham. If he wasn't mistaken, he thought it
was a six- or seven-year period before an English
subject could be declared dead *in absentia*. By
then, Francis would be wallowing in debt.

Of course, Andrew would have made an
appearance well before that. He would deal with
the pugnacious brat in his own way.

For now? He would let the little bastard
sweat. Andrew intended to regain his strength—
and enjoy the company of the lovely Mrs. Smith.

She returned, her eyes warily searching him,
trying to decide if he was a danger to her or not.
Andrew needed to behave himself around her.

This woman had come to the aid of a perfect stranger, despite the fact she thought him to be a criminal. That spoke to her good character. He must show her that he could be trusted. He would start by apologizing.

"Mrs. Smith, I pray you must forgive me if I have offended you in any way. I appreciate the fact that you have played Good Samaritan to me. You will be amply compensated once I am on my feet and I'm able to—"

"No, that's quite all right, Mr. Andrew. Keep your money. My husband left me well off. I am more than happy to share what I have with you and expect nothing in return."

He glanced around the tiny bedchamber and thought her idea of well off differed from every person of his acquaintance. When it came time for him to leave, he would make certain that Mrs. Smith received proper compensation.

She came around to the other side of the bed, setting down a tray on the small table. Andrew saw it contained two basins of clean water, soap, the bottle of brandy, and clean cloths.

"I am going to remove your bandages now," she explained in a motherly, soothing voice. "You're quite lucky, you know. The lead shot missed bone altogether and just damaged the flesh."

He frowned. "I don't feel fortunate. My shoulder is throbbing painfully." He eyed the brandy. "Might I have a drink?"

She sighed. "I suppose that's a good idea. Just be careful. It's all I have. If you drink it, I won't be able to cleanse your shoulder properly."

He grinned. "I suppose I could always get you more." Andrew tilted the bottle and downed a healthy swallow.

Her eyes widened and then she pursed her lips. "That won't be necessary," she said primly. "I wouldn't even have any unless it hadn't already been here when I moved in."

"When was that?" he asked in curiosity as she began unwinding the linen strips holding the bandages in place.

He noticed the scent of lavender in the air and realized it was coming from the strips as much as it was from her skin. She must have torn one of her chemises in order to bind his wound properly. He'd offer to buy her another one but he'd already made her blush enough for one day.

"A while ago," she said vaguely.

"After your husband's death?" he prompted.

"Yes." Her tone was dismissive and Andrew knew that topic was off-limits.

Mrs. Smith placed the strips aside and then gently lifted the bandage from his shoulder. It clung in some places but she carefully maneuvered it instead of ripping it away, as medics in the army would. They didn't have the luxury of time during war. Here in Cornwall, though, it was a different story.

"Hmm." She studied his shoulder—while he studied her.

She had thick, sooty lashes, dark against her cheeks as she glanced down. In the sunlight that now streamed through the window, the various shades of color in her hair became alive, rich browns and warmed honey tones that mingled. His fingers itched to unpin her hair and run his fingers through its silky texture as it cascaded about her shoulders.

"I don't see any red streaks," she murmured. "That's a good sign. Let me wash it."

She dipped a cloth into the water and lathered it with soap, gently moving it across his wound and the surrounding area. Andrew had a glimpse of a memory. Of this woman doing the same to his limbs and chest, bathing them as she spoke soothingly, combating his fever.

"You must be exhausted after nursing me for several days," he said.

"I didn't mind. You were an easy patient. You didn't talk back," she teased. "The most difficult patients are men when they are feeling poorly enough to need attention but still have enough feistiness to protest."

Her fingers moving along his shoulder caused his manhood to begin to stir. Andrew quickly focused on anything other than the beautiful woman who ministered to him. He thought of catching tadpoles as a boy. Mucking out stables. Even charging the enemy on the battlefield.

She finished washing the wound and patted it dry, telling him, "You might want to wash yourself before I secure another bandage. I can heat some water for you but then I'll need to retrieve more."

"Don't bother heating any. Let me just use what you brought."

Andrew took another cloth and dipped it into the large basin. He tried to wring it out and then lather it up but he grunted in pain. Doing it one-handed was impossible. Mrs. Smith claimed the rag.

"Here, allow me."

He let her bathe his arms and chest, his racing heart playing havoc with his common sense. Her very nearness kept his pulse fluttering wildly. It took all the willpower he had not to pull her into his lap and kiss the life out of her.

She pressed a towel to the areas she'd washed and then said, "Lean up and I'll do your back."

He did, squeezing his eyes closed and gritting his teeth, telling himself not to let his willpower crumble. She finally finished, her magic, soothing fingers having worked him into a state where after she glided the towel along his back and arms, he slipped his hands under the bedclothes to hide his erection from her.

She studied his wound, worrying her full,

bottom lip. "I'm not sure we need to use any more of the brandy. I will just to be safe, however."

She held a cloth to the lip of the bottle and poured out a small amount and then carefully placed it against the wound. He inhaled quickly, the place still tender where the alcohol touched it. After holding it there a few minutes, no words between them, she lifted it and washed the place again with soap and water, drying it carefully before she placed a new bandage against it.

"Oh, I forgot. I need new strips. I can't use the old ones. Would you hold this in place for me, Mr. Andrew?"

He reached and placed his hands atop hers, watching how her cheeks pinkened. Slipping her hands from his, she went to a trunk in the corner of the room and dug about a moment before she removed a chemise. He felt guilty that she had to destroy her own undergarments to help him and even more guilty as he imagined her slipping the chemise she wore from her body, picturing her naked.

"I will certainly replace whatever garments you've used in my treatment," he said, thinking that instead of linen, he would buy her ones of the finest silk to rest against her own satin skin.

Mrs. Smith shook her head. "No. I told you that you are my guest and I will care for you as I see fit. There's no need to replace anything."

She sat in the chair and began ripping the chemise into long strips. When it was completely destroyed, she brought the strips to the bed and began using them to tighten the bandage so that it was securely in place.

"It's a good thing I was shot with a pistol and not a rifle," he said, making conversation. "A rifle would have done far more damage." Glancing down as she worked, he added, "Your stitches were quite neat, Mrs. Smith. I'm hoping no scar tissue will form around the site. That would lead to ongoing pain or discomfort."

"Does the scar on your forearm or ribs bother you?" she asked.

He supposed she had noticed them as she'd tended to him. "The arm does upon occasion. A pesky bayonet wound. I threw an arm up to block one man and another sliced me but good."

"In the war?"

He nodded. "In the war. Smugglers aren't nearly as violent as you think them to be."

"Except for the one who tried to murder you."

Andrew grinned. "Well, there is that. Actually, many smugglers in Cornwall are everyday men. Farmers. Innkeepers. I even know of a doctor who dabbles in smuggling, using the brandy to treat his patients' wounds."

She finished stabilizing his shoulder and stepped back. "I do think a doctor should see you."

"No," he said quickly. "You have done everything a doctor would do. Even more."

She shrugged. "You are the one who walked me through the procedure. I haven't dealt with anything more severe than a skinned knee or sprained ankle."

He took her hand and, for the first time, she didn't try to wriggle away.

"I greatly admire your courage, Mrs. Smith. You acted quickly and calmly. Thoroughly. Your stitches were as good—if not better—than any battlefield surgeon. I applaud your efforts on my behalf."

"Was the war so very hard?" she asked softly.

He squeezed her hand. "It was. It's something I do not wish to discuss. I saw enough of my . . . enough of my friends lose their lives."

Andrew had almost called them his men. He didn't want her to know that he was an officer. An officer meant a gentleman. A naked gentleman in Mrs. Smith's bed would lead to too many questions.

He released her hand and she placed it on his shoulder. "You've had a busy morning, what with me dressing your wound and eating. Why don't you try to nap for a while, Mr. Andrew? I'm sure you'll feel more refreshed when you awaken."

"A splendid idea, Mrs. Smith."

"Let me help you."

She had him lean forward and lowered his pillows, plumping them. He lay back against them and she raised the bedclothes to just below his shoulders.

"There," she said and then smoothed his hair back, her touch gentle. "Have a nice rest, Mr. Andrew."

Mrs. Smith gathered her supplies on the tray and then left the room, her footsteps quiet. She was right. Weariness blanketed him. Andrew closed his eyes and willed himself to dream of his angel of mercy.

CHAPTER EIGHT

A FTER PHOEBE PUT away the supplies she'd used on Mr. Andrew's shoulder, she tiptoed back to the doorway. He was already asleep, as she'd suspected. She had much to do while he napped, hopefully for several hours. Though his fever had finally broken, he was very weak. It would take a week or more to build his stamina. She quickly fed Caesar and then left the cottage, pushing the small cart that would hold her purchases, hoping the cat would curl up with their guest while she was away.

Today was noticeably cooler though the sun was shining, peeking from behind the cloud-filled sky. She kept to a quick pace in order to reach the village sooner than she usually did. Her first stop was the Butlers' shop. She removed her baskets from her cart and entered the structure. Mrs. Butler was with a customer so Phoebe loaded her baskets quickly and brought the goods to the counter just as the sale was concluded.

"Ah, Mrs. Smith. I haven't seen you in a few days," Mrs. Butler said. "Have you heard about the duke?"

"No. What duke? Is there one visiting the area?" she politely inquired, doubting it was anyone she knew since she didn't move in lofty *ton* circles.

"Why, the Duke of Windham, of course."

She shrugged. "No, Mrs. Butler, I have not heard of him."

"Why, His Grace has the most gorgeous estate in Devon called Windowmere," the woman said dreamily. "And he's supposed to be quite handsome."

"I wouldn't know," Phoebe murmured and began setting her purchases out on the counter. She wanted to hurry Mrs. Butler along but knew the woman loved to gossip.

"Well, he's missing."

"Missing?"

"Yes, missing!" Mrs. Butler declared. "He has an estate, Moreland Hall, here in Cornwall. It's a little east of here. A good ten miles from Truro, along the coast."

"Uh-huh," Phoebe said, her goods now all spread out, ready for Mrs. Butler to check the prices and total her bill.

"He vanished." The woman snapped her fingers. "Just like that!"

"Oh, dear," she said sympathetically. "I hope it's not serious."

"No one knows. He's been gone several days. Maybe a week or more, from what I hear. His poor brother, who's quite close to him, came to visit him and then His Grace simply disappeared. How can a man—especially a duke—simply disappear, I ask you?"

"I have no idea. Might you ring me up?" she asked politely.

Finally, Mrs. Butler started doing her job but she kept up a steady stream of gossip the entire time. How the duke's father rarely came to Moreland Hall and this was the first time his son, the new duke, had set foot in Cornwall. That he'd gone out for a ride and hadn't come home. How his horse was found but no sign of His Grace was visible.

As Phoebe helped place the items into her baskets, Mrs. Butler said, "The duke is said to enjoy walking. Could he have been attacked by wild animals in the forest and his body dragged off? Or what if he encountered highwaymen—or even smugglers—and they're holding him for ransom? Oh, his poor brother must be distraught, indeed."

Since it was obvious Mrs. Butler had never met the duke, Phoebe couldn't quite understand why the woman was so worked up over the matter. Yes, it was unusual that a duke had vanished without a trace. Maybe he'd tired of being in Cornwall's quiet and simply up and left for one of his many estates. It didn't matter a whit to her. She needed to get home to her patient.

"What do you say to that, Mrs. Smith?" Mrs. Butler demanded.

Since she didn't want to admit to woolgathering, particularly because it had involved thinking about her unexpected guest and his good looks, she said, "I have nothing I can add, Mrs. Butler. You have said it all."

"I have, indeed," the woman said, nodding sagely. "Mark my words, something rotten has occurred. Why, they're talking of calling out the magistrate and hiring men to search for His Grace. I've even heard that his brother wishes to bring in the Bow Street Runners, all the way from London. He's that upset about his dear, missing brother."

"Well, I hope they find His Grace." Phoebe gathered her baskets and made for the doorway.

Mrs. Butler sniffed. "I am praying daily that they will. What is the world coming to when a duke goes missing from his very house?"

"Goodbye, Mrs. Butler," she said, glad to have finally made her escape.

Transferring the goods to the cart from her baskets, she stopped at the bakery and butcher shop and ended at the fish market. By the time she left Falmouth, the cart was heavier than it had ever been. Thank goodness no rain had come for a good week and the path was smooth.

She arrived at the cottage and parked the cart next to it. Going to the well, she drew water into all four buckets and toted them to the door. She would need to bring in enough not only for drinking and cooking but she was desperate for a bath herself after days of nursing Mr. Andrew. He, too, could afford to sit in a tub and soak, as long as he kept his bandage dry.

Phoebe nudged open the door to the cottage and carried two buckets inside.

"Where the bloody hell have you been?" an angry voice shouted.

※》》》《《《※

ANDREW AWOKE, THIS time knowing where he was. His eyes immediately went to the chair, where the lovely Mrs. Smith was usually stationed. She was missing, though. He lay there, his thoughts drifting idly as he waited for her to check on him.

And waited. Then waited some more.

Frustrated, he decided to call out.

"Mrs. Smith?"

At once, he heard how weak his voice sounded. It hadn't projected but a few feet from the bed. The noise had awakened Caesar, though.

The cat, who sat next to him, stretched lazily and began cleaning his front paw. Andrew stroked the gray furball. He wished he had something to drink. His throat felt clogged. He cleared it and tried again.

"Mrs. Smith? I say, are you there?"

No one replied. This time, he was certain his voice could have been heard in the next room. From what he remembered, the cottage only had the two rooms. Guilt swept through him, knowing he'd taken his angel's bed from her and that she'd slept in the chair the past few nights. Having done the same thing himself as he watched over various soldiers under his command as they slept in hospital, he knew her back must be aching and that a good night's rest was the last thing she'd had. Especially since he'd been feverish and she'd constantly bathed him the last several days.

Where on earth could she be?

She might have gone outside, dumping the chamber pot. Or be drawing water from a well. It was obvious the woman had no help and must do everything for herself. Andrew couldn't imagine being responsible for washing his clothes and preparing all his meals and cleaning his rooms. Or his many houses full of rooms, lest he forget he was now a duke and had more estates than he knew what to do with.

He wondered what the staff at Moreland Hall

had done when he hadn't arrived home. Had the authorities been notified? Were search parties with dogs sent out to look for him? Of course, he'd fallen into the sea so if any dog traced his scent, it would be to the edge of the cliffs.

Would people think he'd jumped?

If they did think him a suicide, they must be looking for his body to wash up. Mrs. Smith was right. People might come questioning her as they looked for him.

The thing is, he wasn't ready to go home just yet.

It wasn't only because he needed more time for his injury to heal. To be back at full strength would take him several weeks. Andrew didn't want to confront Francis unless he could thoroughly thrash him. He pictured himself beating the whippersnapper to a bloody pulp. It would take brute force to do so. His rage would do half the job but he needed his fists to do the rest.

Should he go to the authorities? Or challenge his half-brother to a duel? Andrew was a crack shot before the war and years of battle had only honed his skill. Could he actually pull the trigger and kill his own flesh and blood?

Without a doubt.

But what really held him back was the delectable Mrs. Smith. His growing attraction to the young widow needed to be fed. She might not agree to couple with him but he wanted—no, needed—to kiss her. Thoroughly. As if she'd never been kissed. He wondered what her husband had been like. Mrs. Smith looked to be a couple of years younger than Andrew. How old had Mr. Smith been? Was he more her contemporary or closer to her father's age? What had caused the man's death? Had she wed the man willingly or was she forced to do so by her family?

And had she loved her husband?

Andrew had so many questions to ask her and doubted she would answer a one of them, especially since she thought him a man who broke the law. He would like to break through the prim and proper wall she'd managed to erect about her and kiss her all day and into the night. Something told him she'd never experienced passion—and he wanted that for her. He wanted to be the man who brought it to her.

God, he wanted her.

Andrew enjoyed women. He had good looks and easily had many women over the years. Yet there was something about the lovely Mrs. Smith that made her different from all the others. Maybe because she had gone against her nature and better judgment and taken in what she thought was an outlaw, nursing him back to health.

Oh, he truly wanted to kiss her.

Where the bloody hell was she?

He moved to toss the bedclothes back and found that was hard to accomplish. It took three tries before he untangled himself from them. Caesar hissed and jumped from the bed, tossing Andrew a malevolent look as he strolled from the bedchamber. He sat on the edge of the bed, a bit dizzy, trying to center himself.

Gradually, he rose, unsteady on his feet but determined to walk. He found the chamber pot and pissed the longest stream of his life. Bracing his hand against the wall, he glanced around and saw his breeches neatly folded, his stockings atop them. His worn pair of boots rested next to them. He wondered where his shirt had gone. He'd left Moreland Hall without a coat or cravat. If the beautiful Mrs. Smith had found him in those or what he usually wore, she would definitely have known he wasn't a smuggler.

Stumbling to his clothes, his decided the breeches were all he could handle at the moment. He snatched them and then fell to the bed. It took some minutes before he worked them up his legs and over his hips. They were a bit loose on him Not eating for several days made him realize he'd lost some weight.

Finally, he stood and fastened them. Taking halting steps, he made his way to the doorway, which wasn't far away at all but took a good while to reach. He entered the outer room and he was right. It was the only other room in the humble cottage. Looking around the room as he clung to the doorway, he saw a table and its two chairs in the kitchen portion of the room and a small settee and table on the other side. A simple desk sat under a window, pages scattered across it. He was too tired to make it that far, only managing to get to the settee. He collapsed onto it and then raised his bare feet, propping them upon the table. Andrew leaned back, sweat beading along his brow, and waited for Mrs. Smith to come inside.

What could be taking her so long?

The more time passed, the more concerned he grew. The cottage was isolated. Had someone come by and taken her? By God, he would hunt them down and rip out their throats.

He chuckled. Where had all this anger come from? He barely knew a thing about his benefactress, other than she was kind and beautiful and very caring. And that he longed to kiss her in the strongest of ways.

Suddenly, he heard a noise from outside. He was too weak to walk to the window but he peered out it from where he sat.

Mrs. Smith was pushing a cart filled to the brim. How heavy was it? Where had she been? He saw her coming closer and placed his feet on the ground, sitting up expectantly.

She didn't enter the cottage.

Next, he saw her pass by again. She must

have put down the cart. She walked to a well and began drawing water. Four times, to be exact. It hurt him to see her laboring as a servant. She deserved to be waited on hand and foot, wearing fine gowns.

And being made love to. By him.

Suddenly, Andrew knew he had already come to a decision. He needed to wed. Why not this woman? She may not be from Polite Society but she had more attributes than a majority of the women he'd tried to get to know during the past Season. Yes, it would shock some that he took a woman as his bride from her station in society but, by God, he was a bloody duke and could do as he pleased. Mrs. Smith would never want for anything again. She would make for a fine duchess.

The door slowly opened and she came in.

"Where the bloody hell have you been?" he demanded.

The buckets fell from her hands. Water spilled everywhere. She looked tired and frightened—and in need of comfort.

Pushing himself to his feet, Andrew somehow took the few steps needed to close the gap between them. He clasped her shoulders and lowered his mouth to hers.

CHAPTER NINE

PHOEBE FROZE AS Mr. Andrew clutched her shoulders. Suddenly, his mouth was on hers. She ought to pull away. She must. He was a stranger. An outlaw.

But the slow brushing of his firm yet soft lips against hers felt utterly delicious.

She'd only been kissed once. At the close of her vows when she'd wed Borwick seven years ago. Her husband had never kissed her after that. Everything that had occurred in the bedroom between them had been focused on his needs. Not hers.

Not that she would have known she needed this. Goodness gracious. Her first thought centered around what she had missed out on during all those years of marriage. That kissing was a magical experience between a man and a woman when they pressed their mouths together.

Heavenly . . .

Coherent thought ceased after that. His arms held her firmly against his bare chest. Her palms pressed against it. She'd meant to push him away but now the heat beneath her fingertips drew her in. It wasn't the heat of a man struck by fever. No, this was the body heat of a man who desired.

And he desired her.

His kiss grew more urgent, more demanding. Almost harsh. Yet Phoebe reveled in it. Then his lips moved, drawing away, and his teeth sank softly into her lower lip. A frisson of warmth swept through her. He held her lip prisoner and a throbbing began between her legs. Then he released it, brushing his tongue lightly over it, soothing it. He nipped at her again several times, causing the throb to beat wildly. The unknown feeling caused her body to tingle. She slid her hands along his chest, feeling the ridges of muscle dance beneath her fingertips.

Then his tongue traveled lazily along her bottom lip and to her top one, outlining her mouth in a sensual move that had her knees buckle. He must have sensed her shift and held her closer. Her hands slid around his waist. Her breasts pressed against his bare chest, causing the nipples to pucker as her body went hot all over.

This was too much. Her senses were on overloaded. She needed to pull away. Stop this madness.

Yet even as her mind told her to do so, her body betrayed her. Her hands began to stroke his sleek back. Her breasts brushed against his chest. Her mouth never protested, not even when his tongue teased it open. Suddenly, his tongue swept inside, causing a delicious ripple of something to run through her. She couldn't name it because it was unfamiliar.

Phoebe didn't know things like this could happen. He leisurely explored her mouth and she found herself answering his call, her own tongue playfully joining his and tangling for control. Her breath caught and the pounding between her legs became a hard, insistent beat. His mouth. His tongue. The beating of that drum. That was all her world consisted of.

The kiss went on and on. She wanted to wrap herself around him until they were as one person. She couldn't remember anything that had come before this moment. There was only him. His taste. A masculine scent. His heart beating against her breasts.

His arm tightened about her waist and his hand traveled to her nape, massaging it. A moan escaped her as her bones seemed to melt. He tugged on her hair, forcing her head back, and the kiss deepened. Her fingers kneaded his back just as Caesar kneaded his paws against her sometimes. He continued kissing her until all thought had been driven from her mind. Only a pulsing need to get closer to him existed.

Then he withdrew. His forehead rested against hers as they each caught their breath. Slowly, Phoebe came back to reality.

What had she done?

She'd kissed a man. A half-dressed man she barely knew.

And it had been the most moving experience of her life.

She became aware that he now clung to her as much as she did him. He'd been shot and could barely stand.

"We need to get you back to bed," she said breathlessly. Immediately, images of him naked in bed—with her—filled her mind.

"I don't know if I can make it that far," he admitted, his breathing rapid.

"Let's try." She turned him in the direction of the bedchamber. "Take a few steps."

"No. Guide me to the settee," he instructed.

They shuffled toward it and he collapsed. Phoebe merely stared at him a moment. While he had felt large and powerful as she'd been nestled in his arms, she saw the effort he'd put into their kiss had drained him of all his strength.

"I'll make you some tea," she said. "Hot and strong and very sweet. You need it."

She stoked the fire and put the kettle on, glad to have something to do. Though she longed to lose herself in daydreams of their kiss, it was better for her to keep busy. While she waited for the kettle to boil, she brought in the two remaining buckets of water and all the food which she'd purchased. She put away the eggs and then decided to soft boil a couple. Eggs would be good for him.

The kettle whistled and she prepared the tea, letting it steep as she took out cups and saucers and honey to sweeten it. Grabbing the broom, she began sweeping the water which had spilled from the buckets out the door. Whatever remained, she could mop up later.

After she completed her task, she poured out cups for them both, adding a generous amount of honey to Mr. Andrew's and placing two raisin scones on a plate, along with the eggs. She put all the items on a tray and brought it to the table in front of the settee, looking at him for the first time. His face didn't bear the strain she'd seen earlier. In fact, his color was good. She handed him the saucer and a spoon.

"Stir it well. It will take a few moments for the honey to dissolve."

He did as told and said, "I've never had honey in my tea, only lumps of sugar."

"I find honey gives the brew a pleasant taste. Plus, you don't need to use nearly as much of it to sweeten your tea. If you drink it without, I'm sorry. I find when my strength is sagging, a shot of honey does the trick."

He chuckled. "Then perhaps I should down your entire pot of it. It may speed up my recovery."

The thought of him leaving saddened her. Phoebe had thought she wanted to be rid of him. Their kiss had changed her mind. She wished she could think of a way to keep him here longer.

"How long do you think it will take you to recover from your wound?" she asked.

One brow cocked up. "Are you already tired of my company, Mrs. Smith?"

"No, it's not that," she said hurriedly. "I've just never been around this particular problem. I have no idea what the recovery period involves."

"I have. I saw plenty of gunshot wounds during the war. It varies." He paused to sip the tea. "Ah, that certainly hits the spot. But as to your question, it depends upon where the person was shot. A gut wound usually kills its victim or they linger in agony for far too long before death claims them. If the lead shot hits bone, you must factor in the healing of both flesh and bone. Since only skin and tissue were damaged in this instance, I should begin to build my stamina now that the fever has passed. A week after being wounded, I will be up to half my usual strength. By the end of the second week, I will look and feel close to normal but it will probably take a third week to pass before I truly begin to function properly."

"I see."

Would he stay three weeks? Or leave in a few days? She was afraid to ask.

"I'm sorry you had to deal with all the spilled water. I didn't mean to frighten you. I awoke and called out and you didn't answer. When I made my way in here and you weren't nearby, I began to worry about you."

"I was running low on supplies. Eat your scones," she prompted.

He bit into one. "Oh, my goodness."

Phoebe grinned. "They are wonderful, aren't they? The local baker is quite talented." So talented that she wished she could hire him when she left the Falmouth area.

Mr. Andrew frowned. "Aren't you having any?"

"I bought them for you."

"I insist. Take one."

"No, they are for you."

"Then take a bite of one."

He tore off a piece and held it up. Before she could reach for it, he touched it to her lips. She opened her mouth, accepting it, and shivered at the brush of his fingers against her jaw. It seemed quite intimate for him to be feeding her. She took a quick swallow of tea, hoping to hide the blush that heated her cheeks.

"Is town far from here? And where exactly is here?" he asked.

"This is Falmouth Cottage. We're south of Truro but not quite to Lizard's Point. Falmouth is the closest village and it is two miles from here."

"You walked two miles and back again, lugging all those goods?"

"Yes. I've always enjoyed walking, even in my youth. I go into Falmouth a couple of times a week, especially for fresh eggs, bread, and fish."

"You also brought fish?"

"I did and I stopped at the butcher's, as well. I was going to put on a stew for dinner." She sighed. "I may wait and save that for tomorrow. Frying up some fish will be quicker and easier. I prefer a stew to sit for a good while so the flavors blend."

Phoebe had only learned to cook recently, when she'd leased the cottage. Her repertoire was limited. She hoped he would enjoy the simple fare she made.

"I adore fish, no matter how it's prepared," he declared. "I missed eating it during the war."

"How long were you a soldier?" she asked, wanting to glean some information about him.

"Five years." A shadow crossed his face. "I wanted to do right by my country but seeing men die on a daily basis hardens a man. Especially when they are your friends."

She placed her hand atop his. "I'm sorry for bringing it up. I won't mention it again."

Realizing what she'd done, she withdrew her

hand but he caught it and entwined his fingers with hers. She looked at him, puzzled by his action. Nervous. Thrilled.

"Sometimes, it's nice to have human contact. Holding your hand brings me comfort, Mrs. Smith," he explained. "I remember you held it when I was fevered."

"I did," she admitted.

He smiled and her heart skipped a beat. "I am sure it helped see me through the worst of it." He hesitated. "It helps me even now, talking about the ugliness of war." He squeezed her fingers slightly.

"I am sure I could never comprehend what you went through, Mr. Andrew. I do thank you for your service to our country, however."

He continued holding her hand as he finished his scone and the eggs and drank the rest of his tea. Then he yawned.

"You are tired," she said worriedly. "I had wanted to come home and heat water so you could have a bath."

His eyes twinkled. "I would probably fall asleep if submerged in warm water. You'd have to come and save me all over again."

Phoebe giggled. "I fear I am too tired to do that, Sir. Why don't we try again to get you to the bed? You can sleep for an hour or two. By then, I'll have dinner ready for you."

She pulled her fingers from his grasp and took his saucer and plate and placed them on the tray. He pushed himself to his feet and she slipped her arm about his waist. Together, they slowly made their way to the bedchamber. Funny how she'd forgotten he was naked to the waist as they talked over tea. She guided him to the bed and he sat.

"You should take your breeches off after I go," she suggested. "I'll bring your food to you so that you might remain in bed. I believe you've had more than enough activity for one day. Tomorrow, I will see to your bath. You'll feel a world of difference after that."

"Very well."

She went to the door and started to close it. She'd already seen him completely naked once and didn't plan to do so again.

"Mrs. Smith?" he called out.

"Yes?"

He gazed at her a long moment and she worried he was going to bring up the kiss. She didn't think she could talk about it with him or she would turn red to her roots. She didn't know what had gotten into her. It certainly wasn't something that should be repeated. It was best that neither of them acknowledge it had occurred. Best to sweep it under the rug and pretend it never happened.

"I was wondering if it might be possible . . . that is, oh, never mind. I will see you shortly."

Phoebe wondered what he was going to ask of her as she closed the door.

CHAPTER TEN

"OH, BLOODY BRILLIANT, Andrew," he said under his breath as he watched the door close.

He'd wanted to ask what her Christian name was. After all, once you'd kissed someone the way they had kissed each other, it was only fitting to be on a first-name basis. Something told him, though, that the lovely Mrs. Smith didn't want any mention of the kiss, despite how she had responded to it.

He'd known almost immediately that she'd never been kissed before. Or at least not how he had kissed her. It made him even more curious about the deceased Mr. Smith. How old he'd been. How and when he'd died. What their marriage had been like. It certainly hadn't involved much kissing because she did it like a virgin. Somehow, that appealed to him greatly. His beautiful angel almost untouched by a man.

Andrew was glad he'd been the one to introduce her to proper kissing and couldn't wait to do it again with her.

If she'd let him.

She'd been incredibly shy when they'd started. As she'd warmed to him, she became braver. Bolder. She mimicked what he did and it had rocked him to his core. Andrew was used to experienced women, ones where kissing had almost become passé. Mrs. Smith made him feel like a schoolboy again, discovering the sweetness and joy and passion of simply kissing. He longed to spend hours with her doing just that. He'd pull her into his lap and devote a good afternoon to kissing her.

Of course, he wanted more than her lips to touch his. He wanted to kiss the long, elegant throat. Feel the pulse jump there. Kiss her nape. The shell of her ear. Her bare shoulder. The back of her knee. He wanted to spend a good hour on each breast, dining on them as if they were a meal. He wanted to kiss her delicate feet and work his way up her calves, all the way to her core. Once there, he would plunge his tongue deep inside her, tasting her essence. He knew instinctively that no man had ever made a foray there. He would be the first—and last.

Now, he just had to convince her to marry him.

Andrew could be proud at times and this was

one of them. He wanted the delightful Mrs. Smith to want *him*—not the Duke of Windham. He wanted to win her as himself, not as some title he still had a hard time believing was his. He wondered how long it would take. Days? A week or two? How long would she allow him to remain so he could press his suit?

He sighed and stood, unbuttoning his trousers. It was much easier to push them down and work them over his feet than it had been to struggle pulling them up. He almost left them crumpled on the floor but remembered there was no valet to come along and pick them up, much less clean and press them. Because of that, Andrew lifted and folded them neatly. He leaned and tossed them onto the chair. Thankfully, they hit it perfectly and stayed in place.

Leaning back, he stretched out on the bed, remembering to capture the bedclothes and tug them up to his waist. It wouldn't do to have the almost-virginal Mrs. Smith come in with a supper tray and find him sprawled atop the covers, bare as the day he was born. He closed his eyes, thinking of how he could convince her to cast aside her own clothes and come to bed with him. He believed he had sparked need within her. Awakened a sleeping giant of passion that was eager to come out and play.

All he had to do was discover what it would take to persuade her to join him.

He dozed and then came to, smelling the fish she'd promised to make. His mouth salivated at the thought of it. Andrew prepared himself for her visit, slipping his pillows behind his back and sitting up against them. Then he closed his eyes and relived the never-ending kiss. If he'd had his way, it might well have gone into tomorrow—but his damned legs had betrayed him. He was still far too weak and hadn't wanted to go tumbling into the water that covered the floor, taking her with him. Although the thought of a wet, slightly bedraggled Mrs. Smith appealed to him immensely. It would mean stripping the wet garments from her and taking his time to dry her. He could picture her in nothing but a towel, her ivory skin smooth, the swell of her breasts tantalizing him as her long, shapely legs peered out from beneath it.

Andrew imagined a half-dozen ways to remove the towel from her, each involving his hands and mouth and tongue. He shuddered, the thought of her naked more enticing than any experience he'd shared with another woman. Why did this angelic widow have such a hold on him?

It didn't matter. Somehow, some way, he was going to make her his wedded wife.

The sound of footsteps approached and he opened his eyes, drawing in a long, cleansing breath as his hostess opened the door. Although the familiar lavender wafting from her skin had become his favorite scent, the freshly fried fish almost won out. His stomach gurgled noisily and she laughed.

"That's a good sign, Mr. Andrew. I only hope you'll enjoy the fish. I'm not the most talented cook."

His eyes followed her as she entered the room and set the tray down in front of him. He'd gone from battlefield food, which was barely edible slop to having one of the finest cooks in England. He'd attended dinner parties in London, where the fish course was baked with butter and various herbs. These fried pieces of what looked like cod, though, were something he knew would satisfy him. The fish was accompanied by potatoes and two more of the delicious raisin scones. A small pot of tea rested on the tray, as well.

"I'll leave you to your supper," Mrs. Smith said and turned to go.

"No. Please, stay," he encouraged.

She hesitated a moment and then took a seat in the chair by the bed.

"Have you eaten already?" he asked.

"No. I'll do so after you. I wanted to be sure you were taken care of first."

"Would you care to share my meal? There's plenty here for the both of us."

She smiled. "I'd rather you eat it all so you

may return to vigorous health."

Reluctantly, he began eating. The batter on the fish was crunchy and yet the fish inside quite tender.

"You are an excellent cook, Mrs. Smith. This might be the best piece of fried fish I have ever eaten."

Her cheeks pinkened. It was so easy to cause a blush to rise on them. Andrew thought of things he wanted to do to her that would have her turning bright red. He would teach her not to be embarrassed by such things. Rather, she would learn to want them—and ask for them from him.

Caesar appeared, springing onto the bed in a smooth movement. He studied Andrew's plate and then turned away, circling three times and settling against his ankles near the foot of the bed.

"A cat who doesn't like fish?" he asked.

Mrs. Smith's rich, throaty chuckle caused a frisson of desire to run through him. "He prefers sardines and got some just before I brought in your tray."

"How long have you had Caesar?"

"Not long."

It seems she wasn't willing to give away much about herself, which frustrated him. Trying a new tactic, he asked, "How was your trip into Falmouth today?"

"The same as usual. I made many of my familiar stops. Mrs. Butler, who runs the largest shop in town, was in a mood to gossip."

He finished the first fillet off and asked, "What did today's gossip feature? A couple announcing their betrothal? A new baby? Someone who's bought a new boat or horse?"

"None of that. Today's only topic centered upon a missing duke."

Andrew stilled and then reached for his tea, not wanting her to know how her words affected him.

After sipping some, he asked, "So, who is this missing duke? And when did he go missing?"

She thought a moment. "Hmm. Mrs. Butler did mention his title. I'm afraid I can't recall it. I do remember that she said was he was from Somerset. Or maybe Devon. I can't recall. Anyway, he has an estate here which he was visiting. Morefield? Morewood? Something like that. And Mrs. Butler said that he's considered quite handsome."

He picked up a scone and bit into it to have something to do. "Why do they think he's gone missing?"

She chuckled. "I'm afraid I'm not one for gossip. I was also anxious to return here before you awakened. Let me think." She worried her lip and Andrew almost leaped from the bed, hot desire flooding him. "Mrs. Butler said something about his horse being found. Oh, and a brother he's quite close to has now arrived. He's despondent over His Grace's disappearance and wants the local authorities to be called in to aid in the search."

He'd been afraid of that. He didn't want to be found here. Especially not before he told Mrs. Smith who he really was. He needed time to woo her before she discovered his true identity. What angered him most was Francis pretending to be an upset, worried brother. Anger began rising within Andrew. He truly believed if his half-brother walked into the room that he could kill him with his bare hands.

"I hope this duke will be found," he said.

"I do, too. Especially because of his brother. If my sister went missing, I would be out of my mind with worry."

Finally, a piece of information revealed. "You have a sister?"

"Yes, a very pretty, very happily married one. Letty is her name, short for Leticia. She's going to have a baby come January. I am eager to become a doting aunt."

"Where does Letty live?"

Mrs. Smith licked her lips. "London."

"Is that where you are from?"

"No. I come from Somerset." Her tone shifted.

Still, he kept digging. "Will you go see your sister once the baby arrives?"

"Yes, I plan to go to her before the baby is

born. We are very close. I raised Letty. She was only three when our mother died. I was ten. It was left to me to see she had all she needed."

Andrew tamped down his anger. Poor Mrs. Smith had been given a huge amount of responsibility at a young age, being placed in charge of her sister.

"Did your father remarry?"

She shook her head. "No. He wasn't much interested in family. Especially since we were both girls."

"And what of Mr. Smith? Where did you meet him?"

She huffed. "What are all of these questions?"

"I'm merely curious about you and the home I'm staying in."

Mrs. Smith crossed her arms. "Don't you think if anyone should be asking questions, it should be me? For example, why did you leave the army? Isn't that hard for a soldier to do, especially during wartime? And why did you turn to smuggling? Is it really that profitable? Do you make frequent trips to France? And what of your family? Brothers? Sisters?"

Andrew didn't want to lie to her. "I never knew my mother. She died giving birth to me. My brother was killed in an accident. When my father heard the news, he suffered a heart attack. He lingered for a bit but I knew his heart wasn't interested in living anymore."

Tears filled her eyes. "Oh, Mr. Andrew. I am so sorry. I did not mean to pry."

Fortunately, he didn't think she would press him any further about his livelihood. He finished the scone.

"No one truly knows what another person has endured. It seems we've both had our fill of sorrow. You, even more."

"Why do you say that?"

"I have never been married but you have lost a husband."

The tears brimming in her azure eyes spilled onto her cheeks. It gutted him that she had loved her husband so. Selfishly, he wanted her all for himself.

Rising, she moved toward him and lifted the tray. "Get a good night's rest, Mr. Andrew."

Before he could speak, she had vacated the room.

Damnation. He'd wanted to comfort her. He sat berating himself. His curiosity to learn all he could about her had caused him to push her too hard. Mrs. Smith was a very private woman. He had to remember that she still thought him on the run from the law. She might have kissed him—but she certainly didn't trust him.

She'd left the door open. He could hear noises from the other room and recalled that she hadn't eaten. He waited, straining to hear what she might be doing. After an hour, he heard no more sounds. No sloshing of water or pans being scrubbed. He decided to call out to her.

"Mrs. Smith?" Thank goodness his voice already grew stronger.

Footsteps headed his way and she appeared at the doorway.

"Yes, Mr. Andrew?"

"It's about the bed," he began.

She came closer and said, "Don't worry. I will heat water for your bath tomorrow and also wash the sheets. I would have changed them before because I know they have been soaked with the sweat of your fever. Let's get to tomorrow and I will take care of it."

"No. You misunderstand me." He caught her hand and drew her closer to the bed. "I feel guilty because I have taken your bed since my arrival."

"You've been injured. Ill with fever. Where else would you sleep?" she asked, seemingly baffled by his question.

His eyebrows rose. "I am a former soldier, Madam. I will sleep on the floor."

She jerked her hands from his. "I won't allow it!" she proclaimed. "That is utterly ridiculous."

"Then where will you go tonight?" he asked softly.

"You are much better. You won't need me sleeping in the chair beside you. I shall move to the settee."

Andrew snorted. "That was barely large

enough for the both of us to sit upon. No, you must reclaim your bed. I insist."

"You may insist all you like, Mr. Andrew, but this is my cottage." She smiled. "Which means my rules. You are my guest."

"An uninvited one," he quickly added.

"True, but a guest all the same. You will keep the bed until you leave. Whenever that occurs."

Deciding to play on her sympathy, he pleaded, "But I will not get a good night's rest, knowing you're suffering. I have an idea. Why don't you join me?"

CHAPTER ELEVEN

PHOEBE SPUTTERED. "ARE you mad? That's preposterous!" Her hands fisted on her waist. "Just because I kissed you, you think I will now willingly fall into your bed? You may be as handsome as the Devil Himself, Mr. Andrew, but I am not that kind of woman."

Andrew hid his grin. So, she though him handsome?

"My dear Mrs. Smith, you have totally mis-understood me," he said smoothly. He raised his hands, palms up, trying to look as nonthreatening as possible. "I am not suggesting anything untoward occur between us. Lord knows you are beautiful enough to tempt me but, as you can tell, I am weaker than a newborn babe. Even if I wished to couple with you, I would be too exhausted to attempt to do so."

Fire still sparked in her eyes and he added, "I merely thought we could each try to get a good night's rest lying side-by-side in the only bed available. There are two pillows and plenty of room. I can sleep beneath the covers and you atop them. I just can't stand the thought of you cramped on that small settee."

She lowered her hands and folded them in front of her, her temper cooling. "I am sorry I jumped to conclusions, Mr. Andrew. Still, though it is very thoughtful of you to suggest it, I cannot accept lying in the same bed with you."

"Because I am a man—or because you believe I'm a smuggler?" he asked.

She gave him a rueful smile. "A little of both," she admitted. "It is kind of you to think of my health but you are the one who needs to regain his. That means sleeping in a bed."

Andrew shook his head. "That's not going to happen. I feel terrible that I've kicked you from your own bed. The remainder of my time at Falmouth Cottage, I shall sleep on the floor. I can make a pallet. I promise I'll be quite comfortable."

"Did you hear what I said? I refuse to let a guest sleep on my floor." She crossed her arms again, her mouth and posture definitely stubborn—and highly appealing.

He shrugged. "And I refuse to keep a female from her own bed." He crossed his arms over his chest, mimicking her. "It seems we have come to a standstill, Mrs. Smith."

She huffed. "Why are men so impossible?"

Grinning, he said, "Perhaps we like the attention we receive from women when we are?"

She bit back a smile but not before he saw it. Andrew hoped he had charmed her a bit.

"All right. Much to my dismay, I will share the bed." She raised a finger and shook it at him. "But there are to be no antics from you. You are to stick to your side of the bed and not even glance my way. Is that understood?"

"Oh, yes, Mrs. Smith. Thank you for agreeing to the unusual arrangement."

Andrew might not touch her—but she would be close enough for him to see. He'd smell the lavender on her skin and hair. Feel the heat of her body nearby.

It was a start.

"I have a few things to do," she said and abruptly left the room.

He heard noises but didn't care what she was doing. Soon, the appealing Mrs. Smith would be in his bed.

"Caesar!" she called.

The cat's ears perked up and he jumped from the bed. Andrew supposed Caesar would mean there would be three of them sharing space tonight. Several minutes later, the cat returned and curled up at the foot of the bed. Mrs. Smith appeared shortly afterward, wrapped in a dark dressing gown. He wondered what she wore underneath it.

She sat in the chair and began to remove the pins from her hair. Strands of it had already come loose. He doubted she'd attended to it the entire time he'd been there. He removed one pillow from behind him and placed it on her side of the bed. The other he lay flat behind him and then scooted down so he was prone, his head atop the pillow.

Mrs. Smith had finished unpinning her hair now and was working the braids loose. Once it was free, it hung to her waist. She reached for a brush which rested on the table and spent a good five minutes working the tangles from her hair. Then she plaited it into a single braid and stood. Making her way to the small wardrobe, she opened it and withdrew a blanket, then came to her side of the bed. She unfolded the blanket and as she lay down, still wearing her dressing gown, she shook it out. It fluttered in the air a moment and then fell to cover her.

Now, they lay side-by-side. Andrew was afraid to breathe, lest he scare her off.

"Could you please blow out the candle, Mr. Andrew?" she asked primly.

"I'd be happy to, Mrs. Smith."

He leaned up and did so. The room now was dark except for the faint moonlight that streamed through the open window. His eyes adjusted to the darkness. He kept his breathing even. He knew this was a test of her trust in him. Much as he would like to roll over and kiss her, he knew it would be the kiss of death and end any future he might have with her.

"Thank you for humoring me, Mrs. Smith," Andrew said softly.

"How so?" she asked, her voice low and still filled with a shade of doubt as to whether or not she had made the right decision by joining him.

Longing to reassure her, he said, "For agreeing to sleep in your own bed. I still feel guilty I have kept you from it as long as I have."

"You have had a far greater need of it than I, Mr. Andrew. Rest is important in your recovery."

"And that recovery never would have occurred without you, Mrs. Smith. You saved my life. I will forever be in your debt."

"I would have helped anyone in your position."

He grinned in the dark. "Yes, even someone whose morals don't quite align with your own."

He sensed that she stiffened. "If you are referring to your occupation, Sir, you know where I stand. On the side of the law. Still, it is not my place to judge you. Perhaps this experience will help you to turn over a new leaf."

"I do have my own code of morals, Mrs. Smith. I am grateful to you for rescuing me. Let me assure you again that I would never take advantage of any woman, much less the very woman who saved my life. I hope you get a good night's rest, Mrs. Smith. Pleasant dreams."

For a moment, only silence filled the air. Then she said, "I hope you, too, will get a good deal of rest. Goodnight, Mr. Andrew."

Andrew closed his eyes and enjoyed the fact that she was next to him. The bed wasn't as large as he'd made it out to be. He was two inches over six feet and broad through the shoulders. In fact, their shoulders almost touched. She must have been aware of that because she shifted, rolling onto her left side so that her back was to him. It didn't matter. This was a tiny step of progress in what he thought would be a most unusual courtship.

He listened to her breathing and knew the minute she fell asleep. Her breath softened. Her body relaxed. Though he longed to reach out and touch her, he forced his hands to remain by his sides. He'd made headway today with Mrs. Smith. He'd kissed her. Thoroughly. He'd learned that she had a sister in London. That his angel was from Somerset and would be joining her sister during her confinement. That she looked forward to becoming an aunt. It was a shame that she didn't have children of her own. She certainly had a nurturing nature. Andrew would see to it that they had a child soon. Not that he was eager for an heir but he thought it would please her if they did.

Finally, he slept.

When he awoke, Mrs. Smith was curled up next to him, much as Caesar was on his far side. She must have rolled his way during the night. Her head was pillowed just below his bandages, her cheek resting against his heart. An arm was tossed across his bare waist and the bedclothes were perilously below that. One leg was bent, its knee resting atop his leg.

It was the way Andrew hoped to wake up every day. With his duchess warming him and his bed.

He lay perfectly still, hoping that his hammering heart wouldn't rouse her. He wanted to enjoy the feel of her against him. The soft, even breath that tickled his chest. The curve of her leg pinning his. Everything about this delightful woman appealed to him. Andrew longed to kiss her awake but continued to lie unmoving. His arm must have been around her for a long time because it was numb. She must have gravitated to his body warmth because the room was chilled this early in the morning. How he wished he could rise and close the window and then come back to bed and make sweet love to her.

She began to stir and he slowed his breathing, trying to make his racing heart behave. If she knew he was awake, she would be as mad as a wet hen at him—even though she was the one who clung to him in sleep. Andrew turned his head to the right, not wanting to be more aware of her movements than he already was.

A soft sigh spilled from her lips. It was maddening having her so close. He must be made of truly stern stuff to exhibit this much control. His patience would be rewarded.

When he made her his duchess.

PHOEBE SIGHED AND stretched. Immediately, she froze. Her eyes popped open.

Oh, no. She was lying snug against Mr. Andrew. She listened and heard his breathing. Felt the rise of his chest. Heard his heartbeat against her ear.

Her body had betrayed her in sleep. It had sought him, wanting him after that amazing kiss. She glanced down and saw her arm against his bare skin. He radiated an enormous amount of heat, which is why she must have turned to him. The bedchamber was chilly. She should have closed the window last night with the nights becoming cooler.

She should also move. Now. Yet something compelled her to remain in place. When would she have a chance like this again to be so close to such a wickedly handsome man? Even when she returned to society and made known her wishes to wed again, she was certain her husband would be similar to Borwick. He would be a man of the *ton*, one who only cared for his own needs and never gave a thought to his wife. He would come to her bed for brief visits and be gone, no lingering such as this.

Phoebe wondered what it would be like having Mr. Andrew make love to her. Instinct told her that he would take care of her in a way most men wouldn't. She loved the feeling of being close to him. It made her realize she hadn't felt safe since her mother had passed away over fifteen years ago. She used to love to climb into her lap and have her mother read to her. That spot felt like the safest, most wonderful spot in the world.

Until now. Being next to Mr. Andrew made Phoebe believe nothing wrong could ever happen to her. That was utterly insane. She barely knew anything about him, other than he broke the law for his living and someone had wanted him dead.

No, that wasn't true. He was well-spoken. Polite. Intelligent. And he loved to tease her. Half the time, she thought he said something outrageous just to see her blush.

He also was the most handsome man she'd ever come across, and that included all the many gentlemen she had encountered in London's ballrooms. It would be a bit of a disappointment once she did return to Polite Society because her heart told her no one would live up to Mr. Andrew.

Especially when it came to kissing.

She couldn't lie abed all day, though. They both needed to eat and she'd promised him a bath. She wanted one, as well, and that would take a long time to prepare. The sheets on the bed also needed changing. Only the one set had come with the cottage so she really needed to get them washed first and hung to dry so they could be put back on later today.

Slowly, she removed her arm and leg, rolling away from the delicious warmth and onto the floor. The blanket she'd covered herself with lay on the ground and she picked it up and began to fold it—when her eyes returned to the bed.

Good God in His Heaven . . .

The bedclothes rode low on the smuggler's hips, so low that if he moved an inch she would see more than she was intended to. Caesar stood and arched his back, moving the covers a tad. Phoebe forced herself to look away. She finished folding the blanket and set it on top of her trunk and then came around and lifted the covers by their edge, drawing them up over his perfect form. God had certainly done a wonderful job creating this man. He was all hard planes and muscles and total perfection.

She motioned to Caesar, who sprang from the bed and landed silently on the floor. Once he strolled from the room, she eased the door closed behind her and set about making them breakfast. She scrambled some eggs and fried bacon along with it, cutting a few slices of bread from one of the loaves she'd purchased and gathered a pot of jam.

"That certainly looks good."

Phoebe glanced up and saw Mr. Andrew coming toward her. He wore his breeches again without his shirt. She made a mental note to make sure she repaired the hole in it today. She'd already washed out as much of the blood as she could. She couldn't have him walking around half-dressed any longer. It made her insides do strange things.

"Should you be up?" she asked.

"The answer is a definite yes." He sat at the table. "I've lain in bed long enough. It's time I start using my limbs again. I'll never regain my strength if I don't."

"As long as you rest in-between those times, I think you are right."

She removed his plate from the tray and set it on the table in front of him. He began spreading jam across the bread. Returning to the skillet, she spooned the remainder of the eggs and the single piece of bacon onto another plate and joined him.

"You need another cup and saucer," he said. "For your tea."

Phoebe retrieved that and he poured out the

tea for her.

"Thank you. I don't ever recall a man pouring tea for me."

He looked about. "I don't see any honey."

"Oh, let me fetch some." She got the pot and set it on the table. "Use a nice amount. It will do you good."

He spooned some into his cup and stirred it.

They ate in companionable silence. She thought how easy it was between them. Though Borwick had been polite, he had always remained distant with her. After a handful of days, she felt more comfortable in Mr. Andrew's company than she had with her husband of several years.

"May I help you wash these?" he asked once they were done eating.

"No. You may continue sitting up, though. It will do you some good. I've work to see to. I must wash the sheets first and then will see to your bath."

Phoebe busied herself, making several trips to the well and heating water. She stripped the bed and scrubbed the sheets. Ever since she'd rented the cottage, she hadn't minded hard labor but she hated what it did to her hands. The lye she used caused them to grow red and rough. She would have to use some of Letty's lotions once she left Cornwall and hope her hands would lose their calluses in time. If not, she could always hide them with her gloves, which she would wear to

ALEXA ASTON

every social occasion.

After the sheets were hanging in the sun, she began drawing more water from the well for Mr. Andrew's bath. It was then she heard the hoofbeat of horses coming. Fear caught in her throat, tightening it.

Would they be looking for him? Would it be the law—or the man who tried to murder him?

She continued pulling on the rope as three men rode into the clearing in front of the cottage. She glanced at the door and saw it was still open. Phoebe only hoped Mr. Andrew would stay out of sight.

The bucket reached the top and she lifted it and placed it on the ground before facing her company.

"Good morning, gentlemen. How may I help you?"

She noticed they were all well-dressed and rode mounts that were sturdy.

"Be you Mrs. Smith?" the oldest of the three asked as he dismounted. The others did the same.

"I am. And you are, Sir?"

"I'm happy to introduce myself to you. I am Sir William Rankin, magistrate for this area. I was told that you are a widow and renting Falmouth Cottage."

At least it was no one searching for Mr. Andrew. These men had to be here about the duke who'd vanished. Still, she hoped her guest would keep out of sight. As Mrs. Smith, she still had a reputation to maintain. A man spotted in her cottage, especially one half-dressed, wouldn't do.

"Yes, Sir William. I have a six-month lease and will leave at that time and return to my sister. She is expecting her first child and I want to be present for that event." Phoebe hoped her voice was steady as she asked, "Might you be here looking for the missing duke?"

His eyes lit with surprise. "You've heard of the situation?"

She chuckled. "Anyone who has been in Mrs. Butler's presence will have heard the tale, Sir William."

"Oh, yes. I see. Mrs. Butler has . . . spread the word, so to say. Have you by chance seen His Grace?"

"Not at all, my lord. You can tell I'm a bit isolated here. I like it that way. No misplaced dukes have wandered into my cottage. Have you been searching long?"

"For two days now. His Grace's brother is worried sick about this disappearance. He fears highwaymen may have taken the duke. If so, it would be to ransom His Grace, no doubt. No note has been forthcoming, though. Mr. Graham has sent all the way to London for Bow Street Runners to aid in our search."

"I'm sorry to hear His Grace is missing. I do wish you luck in finding him. He and his family will be in my prayers."

"Thank you, Mrs. Smith. And if you see anything noteworthy?"

"I'll be sure to speak up, Sir William."

"Good day."

The other two men, who'd never said a word, nodded politely at her. All three men mounted their horses and rode off. Phoebe finished filling the last bucket of water. She said a prayer for the missing man and entered the cottage.

Mr. Andrew stood just behind the door. "They're gone?" he asked, concern on his face.

Phoebe knew he must have been worried that the men were there for him. It still amazed her that she had a fierce need to protect this outlaw.

"Yes. Please, have a seat."

Instead, he took the buckets from her hands and took them to the stove, pouring them into the large pots on top. He shouldn't be doing anything so physical yet but she sensed he was becoming restless so she didn't say a word. She did retrieve the other two buckets and poured one of them into the wooden tub.

"Once the water has heated, you can bathe. Try to keep your bandage from getting wet, though, because I'd like to leave it on one more day before changing it."

"I may need your help, Mrs. Smith. My

shoulder is still stiff and somewhat immobile. You've secured it well. Tomorrow, when you change the bandages, I think I can fashion a sling to support it."

"All right. When I washed the bedclothes, I also cleaned the strips of linen I used the first time. You may use some of them to make this sling."

She washed the breakfast dishes as she waited for the water to simmer and had just finished drying the last plate when she noticed the water was almost ready.

"Let me get you a bath sheet, Mr. Andrew."

Phoebe went to the bedchamber and withdrew one from the wardrobe, placing it on the bed. She turned and found him right behind her.

"You may use this. I'll need to wash your breeches. I've already done so with your shirt and stockings though I need to sew closed the hole the bullet caused. I'll go prepare your bath now."

She closed the door firmly behind her, fighting the images of a naked Mr. Andrew from coming to mind as she poured the steaming water into the bath and swirled her hand around to mix it with the cool water already there. By then, he emerged, the towel slung low on his hips. He carried his pants and handed them to her.

"I'll wash them in the tub once you finish with your bath. I'll go fetch more water to heat in case you need more."

Two more trips later, Phoebe was wearing down from all the morning's physical activity. Mr. Andrew was in the tub, scrubbing himself. She avoided looking anywhere near him as she bustled about.

"I seem to be doing fine, Mrs. Smith, but I would like to have your help washing my hair."

"Oh, of course. I'd be happy to do so."

She set a large pan behind the tub, wishing she'd thought to move the tub outside. It was too late now. She sat to rest for a few minutes until he turned toward her.

"Can you help me now?"

"Certainly."

Phoebe had him lean back as she poured fresh water over his dark brown hair. It was thick and slightly wavy. She took the soap and worked up a good lather, running her fingers through his hair and massaging his scalp. He let out a little noise of pleasure and she smiled, remembering how Nathan used to do the same. Tears misted her eyes. She missed her little boy so much. And the child she'd lost. She had to hold fast to the idea of one day having others.

"I think that's good. I'll rinse it now."

"You have magic fingers, Mrs. Smith."

"That is a lovely compliment, Mr. Andrew."

After Phoebe finished rinsing his hair, she reached for the bath sheet he'd draped across a chair.

"Here you go. It might do you some good to sit in the sunshine for a few minutes."

"Would you sit with me?" he asked softly.

She had far too much to do but the thought of resting next to him was hard to pass up.

"I will for a while. I will meet you outside."

Two chairs sat just outside the door to the cottage and she sat in one of them. She could hear him stand, the water splashing, and thought of him drying that magnificently muscled body of his. Her throat went dry. Then he appeared in the doorway, the sun streaming down on him, like a Greek god chiseled into human flesh. Her breath caught as her eyes roamed his torso and then she quickly turned away as he took the seat next to her. She stared out across the clearing.

He took her hand again, his fingers threading through hers. Phoebe didn't protest. She couldn't. It felt too right. Besides, it brought him comfort.

She wasn't about to admit what it brought her.

"I know how hard you have worked on my behalf," he said, his voice low and rough. "I feel especially close to you. Might I . . . might we call one another by our first names?"

She faced him. "I can agree to that. I am Phoebe."

A beautiful smile touched his mouth. Unlike so many in Polite Society, his smile reached his eyes. She stared into them, losing herself for a moment in their deep warmth.

"And I am Andrew. Not Mr. Andrew. Just Andrew."

CHAPTER TWELVE

I T HAD BEEN the best two weeks of Andrew's life.

Even if he'd had to be shot to experience them.

As the days passed and his strength grew, he and Phoebe had come to know quite a bit about each other. They still danced around specific details but he believed they were meant to be, despite their class difference. He knew she enjoyed strawberries and walking in the rain. That her father couldn't abide pets in the house and her husband had been allergic to them, so Caesar was her first pet. He knew she had a quick wit and a strong grasp on current issues of the day, which had surprised him to no end.

He'd also learned she was a talented artist. As he'd moved about the small cottage, he'd come across drawings she'd done resting atop the desk. When asked about them, Phoebe said she enjoyed making up children's stories and illustrating them. He had her tell him a few and found them delightful. She had been working on a story of two fish in the sea, Freddie the Flounder and Walter the Whale, who became close friends. Both her tales and drawings had the right touch of whimsy and he thought them worthy of publication. She admitted she had thought of trying to see them published and Andrew encouraged her to pursue the matter.

With each passing day, he began moving about more, helping her with household chores. They began walking to the beach and along the shoreline, each day going a bit further. She always allowed him to take her hand. He supposed she told herself that it was to make sure he didn't lose his balance and hurt himself. Still, walking hand in hand with Phoebe Smith was the highlight of his day.

Andrew now felt physically fit and had abandoned the sling this morning. His shoulder was still stiff but he believed there were no lasting ill effects from the bullet wound he'd suffered. His mind told him it was time for him to confront Francis yet his heart wanted to avoid going home and stay with Phoebe in the cottage that had become more a home to him than anywhere he'd ever lived.

He determined that during their afternoon walk along the beach today that he would tell her who he was—and ask her to marry him. It would certainly be a shock but he sensed her trust in him. If Andrew the smuggler had won her over, surely Andrew the duke could keep her.

Restless, he paced the small cottage while waiting for her to return. She'd walked into Falmouth again for fresh supplies and planned to post a package of her stories and drawings to someone associated with her husband. She'd confided how nervous she was to do this but Andrew had encouraged her, telling her how talented she was. He could imagine them both going to the nursery one day, one of her books in hand, and reading it to their child. It should seem odd that he was so willing to settle into such a domestic life after his years at war and then time spent in the glittering ballrooms of London.

Andrew knew his own mind, though. Phoebe Smith was the one for him.

He followed Caesar out the door. The cat strolled across the open space and settled in a patch of grass, the sun shining on his glossy coat. Having never been around a cat before, it surprised him how much he'd taken to the tabby. When they left Falmouth Cottage, Caesar was certain to accompany them.

Glancing in the distance, he saw Phoebe coming, pushing her small cart. Eagerly, he went to meet her and took over, bringing the cart back to the cottage. Once there, he unloaded its contents as she put the items away.

"Are you hungry?" she asked.

For you.

"I could certainly stand to eat," he replied. "Shall I put on the tea?"

They prepared a simple meal together, sandwiches on fresh rolls from the bakery, slices from a small round of cheese, and sliced pears. Thinking how happy he'd been here, getting to know her, Andrew decided to purchase Falmouth Cottage. Perhaps once a year, during the summer, they could return and spend a few weeks. Just the two of them.

"How was your trip into the village? What did the gossiping Mrs. Butler have to say?" he asked.

She chuckled. "Full of news, as usual. More on the missing duke with whom she is endlessly fascinated with."

"Oh, really?"

"Yes. A body washed up on shore, found by none other than His Grace's brother."

His gut tightened. "Go on."

"I feel terribly sorry for this brother. To be so close to a beloved sibling and then to lose him— and then to be the one to discover the body." She shuddered.

"Where was it found?"

"Not far from where they found His Grace's horse. The body had been in the water some time. From what Mrs. Butler implied, it was rather bloated. Still, Mr. Graham, I believe that's his name, was able to identify the duke from a scar on his back. Something that remained from a childhood accident, Mrs. Butler surmised."

Rage rippled through Andrew. A so-called body being produced and identified by Francis meant a dead Duke of Windham.

And his title passing to his nearest relation. Francis.

Andrew would have to reappear sooner than later. It was a good thing he'd decided to tell Phoebe who he was today. It would allow him to return to Moreland Hall and confront his half-brother. He wondered if he should summon the magistrate first. If there was a body, then Francis had most likely murdered some poor fellow in order to claim he was Andrew. It appalled him how vile Francis was. He also hated that Phoebe would be mixed up in the affair. Perhaps he would tell her who he was and explain what had to be done, confronting Francis and seeing him handed over to the authorities.

Then once things calmed down, he could introduce her as his fiancée and they could wed.

"Are you going to nap?" Phoebe asked.

"No. I'd like to stroll on the beach."

"Let me get my bonnet."

They set out, the September day cool but the sun plentiful. Andrew was grateful the cottage and surrounding beach was as isolated as it was because they had yet to see anyone along the stretch of the beach they walked. Because of that, he sought her hand and threaded his fingers through hers, amazed at how right the simple gesture seemed. He would want to hold this woman's hand half a century from now, happy to look back at the decades they had spent together.

They reached the beach and stopped for several minutes, watching the waves roll in and out. Andrew gave thanks to a God that had allowed him to live. To wash up on this shore and be found by this woman. Francis had no idea that his attempt at murder would lead to Andrew finding a wife.

Slowly, they made their way to a grouping of rocks where they stopped every day and removed their boots and stockings. Usually, they did for themselves but as Phoebe sat today, Andrew knelt before her.

"Allow me," he said, propping her foot against his thigh.

She hitched her gown up slightly and he unlaced and then slipped off her boot. One hand held firm to her ankle as he set the boot aside. Her eyes were as round as saucers as she gazed at him. Andrew smiled and slipped his fingers under the hem of her gown, unfastening her stockings and rolling them down. He knew she held her breath because he did the same, their gazes focused on one another. Her tongue darted out and licked her lips nervously.

He planned to lick them soon.

Removing her other boot and stocking, he rose and reached out his hands. She took them and he pulled her to her feet. They stared at one another a long moment. He saw desire in her eyes and knew they would be fortunate to always keep the blaze lit between them.

It was time to test the waters. Slowly, Andrew lowered his mouth to hers for a sweet, tender kiss. Her soft lips were the perfect match to his. Instead of pressing forward, he broke the kiss and merely smiled, releasing her hands and sitting on the rock.

"Let me help you," Phoebe said, bending to pull his boots off, giving him a nice view of her cleavage.

She rested both boots next to one another and then pulled his stockings down. The feel of her fingers against his calves heated his blood. He told himself to be patient. It had worked so far. He didn't want to frighten her off.

Folding each stocking, she placed them atop his boots and rose. He did the same and took her hand in his. Together, they strolled silently down the beach. When they reached a pair of seagulls diving into the water, they paused. Phoebe delighted in seeing seagulls hunting for food or playing together. She'd revealed she could watch them for hours.

The gulls got lucky and recovered several fish, swallowing them whole, and then they rose through the air and flew out across the water.

"They mate for life," she said. "So do wolves. Beavers. Swans."

"I didn't know that."

She shrugged. "Sometimes, I retain the oddest of facts."

He released her hand and slipped his arms about her waist. "It's one of the things that makes you so interesting."

"Me?" Color rose on her cheeks. "I don't believe I am interesting at all."

"You are to me, Phoebe," he said huskily and lowered his mouth to hers.

His kiss was gentle, once again not wanting to startle her. Giving her time to pull away and tell him no if that's what she wished. Instead, her hands touched his chest. Slid up it. Gripped his shoulders.

And her lips parted.

Andrew needed no further invitation. He slipped his tongue inside her mouth, tasting her sweetness—and goodness. His friends would have laughed about that but Phoebe did taste both sweet and good. Better than any woman ever had. She was good for him. He wanted to be the same for her.

He pulled her to him, his arms imprisoning

her. She had answered his call. Made her decision. There would be no going back. She was to be his.

His hands roamed her back and slipped to her buttocks, cupping them. She gasped into his mouth but didn't protest. He squeezed and kneaded them, thinking of the time he could do so with no clothing in the way. His hands moved back up her back, one arm going about her waist, securing her to him, as his other hand found the long, single braid and tugged on it, tilting her head back so that he could deepen their kiss.

Andrew didn't know how long they stood on the beach kissing. It didn't matter. Time was now theirs to make of it as they chose. If he wanted to spend hours each day kissing her, that's what he'd do. Of course, there were other things he wanted to do with her but he would wait until they were wed. Widowed or not, Phoebe had a sense of propriety about her and he wouldn't ask more than she was willing to give.

She broke the kiss, her palms coming to his cheeks, cradling his face.

"I want you, Andrew. All of you. Not just your kisses. I need you inside me."

Her words shocked—then delighted—him. "Are you certain, Phoebe?"

"More than I have been about anything in my life," she told him.

"You would have us make love," he said, wanting to be certain there was no misunderstanding between them.

She grinned. "Was I not clear, Andrew? I thought I was speaking the King's English though he might be uncomfortable hearing what I am saying." She gazed into his eyes. "I want to know everything about you. I want to discover things I've never known. With you. I have a knot of need gnarled inside me and only you can untangle it."

"Oh, Phoebe, darling."

He seized her mouth again, his kiss urgent and fevered. The hunger he felt for her was returned. Joy filled him. He kissed her until they both were breathless and then he swept her into his arms and began carrying her back the way they'd come.

"Andrew! Put me down. Your shoulder. You'll injure it again."

"My shoulder is fine. I am fine." He kissed her. "I will be even better once I've made sweet love to you."

He didn't bother stopping at their boots and stockings and went straight to the cottage instead. He'd thought to tell her who he was and then offer for her—but this was even better. She wanted him as a man. As Andrew. She would make love with Andrew. Learning he was the Duke of Windham would be an afterthought.

Reaching the cottage, he bent and she turned the latch, nudging the door open with her foot.

He closed it behind them and carried her to the bed, placing her on it.

"I am going to love you thoroughly, Phoebe Smith. Be prepared. It will take the rest of the afternoon and most of the night."

CHAPTER THIRTEEN

PHOEBE GAZED UP at the man who had slipped into her heart and become her world. She hadn't known him a month ago yet now he was everything to her. She had always been her mother's good girl and later aimed to be a good example to her sister. Even though Borwick wasn't her choice of a husband, she'd tried to be a good wife to him and an excellent mother to Nathan.

Now, though, in this moment, she wanted to be wicked. Very, very wicked with this sinfully handsome man. She had lived for others her entire life. For one afternoon—or into the evening—she was going to think only of herself.

In her heart, Phoebe knew she could never be anything to this man. He lived life on the edge as a smuggler. Someone who broke the law for profit. Once he healed—and she believed he had enough that he would be leaving soon—she couldn't go with him and he certainly wouldn't think to take her. That was why she had decided today was the day she would give herself to him because he might be gone tomorrow. When he'd kissed her so tenderly on the beach, she'd known she owed it to herself to have one glorious session of making love with this man. He would return to his life and she would to hers.

But she'd always carry the memory of what they did in this bed together.

He reached up to pull his shirt over his head and winced. She immediately came to her knees and caught his wrists, lowering them. Then she captured the edge of the garment and began lifting it over his head. Once he was freed from it, he took it from her and tossed it aside. She gazed upon his bare chest, one she'd gotten to know quite well. The beauty of it never ceased to amaze her. Except now, she could touch it all she wanted.

Phoebe ran her hands over it, feeling the hard muscles and the flat belly, grazing the soft hair that tapered downward and disappeared into his breeches. She slid her fingers up again to his nipples and circled them with her fingertips before tracing them with the pad of one finger. Andrew sucked in a breath and caught her wrists.

"I can't let you have all the fun," he said, his eyes darkening with desire.

His hands went to her waist and he lifted her

from the bed. With deliberation, he began to undress her, taking so much time with the first layer that she wanted to help him. He must have seen the frustration in her eyes.

"No. We will do this my way. Slowly. I want the desire to build within you until you are ready to scream it aloud."

She couldn't imagine screaming at all. When Borwick had come to her, her night rail had remained on. He'd merely raised it and jabbed his cock into her. It had always hurt but she'd bitten back her cries. No desire ever flickered through her as they coupled. The only time she'd felt it was when Andrew kissed her.

He did so now with each layer he peeled away. His kisses grew longer and wetter and more heated until, finally, she stood before him with nothing on. The old Phoebe would have been embarrassed and tried to cover herself. The Phoebe she'd become with him stood proudly before him, waiting to see what his next move would be.

It didn't take long to find out.

He pulled her to him, her body soft against his hard one. He devoured her mouth with a hunger that spiraled into flames within her. His lips went lower, nipping her throat and then reaching the swell of her breast. His tongue lazily outlined it and then moved to her nipple, teasing it. The throbbing she'd experienced before between her legs pounded heavily as his teeth grazed her nipple. Then he was sucking on her, pulling her into his mouth. Her arms went about his head, holding him close to her breast, not wanting him to stop. He feasted on it and then did the same with the other. She heard herself sighing, moaning, groaning in pleasure.

Andrew finally lifted his head. "You are so beautiful," he exclaimed in wonder. His hands slid from her breasts to her waist and traced the curve of her hips. "There's so much to discover about you."

In reply, she kissed his throat and let her lips trail lower to his nipple. She imitated what he had done to her, feeling brave and strong as she heard the sounds of pleasure coming from him. Suddenly, they fell against the mattress and his mouth sought hers once more. As they kissed, his hand danced along her belly and went lower. She stiffened.

"It's all right, love," he assured her. "I won't hurt you."

Phoebe saw sincerity in his eyes and knew she could trust him.

He kissed her again and his fingers teased her curls. Then his hand cupped her pounding mound and she cried out.

Andrew chuckled. "Oh, you are a delight, Phoebe. My delight."

He hovered above her as one finger trailed

up and down her sex. She swallowed. Whimpered. Melted. He pushed it inside her and she gasped in pleasure.

"You are so wet for me, my love. So very ready. But I want to pleasure you first."

She smiled. She had known he would think of her. What he did to her after that was indescribable. He toyed with her over and over, bringing her to some precipice and then backing away. The throbbing consumed her. Need bubbled within her. He kissed her until they both were breathless and then he broke the kiss.

"I want to watch you come, Phoebe. I want to see your eyes."

She looked at him blankly.

"You have no idea, do you, dearest?"

"No," she said hoarsely.

He smiled, his satisfaction evident. "Come with me."

His fingers began caressing her again and it was as if a dam was about to burst within her. As he stroked her, tension built and built and built and then spilled over. Glorious waves of pleasure flooded her and she kept saying *yes* over and over. Her hips bucked and light poured from her. All the while, Andrew looked down upon her and she couldn't look away.

Her body finally stilled and he moved from the bed. She would have cried out but she had no voice. No strength. She watched him shed his breeches, his manhood springing from them, and then he came back to her.

His hand brushed her hair from her brow. "I will always remember this moment, Phoebe. When we came together as one."

With that, he pushed into her. For a moment, she tensed, waiting for the usual pain to come. When it didn't, she relaxed.

"We are meant to be," Andrew murmured into her ear, kissing her neck as he thrust into her.

Phoebe found herself wanting to meet each thrust and did. Her arms went around his waist and she rose each time he entered her, wanting to be as close to him as possible. It became like a dance in which they were perfect partners. Then the same feeling from before built within her and she did scream as he'd said she would. She cried out his name and he did the same, calling hers over and over as they collided and shuddered and then fell to the bed.

Immediately, he rolled to his side, still inside her. His forehead touched hers.

"That was ... incredible," she managed to get out.

Andrew's arms tightened about her. "Yes. It was." He pushed her head to his shoulder. "I need that nap now, Mrs. Smith. And you're just the one to take it with me."

He wouldn't get any protests from her. Phoebe snuggled close and shut her eyes, overwhelmed by what had just happened between them.

She awoke to him kissing her neck, not knowing how much time had passed.

"I was too hurried the first time," he told her. "This will be different."

It was. By the time he finished, she didn't think he'd missed kissing any part of her. He'd explored every curve with his hands, mouth, and tongue. Even a place where she never would have expected him to seek out. He told her she tasted the sweetest of all in that spot and laughed as she felt herself turn bright red.

"Never be shy or embarrassed," Andrew said. "You were meant to be loved this way."

They slept again and he made love to her a third time in the dark since night had fallen. They lay exhausted, their limbs entwined.

"You have worn me out, Phoebe."

She stroked his cheek. "I could say the same but, then again, I haven't been shot recently. I know you are tired. Let me get us something to eat."

"No. That would mean I have to let you go."

"I promise to return."

His stomach growled. "All right then. But hurry else I'll come looking for you."

She slipped from the bed, not bothering to put on her dressing gown. She didn't want to take time to make tea so after she sliced bread and cheese and a couple of apples, she took the bottle of brandy and placed it on the tray with the food.

Andrew had the pillows propped up by then and she climbed into bed with him. They dined on what she'd brought, feeding one another and taking sips of brandy between kissing.

It had been perfect. He was perfect. She could let him go now for she would always hold a piece of him in her heart.

PHOEBE AWOKE TO hot kisses pressed against her belly. Rays of sunshine streamed in the window so she knew it was morning. Andrew made love to her tenderly. She felt treasured.

He told her to remain in bed while he prepared breakfast for them. Since he'd become quite helpful, she allowed him to wait on her. She heard him banging about in the other room as she stroked Caesar.

He returned with slices of ham and toasted bread coated in honey. Soft-boiled eggs and tea.

"If you ever decide to leave smuggling behind, you might work in a great house in the kitchen," she teased.

He frowned and she knew it was because she brought up his illegal activities.

"Phoebe, I need to tell you—"

"I'm sorry," she interrupted him. "We've been good about drawing the lines between what we should and should not speak of. I crossed it. I won't do it again."

She placed the last bite of bread into her mouth. "I also know you will be leaving soon."

Andrew nodded. "Yes. I will."

Taking his hand, she brought it to her lips and kissed his knuckles. "Thank you for giving me the gift of yesterday. You have made me feel different about myself ever since you have been here. I am glad I got to know you, Andrew."

He leaned over and kissed her. She could taste the honey and salted ham on his tongue. She would focus on the here and now and not the fact his departure was imminent.

"I have something to do," he said mysteriously.

"What?"

"It's a surprise. Once I've completed it, I'll return for you. We'll take a walk along the beach." He gazed into her eyes. "And then I will have to go."

Phoebe nodded. He got up from the bed and took the tray back into the other room. She padded naked behind him and wrapped her arms around his waist from behind him.

"I'll wash up after you're gone. Go and do what you must."

He turned and kissed her and then returned

to the bedchamber. She followed him and they both dressed in silence. She noticed he remained barefoot and recalled they'd left their shoes and stockings near the water yesterday. She waited until he left and then made the bed.

So, today he would leave. Rationally, she'd known this time was coming. After making love with him, though, it would be hard to let him go. Still, he had a life she knew nothing about, just as he had no idea she was Phoebe Smythe, Dowager Countess of Borwick. They would never cross paths again.

Only in her dreams.

She went into the other room and fed Caesar as she washed their dishes. When he finished eating, the cat rubbed her legs a few times and then walked to the door. She let him out and heard a loud, rumbling noise. It sounded like a carriage. Phoebe watched and then saw she was right. As it pulled up into the clearing, she recognized the driver and waved. She wondered what Ernest would be doing here. Perhaps Letty had some packages that she wanted to send to Phoebe and hadn't trusted they would be delivered properly. It would be just like her sister to have their coachman come all this way.

He climbed down and hurried to her. "My lady, you must come at once. It's Lady Burton."

Alarm filled her. "What is wrong with my sister?" she demanded.

"It's both the viscountess and the baby," Ernest said.

"Has she lost it?" she asked, her voice breaking.

"No, not yet, but Lord Burton fears for her health. She's come down with a monstrous fever and is delirious. There's been some . . . spotting." The driver reddened at mentioning that. "The doctor is terribly worried about her. Lord Burton said I must fetch you. That Lady Burton needs you. He believes you are the key to making her whole again."

"Of course. Give me a few minutes to pack, Ernest."

Phoebe raced into the cottage and went straight to her trunk. She opened it and then the wardrobe, removing the dresses there and folding them quickly, placing them inside the trunk. Closing it, she summoned the driver so he could take it to the carriage.

"I won't have time to speak to the rental agent who leased the cottage to me. Let me leave her a note," she explained and hurried back inside.

Instead, she dashed off a quick letter to Andrew. She hated leaving without seeing him but he already had plans to head out today. Perhaps it was best that there would be no tender goodbyes between them. In fact, Phoebe would probably have sobbed through their parting. This way, the break would be clean and she wouldn't make a fool of herself, blubbering over him.

Finishing the note, she folded it and scrawled his name boldly across the front. She placed it on the table in front of the settee. Propping it up, he would see it immediately when he entered the cottage.

Without wasting any further time, she hurried outside. Ernest handed her up and returned to his seat. As they pulled away, Phoebe touched her fingers to her lips and then held them up as they passed the cottage. Then she settled against the cushions and wept.

CHAPTER FOURTEEN

ANDREW MADE HIS way to the beach, smiling as he passed their boots and stockings from yesterday. It had been less than a day since he'd removed them from Phoebe. In that time, he'd touched her in every place imaginable. They had made passionate love several times and he knew a bright future was in store for them. He couldn't wait to have her meet Aunt Helen. He knew his aunt would approve of the match, as would his friends when he introduced Phoebe to them. Sebastian would be the only one that wouldn't meet her before the wedding since he was still away at war.

As he walked along the shoreline, he continually knelt to retrieve shells. Since this beach had played an instrumental part in bringing them together, he'd had the idea to propose to Phoebe here. It was important to him that it be a grand, romantic gesture. From her reaction yesterday when he'd started to enter her, he knew that sex had been just that between her and her husband. Nothing sweet or tender or meaningful. Andrew wanted Phoebe to know she was loved.

He came to an abrupt halt.

Love?

Then he grinned. Yes, that was what he felt in his heart. Love for his angel of mercy. Though he hadn't realized it—and certainly hadn't uttered the words to her—his heart told him he did love her. Realizing it, a lightness of spirit overwhelmed him. Yes, there would be a few dark days ahead as he dealt with Francis but he would always have Phoebe to come home to. She was his home. His life.

It took him more than an hour to gather enough shells for what he had in mind. Since he loved her, that had to be part of the message. Painstakingly, Andrew spelled out *Will you marry me?* and surrounded the words with a heart. He stepped back, proud of his work, hoping she would be delighted when she saw the question. It would surprise her but he believed she already knew in her heart as he did that they belonged together and deserved to spend a lifetime side-by-side.

He returned to where their boots and stockings lay and sat a moment, winded from all of his work. He was still weaker than he should be but he couldn't delay any longer. It was important to stop the farce of a funeral before it took place and have Francis taken into custody. No longer did Andrew feel the need to beat his half-brother to a bloody pulp. He merely needed him taken away to prison. Better things lay ahead for Andrew.

His life with Phoebe.

Gathering their items, he made his way back to Falmouth Cottage. He had overheard her tell the magistrate that she'd rented the cottage for six months. He wondered when she had arrived in Cornwall and why she'd chosen this spot to put down roots for a short while. It didn't matter. Soon, she would the Duchess of Windham and have numerous places to call home. Of course, when her sister's time drew near, Andrew would accompany Phoebe to London so she could be with Letty. He sensed the close bond between the women and knew his darling had served as a mother to her sister. As long as he could accompany Phoebe, he didn't mind being in London.

Andrew arrived at the cottage and saw Caesar pacing in front of the house. The cat was a creature who enjoyed the sun and today was overcast and cool.

"Are you locked out, my friend?" he asked jovially. "You should have yowled. Your mistress would have let you in."

Scooping up Caesar, he marched to the door and opened it. The cat sprang from his arms.

"Phoebe, I'm back," he called and went straight to the bedchamber, a small part of him hoping she awaited him naked in bed. Never had the need for one woman enveloped him so.

She wasn't there, though. He started to set their things down on her trunk and stopped.

It was gone.

Alarm filled him. He dropped what he carried and opened the wardrobe.

Empty.

Panic rippled through him.

"Phoebe!" he shouted, hurrying back to the other room, turning in circles.

Then he spied a page resting on the table, his name scrawled across it. With apprehension, he reached for it and opened it with trepidation.

Andrew –

I've just received news that my sister is gravely ill. Both she and the baby are at risk and her husband asks that I come at once.

I wish I could tell you goodbye in person but perhaps this is for the best. The sweet memory of our time together will always be in my heart.

The cottage is rented through the end of the year. Stay as long as you need.

Phoebe

Andrew sank to his knees. Tears stung his

eyes.

Phoebe was gone. Gone. London was a good five or more days away and who only knew what route she might take. He couldn't go charging off after her. Not with Francis deep into his horrible scheme to steal the dukedom away from him. He would need to confront his half-brother and clear up that grisly mess. Only then could he search for Phoebe. If he had to knock on every door in London, he would. He had to find her. Life without her would be no life at all.

Caesar came and rubbed his cheek against Andrew's leg. He petted the cat.

"She left us both," he said sadly and stood. Folding the note, he slipped it into his pocket and picked up the cat. "I don't care if you came with the cottage or not. You're coming with me, Caesar. I promise you no matter what it takes, I will find her. She'll not be rid of the both of us so easily."

Andrew returned to the bedchamber and placed the tabby on the bed. He sat and put on his stockings and worn boots for the long walk ahead. His breeches and shirt were ragged from wearing them so much. Once he returned to Moreland Hall, he would burn everything he wore.

Then he went and picked up one of Phoebe's stockings. He lifted it to his nose and caught the subtle fragrance of her. Slipping it into his shirt, he picked up Caesar again and placed him in one of Phoebe's baskets. It would be easier to transport the cat that way.

He looked around the cottage one last time, remembering his thoughts on buying the place. Once he solved his problem regarding Francis, he would meet with the leasing agent. Surely, the man would have a record of information regarding Phoebe, even her previous address or that of her sister's. Satisfied that he could trace her that way, Andrew set out for Falmouth. It was the closest town and he knew just where to go.

Half an hour later, he'd arrived and went straight for a place he knew well from Phoebe's colorful descriptions. He entered the emporium and marched straight to the counter, where a woman waited on a customer.

"Forgive me for interrupting," he said in his most haughty tone, placing the basket with Caesar on the counter. "Might you be Mrs. Butler, wife of the proprietor?"

The woman behind the counter looked him up and down with curiosity. "I am. What's it to you?"

"I am His Grace, the Duke of Windham."

Mrs. Butler fainted.

Andrew hurried behind the counter and lifted the woman in his arms, placing her prone on the counter. The customer gaped at them.

"Fetch Sir William Rankin at once, Sir. He's the local magistrate."

Jaw still dropped, the man turned and ran from the store. Andrew only hoped the man would bring back Rankin. He quickly perused the store and found a bottle of smelling salts. Opening it, he waved it directly under Mrs. Butler's nose.

Her eyes flew open and she sputtered, choking and coughing. He raised her up and gave her a few whacks on her back.

"There you go, Madam. You'll be fine."

She regarded him with wide eyes. "You really are His Grace? You aren't dead?"

"I am Windham and I've never been dead. I don't plan to be for some years."

"It's just that—"

"I know. There was a terrible misunderstanding. I've sent for the magistrate and he will help iron out the situation." He glanced around. "My, you have a wonderful store. Moreland Hall is near here."

"I know, Your Grace. I've been by it before. Prettiest estate around. I hear you've another one even nicer in Devon."

"Yes, Windowmere is where I grew up. But I do like this village. Who is your mayor?"

Andrew kept asking her questions until he slipped in the question he desperately needed an answer to.

"I think I will recommend this area to my friends. Is there a leasing agent that rents properties?"

"Oh, yes. Mr. Booth handles rentals in the area. Everything south of Truro and to Lizard Point. He's your man."

The door swung open and the same customer from before hurried in, pointing to Andrew and saying, "That's the one, Sir William. He's mad!"

An older, staid gentlemen entered and came toward Andrew. "You claim to be the Duke of Windham?"

Andrew helped Mrs. Butler from the counter and to her feet and replied, "I don't claim to be. I *am* Windham, Sir William. I have things to share with you." He looked to Mrs. Butler. "Might you have a room where Sir William and I could speak privately?"

She looked torn, as if she wanted to be a party to any conversation between the men but knew the polite thing to do was accommodate him.

"Well, Mr. Butler and I live upstairs. I suppose you could go there. You can reach it through the storeroom. Past those curtains."

"Splendid."

He took her hand and raised it to his lips. She tittered nervously, blushing like a schoolgirl.

"We won't be long, Madam."

Instead of turning to the magistrate, Andrew passed through the curtains and marched up the staircase, arriving in a cramped parlor. He took a seat and prayed Rankin had followed him.

The magistrate appeared and said, "See here, Sir, I—"

"Sit, Rankin," he ordered in his most ducal tone.

The man obeyed him, resting his hands on his knees. He started to speak and thought better of it.

"I am the Duke of Windham," Andrew assured him.

"You're certainly not dressed as any duke I've seen," Rankin said testily.

"I had gone out for a ride in old clothes," he began. "I decided to walk for a bit and when I returned to my horse, my half-brother, Francis Graham, awaited me. Unlike my father, who regularly bailed Francis out of debt, I gave him a quarterly allowance and a property to manage to teach him responsibility. Francis begged me to pay off his numerous markers in London, which I refused. Then he shot me."

"What?" the magistrate roared, coming to his feet.

Andrew unbuttoned his shirt and pulled it over his head. Only a small bandage remained and he ripped it off. Sir William took a few steps toward him and leaned close, frowning.

"My half-brother wanted to be the next duke so much he would kill for it," Andrew said quietly. "Twice."

"Twice?" Rankin asked, his expression puzzled.

"My valet is a former soldier under my command," he explained. "He was wounded in the war and is recovering at Windowmere, my country seat in Devon. Francis knew that. The body he claimed to be mine? I'm afraid it's someone he killed. Since the poor victim had a scar on his back, Francis invented a scar for me. With no valet to challenge this identification, you and everyone else took him at his word."

"This is quite a tale you tell," Sir William said. "And if you are His Grace, then where the devil have you been?"

Andrew didn't want Phoebe's reputation dragged into this and said, "A fisherman found me. When I was shot, I fell into the water. This man pulled me to safety and cared for me. I remained on his boat while he made a run and then he returned me back to this area. If you still doubt me, take me to Moreland Hall. My servants will be able to confirm my identity."

The doubt that had flickered in the magistrate's eyes lessened.

"I will do just that. Come with me and I'll have my driver take us there now."

The two men returned to the ground floor

and Andrew said, "Thank you for your hospitali- ty, Mrs. Butler. Once things are settled, I will have you and Mr. Butler come to tea at Moreland Hall."

"Oh, thank you ever so much, Your Grace." She beamed at him as he collected his basket.

He accompanied Sir William outside, where a carriage awaited. The magistrate ordered the driver to take them to Moreland Hall and both men climbed into the carriage.

"If what you say is true, then Mr. Graham is guilty of attempted murder—and murder."

"What would be his punishment?"

"For attempted murder, life imprisonment since he's not a peer. You would have to testify, of course, as to the circumstances. If your theory is correct and can be proved and Mr. Graham killed a man and substituted his body for yours, then he would hang."

Either way would satisfy Andrew. Francis would be gone from his life.

They remained silent the remainder of the short ride to Moreland Hall. The carriage pulled up to the front of the house and the butler opened the door to greet them. Immediately, the color drained from his face.

"Your Grace! You're . . . alive?"

"Yes, Martin. Very much so."

"But . . . Mr. Graham . . . he said . . . he found . . . oh, dear."

By now, the housekeeper and two footmen had appeared. The housekeeper shrieked and the footmen looked as if each had seen a ghost.

He turned to Rankin. "Believe me now, Sir William?"

The magistrate nodded. "I do, Your Grace. Perhaps we should go inside and discuss this further."

They entered the foyer and the housekeeper, who'd recovered her composure, said she would have tea sent at once. Andrew led Sir William to the study, asking that Martin remain. He rested the basket on the ground and Caesar jumped from it, happily exploring the room.

"Fill in the gaps for us, Martin. Tell me everything that has occurred since I've been missing. Especially where Mr. Graham is now."

The flustered butler began to speak but he was rattled. Andrew fetched him a brandy and had him drink it before continuing.

Martin walked him through everything. Francis' arrival at the hall. The duke not returning from his ride. His horse being discovered. The wait and everyone realizing something had happened to their master.

"Search parties were sent out, Your Grace. Sir William was notified and he and his men also searched for you. Mr. Graham even sent to London and a Bow Street Runner came to investigate. Then Mr. Graham went for a walk along the beach and found a body had washed up. He claimed it to be yours."

"Because of the scar on its back?"

"Yes, exactly." The butler paused. "You don't have a scar there, do you, Your Grace?"

"No. I never have. I believe the dead man did and that is why my half-brother lied about it."

The servant looked aghast. "Do you think . . . that is, do you believe Mr. Graham had something to do with the man being dead?"

"Since he shot me and left me for dead, it wouldn't surprise me," Andrew said calmly.

The butler blanched. At that moment, the tea cart arrived and they ceased their conversation until the housekeeper had poured out for the three of them and left, closing the door.

"Mr. Graham has massive debts, Martin. I wasn't willing to pay them. He decided he needed to be Windham."

Martin's eyes narrowed. "I would shoot him full of lead myself, Your Grace. What a coward."

"Where is he now?" Andrew asked.

"He's gone. Back to Windowmere with you. That is, with the body we placed in a pine box."

Andrew looked to Sir William. "Then we must journey to Devon at once."

CHAPTER FIFTEEN

SIR WILLIAM RETURNED to Falmouth to
retrieve a couple of men, worried that Francis
would give them trouble and wanting to have
extra support. The magistrate also noted that he
wished to call on his counterpart in Devon and
bring him to Windowmere when they confronted
Francis. Though the crimes had been committed
in Sir William's jurisdiction, he thought it best to
inform the local magistrate of the crimes Francis
had been accused of and explain that he would be
taken back to Cornwall.

Andrew changed clothes, shedding those he'd
worn for over two weeks, and instructing Martin
to burn them. In a way, he hated to see his so-
called smuggler's clothes gone. They were how
Phoebe knew him, not in his superfine coat and
buckskin breeches that he now donned. He asked
for his carriage to be readied and learned Francis
had taken it to Windowmere. It stuck in

Andrew's craw that the blackguard had claimed the ducal coach and the title and how he now tried to take everything away from the true Duke of Windham.

"Saddle Mercury for me," he ordered, not willing to wait on Rankin and his men. He also instructed the housekeeper to care for the cat he'd brought home, telling her he would send for Caesar once things were more settled.

It would take a good day to reach Windowmere from Moreland Hall. It was almost three o'clock in the afternoon now and he'd have to stop for the night on the road. It didn't matter. The sooner he reached home, the sooner he could end the fraud being perpetrated upon his family.

As the leagues went by, his thoughts continually returned to Phoebe. How distressed she would be, learning of her beloved sister's illness. He hoped she reached London in time and was able to nurse Letty back to health as well as she'd nursed him. Phoebe had never spoken of any other family. She would be devastated if she lost her sister.

He also thought of ways to find her. The leasing agent would have the contract she'd signed. Hopefully, somewhere on the document it would list her former residence or next of kin. If it didn't, the task of finding her in a city the size of London would prove to be monumental. It didn't matter, though. He *would* find her. No matter where she was. He might even use the Bow Street Runners to do so, amazed at Francis' gall of calling them in to look for the very man he had murdered.

Andrew arrived late at an inn and took the only room available. He ate in the tavern downstairs, a thick chowder and roasted chicken leg, along with half a loaf of dark bread and a tankard of ale. When he finished, he visited the stables again, checking on Mercury. The horse had held up well, despite the fact he'd been pushed hard by his rider. By getting to rest overnight, he should be able to ride the mount all the way to Windowmere in the morning.

Sleep eluded him. After having spent every night by Phoebe's side, he was used to her scent. Her breathing. Her warmth. He let his thoughts linger over yesterday and the times they'd made love. The beautiful widow was everything and more he could have hoped for in a wife. He fell asleep thinking of her soft skin and alluring curves.

After a quick breakfast the next morning, Andrew was back in the saddle. He thought he could make it to Windowmere by two that afternoon. He came close to the time, riding up to the stables at half-past two and leaping from the saddle as another rider shot past him. He only got a glimpse of him and thought the man looked vaguely familiar. Shrugging it off because he had more important matters to deal with, Andrew tossed his reins to a dumbfounded groom. He strode toward the house and entered through the back door, cutting through the kitchens. A roasting pan crashed to the ground, dropped by an astonished scullery maid. Several others gaped at him as he hurried through.

As he exited, Mrs. Hanks, the Windowmere housekeeper, nearly ran into him. Andrew assumed she came to investigate the noise coming from the kitchen.

"Your Grace!" she exclaimed. "What on earth?"

"I'm alive and well, Mrs. Hanks, as you can see. Where are my aunt and Mr. Graham?"

She shook her head and took a seat in a nearby chair, clutching it to steady herself. "Most of the guests have left, Your Grace."

"Guests?"

Her face scrunched up. "Those who came for the funeral."

"How is my aunt?" he asked, having worried about her, too, during the ride home.

"Lady Helen has been stoic but is grieving. Your friends have helped comfort her. As for His . . . I mean, Mr. Graham, he left the house an hour ago. Said he had business in Exeter."

"Thank you, Mrs. Hanks."

Andrew moved toward the stairs, imagining

everyone was in the drawing room.

"Major! I mean, Your Grace!"

He glanced up and saw Private Bagwell, his valet-to-be, hurrying toward him. Obviously, the prosthetic leg he'd been fitted with in London seemed to be working well.

"You're moving about quick as always, Bagwell."

The former soldier threw his arms about Andrew. "Oh, we all thought you were dead." Then he sprang away. "Forgive me, Your Grace."

"No, a hug feels quite right between old comrades."

Bagwell's eyes narrowed. "I knew that slimy, no-good bastard was a bald-faced liar."

"I assume you mean my half-brother."

"That's the one. He told us you were dead."

"He thought I was—because he shot me."

"What?"

"Come along, Bagwell," Andrew urged. "You'll want to be a part of this."

They went to the drawing room as Pimmeline emerged. The butler, ever stoic, showed little emotion beyond his eyes slightly widening.

"It is very good to see you, Your Grace," he said evenly. "Your aunt and some of your London friends are inside. They will be delighted you have returned to Windowmere."

"Thank you, Pimmeline," Andrew said.

"He didn't even bat an eye," Bagwell proclaimed in amazement.

"It seems you have a lot to live up to," he said, suppressing a smile as they entered the room.

His eyes went straight to Aunt Helen. He saw her seated next to George, with Weston sitting nearby and Jon across from her. A man he was unfamiliar with stood apart from the others.

She caught sight of him before the others and rose, as if in a dream. "Is that truly you, Andrew?" she asked as gasps filled the room.

He hurried to her and embraced her. "It is, Aunt Helen. I have come home."

She pulled away and looked him in the eyes. "Where the devil have you been? Francis brought home a body and told us you'd drowned."

"Francis is a bloody liar. He shot me and left me for dead."

He led her to her seat and she collapsed. One by one, he greeted his three friends with tight hugs.

"I knew you couldn't be dead," George said. "If Boney's men couldn't kill you, nothing could."

"It would be just like that weasel to shoot you," Weston said, anger sparking in his eyes.

"Where have you been all this time?" Jon asked.

"Sit everyone."

As quickly as he could, Andrew recapped the events of the last few weeks, skipping over

Phoebe's role. Later, there would be time to tell them the entire truth.

"If ever there were a bastard, it's Francis Graham," George proclaimed.

"Where is my half-brother?" Andrew asked.

Jon shook his head. "He said he had business in Exeter. Left all the funeral guests after we came back from burying you. Or whatever poor soul now lies in the grave meant for you."

"Business, my ass," Weston proclaimed. "He and that spineless friend of his are probably whoring away."

"Parks!" he exclaimed. "I thought I knew him. He rode by just as I arrived. I'm sure he'll warn Francis that I've returned from the dead."

"I might be of help, Your Grace." The stranger stepped forward. "I was summoned by Mr. Graham to investigate your disappearance and accompanied him and the body back to Windowmere. I am Brock, a Bow Street Runner."

"I could certainly use your help, Mr. Brock, in tracking down the scoundrel."

"Brock is the best of the Bow Street Runners," declared Weston. "I've used him on a few occasions myself."

"I don't think it wise for you to wait for the magistrates and their men, Your Grace," Brock said. "If Mr. Parks rode off to warn Mr. Graham of your arrival, time is of the essence."

"Then we should head to Exeter immediately," Andrew said.

"Must you go, Andrew?" his aunt asked anxiously. "You just got home. If Francis tried to kill you once, he might attempt to do so again."

"I want to see the look on his face when we confront him, Aunt Helen. Besides, I couldn't be in better company than these men."

"We will protect His Grace with our lives," Bagwell proclaimed.

The group of men left the house just as a carriage pulled up. He recognized it as Sir William's. The magistrate and three others exited and introductions were quickly made.

"This is a criminal matter. Let us handle things," Sir William suggested. "There are four of us. Mr. Brock, as a Bow Street Runner, is also welcome to come along with us."

"And have us miss out on all the fun?" Weston asked. "Not a chance, Sir William."

"But Your Grace—"

"You have four dukes here, Rankin," George pointed out. "You're not in any position to say no to us."

Sir William looked disgruntled but said, "Very well. We shall head into Exeter. If Graham is drinking and wenching as you claim, we'll find him."

"Remember, though, that his friend left half an hour ago and will also be hunting for him to warn him of my appearance at Windowmere,"

Andrew said. "I think it best if we split up and cover more ground."

The men briefly discussed how to divide up the town, with the four dukes, the runner, and Bagwell combing the east side of town and the two magistrates and two deputies the west side. The carriage with Sir William and company took off as the others went to the stables. All but Bagwell had horses saddled. The valet would follow in the carriage so they would have a place to keep Francis and transport him back to Cornwall immediately. Andrew had suggested the plan, knowing his man wanted to be a part of things and knowing he couldn't ride a horse with his false leg.

They set out, hitting up a few taverns and whorehouses, describing Francis to the proprietors. At the fourth stop, the madam in charge knew exactly who they meant.

"Yes, His Grace is here," she confirmed.

"Mr. Graham is not His Grace," Andrew said. "*I* am."

She lowered her eyes demurely, despite her decades. "Of course, Your Grace. Allow me to show you and your friends upstairs. I know exactly where Mr. Graham is being entertained."

With that, she cut through the gaming parlor, whores wearing next-to-nothing sitting on the laps of gentlemen as they tossed dice and held cards. They followed the madam up the stairs and down a corridor with thick carpeting.

She stopped in front of a door. "This is the room." Sighing, she said, "I expect he won't be paying again, will he?"

"He never does," Andrew confirmed, drawing out banknotes from his pocket and handing them over. "This should more than cover his expenses."

The woman gave him an enigmatic smile. "Thank you, Your Grace. You—and your friends—are welcomed back anytime." With her skirts sweeping, she left the men.

"I say we crash through the door," Jon said. "Don't give him time to think."

"That sounds reasonable," Mr. Brock said— and kicked in the door.

A scream erupted. Bedclothes flew. A whore pushed a man from the bed. He fell to the ground, stark naked, and glanced up at them.

It was Francis' friend.

"Hello, Parks," Andrew said, strolling up to the man. "You do remember me, don't you? The Duke of Windham?"

"Yes, Your Grace," the man mumbled, his head dropping so he wouldn't have to look Andrew in the eyes.

"Where is he? My half-brother? We were told he was in here." Andrew paused a beat and then reached out, grabbing a fistful of Parks' hair and jerking the man's head up so their gazes met. "I asked where that weasel of a bastard is, Parks."

He tightened his grip and Parks yelped. Instead of letting go, Andrew yanked Parks to his feet and slammed him against the wall twice, hoping it would knock some sense into the fool.

He stepped back as Parks slid down the wall, looking slightly dazed.

And afraid.

"Shall we try it again?" Andrew asked. "Tell me where Francis is. Now. Else my friends and I will dice you finer than mincemeat."

Fear filled the younger man's eyes. "Francis saved me a time or two. I owed him," he began. "I wanted to return the favor, that's all."

"Not good enough, Parks," Andrew ground out.

"Let us at him," Jon said, his tone deadly. "When we are through with him, no one will want to look at him. Not even his own mother."

Parks whimpered, his mouth quivering.

George added, "And after we beat him beyond recognition, we must hand him over to Sir William. The magistrate will charge him as an accomplice." George squatted before Parks. "Not only because you aided Francis' escape just now—but for the attempted murder of a duke of the realm."

"No!" cried Parks. "I had nothing to do with that. Nothing at all. You can't—"

George slammed his fist into Parks' nose.

Blood shot everywhere. "I can do anything I like, you sniveling fool. I am a duke. We all are dukes. And you are a pathetic loser who chose the wrong side. You will hang, along with Graham. And burn in Hell with him."

Parks burst into sobs.

The whore cleared her throat. "*This* bloke came in while I was servicing the other one, Your Graces." She sniffed. "He told the man I was with that the duke had returned and was out for blood. That he better leave the country else he'd hang from the gibbet." She crossed her arms and glared at her former bed companion.

"Where would he go from here?" Weston demanded.

"Bristol," the whore said. "I heard them mention Bristol."

Andrew nodded. "He could make his way there to catch a boat and go just about anywhere." Disappointment filled him. "The magistrates can't do anything if he leaves England. They have no authority beyond our borders."

"I'll head for Bristol," Brock said. "If you'll allow me the mount."

"Of course." Andrew emptied his pockets and handed over what money he had to the runner. "Bring him back to Windowmere if you find him. If you don't, report to me anyway. I have another job for you once this one is completed."

"Yes, Your Grace." Brock left the room.

"Thank you for your help," Weston told the whore, reaching into his pocket and withdrawing several banknotes.

"Anytime, luv," she replied, eyeing Weston with interest.

"What do we do with this one?" Jon asked, indicating the sobbing Parks.

"Leave the little coward. He isn't worth our time." He looked at Francis' friend. "Don't come back to Windowmere. And you better hope I never lay eyes on you in London."

Andrew left the room, followed by his friends. They went to the center of town, where they'd arranged to meet up with Sir William. Once the magistrate and his men arrived, they explained how Francis had been warned and fled Exeter.

"You're right about our jurisdiction, Your Grace," Sir William said. "If Graham makes it to a boat and it pushes out to sea, it's out of our hands. Of course, if he returns, then we can see that justice is done. For now, we can take your sworn statement so that it is on record. Just in case Francis Graham is ever foolish enough to enter England again."

He rode with his friends to the local magistrate's offices and his statement was recorded and signed. Once finished, they returned to their horses.

"I feel as if you're the lost sheep of the Bible, Andrew," George proclaimed. "You were lost and now found. Alive and not dead. I think this calls for a celebration."

"Hear, hear!" echoed Jon and Weston.

Andrew returned with them to Windowmere, feeling at loose ends. His aunt had a large dinner awaiting them and they dined in style before retiring to the library after dinner.

Weston said, "We will be respectful of your aunt and wait and do our true carousing once we return to London. Once we hear from Brock, that is."

He shook his head. "I don't see much of that in my future, gentlemen. I have met the woman who will be my duchess."

"Who? When is the wedding?" George asked, his face betraying the thought that a wife for Andrew seemed impossible.

He sighed. "It seems I've misplaced her. I must return to Falmouth to search for clues as to her whereabouts."

"Misplaced her?" Weston asked. "Oh, I sense a story here. And that calls for a brandy."

Weston went to the decanter and poured snifters for the four of them, passing the drinks to his friends.

"Tell us, Andrew," Jon encouraged.

He cleared his throat. "Her name is Phoebe Smith. She is a widow—and the reason I am alive today."

Andrew explained how Phoebe had found him barely alive after he had washed up on the beach.

"She took me home, a complete stranger, and tended to my wounds. Dug the ball from my shoulder and stitched me up." He chuckled. "She thinks that I'm a smuggler."

"A what?" George exclaimed. "Why, you are the least likely man to ever do anything lawless, much less smuggle goods. Now Weston, on the other hand, would be my prime candidate for the role if you ask me."

"I'll take that as a compliment, George," Weston said. "But truly, Andrew—she thinks you are a criminal—and you still wish to make her your duchess?"

"She doesn't know you're a duke," Jon said.

"No," he admitted. "I wanted her to want Andrew, the man. Not Andrew, the duke." He paused. "Phoebe is everything to me. I must find her and make her mine."

"So, what is this about misplacing her?" Weston asked.

Andrew explained about Letty and how Phoebe had raced off to London to tend to her sister.

"Unfortunately, I do not know Letty's last name or even the area in London where she lives. From Phoebe's note to me, she planned to remain with Letty and not return to the cottage. I will start in Falmouth, with the leasing agent for the cottage, and then go from there. That is, once this business with Francis is cleared up."

"You know you have our support," George said. "We can help you locate Phoebe, either here or in London."

"That's right," Jon said. "Four of us looking is better than one."

"We will do whatever you ask of us, Andrew," Weston added.

Andrew's throat tightened with emotion. "Thank you. I am grateful to have your friendship and support."

Weston raised his snifter. "To finding Phoebe," he said and the others echoed his words.

Andrew prayed the situation with Francis would be resolved quickly so that the search for Phoebe could begin.

CHAPTER SIXTEEN

PHOEBE WRUNG HER hands, anxious to be so close to Hearthstone Manor and still not there yet. From what Ernest had told her at their last stop, they should arrive in the next hour.

She needed to focus now on Letty. Her sister had to be her priority. Phoebe had spent far too much of this journey thinking about Andrew and their time together. It angered her that she had lied to herself. She'd thought giving herself to Andrew and taking a piece of him would be enough. All that had changed, though. She'd foolishly given her heart to him. A criminal whom she would never see again. She worried that the man who'd shot him would find out Andrew hadn't died and return to ensure he did kill him this time. Images of him shot, bleeding, dying were too much to bear.

"Get a hold of yourself, Phoebe," she murmured aloud.

She stared out the window at the passing countryside. Oxfordshire was very scenic this time of year. She had enjoyed living with Burton and Letty after she'd been widowed and watching the change in Letty. Her sister had blossomed after her marriage, becoming prettier and more confident. Phoebe prayed she would find Letty alive when she arrived at Hearthstone Manor though she knew it was possible that she would arrive to find her sister gone. Her heart refused to believe that, though. The many hours of fervent prayers in this carriage must count for something. At least she hoped they did.

The scenery became familiar and she knew they were only minutes from reaching their destination. She composed herself, knowing that no matter what circumstances had occurred, she would need to be strong. She had survived what had come before and would do so again. Losing Nathan and her unborn child had been the greatest tragedy of her life. She steeled herself, resolving to contain her emotions once she arrived.

They drove up the lane and the manor came into sight. The carriage pulled up next to the house and the door opened immediately. Moments later, her brother-in-law opened the door to the carriage and stuck his head inside the vehicle.

"Thank God you've come, Phoebe." He took

her hand and assisted her from the coach. "The doctor is here. He'll want to speak to you."

"How is Letty?"

"She's improved a bit since I sent for you. Thank you for coming."

"Of course, I came." She embraced him. "I know this has been difficult for you, Burton."

Tears swam in his eyes. "I love her, Phoebe. More than I ever dreamed possible."

She touched his cheek. "Together, we will see she returns to us."

The viscount led her inside, where the housekeeper and butler greeted her. She was to be given her former bedchamber and saw her trunk already headed up the stairs, carried by a footman.

"Would you care to wash first and then speak with Dr. King?" Burton asked.

"No. I want to see him immediately," she replied. "Where is he?"

"I had the doctor wait in the drawing room, Lady Borwick," the butler said.

"Let us go to him at once," she told her brother-in-law.

As they walked, she asked, "I don't know Dr. King. There was no need of his services when I was here. What do you think of him?"

"He is in his mid-thirties. Very capable. Not one to act rashly."

"That's good to know."

The physician rose when they entered the drawing room. Burton made the introductions.

Phoebe said, "Speak frankly, Dr. King. I want to know everything that has been done for my sister and her prognosis."

"Lady Burton is still feverish," he said. "Fortunately, the spotting has stopped on its own."

"Then the baby is fine?"

"I believe so. We need to quell the fever, though, because she needs to eat. She is more than five months along with child now. While many women are nauseous and can't eat during those first few months, this is a time when it's important that the baby receives nutrition from its mother."

"What about bloodletting?" she asked. "Have you used leeches on her?"

"I know it's common to do so but I have never found it very effective with my patients."

"Good. I feel the same."

"I think your presence will help, Lady Borwick," Dr. King continued. "Be sure to speak to her. She may not be conscious but will still know your voice and that you are present. Lord Burton has spent much time at his wife's bedside and I feel that has helped her improve. She was delirious before. Now, she has calmed but the fever is still spiking higher than is considered safe. Not only for her but the baby she carries."

"I will go to her now. Will you be back,

Doctor?"

"I come every day about this time, my lady."

"Then I will see you tomorrow."

Burton escorted her to Letty's rooms. The bedchamber was dark and the smell of sickness hung in the air. Going to the bed, her composure crumbled when she saw her little sister lying there, looking so vulnerable and ill. Her skin was flushed bright red. Sweat beaded her face. She mumbled incoherently. A maid sitting by the bed rose.

"I want the drapes drawn and the windows opened at once," Phoebe instructed. "New bedclothes are to be brought. They are to be changed every day."

"The doctor didn't want her moved," Burton said anxiously.

She looked at him steadily. "Trust me. I have experience with this."

"Whatever you need, Phoebe," he assured her, his brow still creased with worry.

Turning back to the maid, she said, "Bring me fresh strips of linen and cloths and several bowls of cool water and place them beside the bed. Also, Lady Burton will need a cool bath, as well. Have the buckets brought up immediately. And find a fresh night rail for her ladyship, as well."

The maid bobbed a curtsey and opened the drapes and the windows. Later, when the temperature fell tonight, Phoebe would see they were closed. For now, Letty needed fresh air and the chamber desperately needed airing.

Burton insisted being the one to lift Letty from the bed when it came time to change the linens. He cradled her in his lap as two maids quickly readied the bed. By now, the water for the bath had arrived. Phoebe supervised the buckets being poured in, wanting the temperature of the bath somewhere between cold and tepid. When the mix satisfied her, she signaled to Burton.

"Bring her here. Set her into the bath, night rail and all."

He did as she asked and she touched his arm. "Go now. I will take care of her."

Once the viscount left the room, she had scissors brought and cut the night rail from Letty. Who only knew how long she'd been wearing it? While Dr. King had been wise not to bleed her, it took a woman to think of things such as this.

Phoebe bathed Letty herself, tenderly washing her limbs and hair, though she had one of the two maids help hold her up. Letty didn't seem aware of what went on and needed to be steadied so she didn't slide down into the bath. The servants helped get Letty to her feet so that Phoebe could dry her. Between the three of them, they got her dressed in fresh clothing and back in the bed.

"There, dear. That's all better," she said soothingly, kissing her sister's warm cheek.

At least Letty was clean now and didn't look so flushed. Phoebe dismissed the maids and sat on the bed, holding Letty's hand and kissing it.

"You are going to be fine, my darling girl," she cooed. "Your Phoebe is here."

⋙⋘

A WEEK LATER, Letty smiled at Phoebe weakly. "You have been the best medicine for me. My fever is gone. I am growing stronger every day."

She kissed her sister's brow. "I told Burton I would nurse you until you were whole again. You are going to be fine. And this baby will be so very loved."

"You have always taken care of me, Phoebe. You always knew when something was wrong."

The viscount, who sat on the other side of the bed, pressed kisses into his wife's palm. "Sending for Phoebe was the best decision I've ever made. Except for marrying you, of course."

Letty sighed. "I'm sorry I've been such a bother."

"Never say that," Burton said, bringing her hand up and placing it next to his heart. "You are no trouble at all, my love."

"But poor Phoebe had to cut short her holiday to come home and take care of me."

"I didn't mind, dearest."

"How was Cornwall? Tell me about it. Now that I am awake and can listen," Letty chuckled.

"It was lovely."

Phoebe described Falmouth Cottage and her daily walks along the beach. Watching the waves roll in and out and the gulls swooping through the air. She told Letty about the town and how vibrant the fish market was. She even mentioned Caesar, the cat who'd come with the cottage. Her biggest regret besides having to part from Andrew had been that the cat was nowhere in sight as she left Falmouth Cottage, else she would have taken the tabby with her.

"It seems you enjoyed your time there," her sister said.

"I did. I started drawing. You know how I used to tell Nathan stories?"

"I remember. He would beg for them. I loved them, too."

"I thought I would write some of them down. I even did little pen and ink sketches to accompany them."

"Oh, I want to see them."

"Maybe later."

Phoebe had sent the bulk of her work to Sir Winston Barnaby, the friend of Borwick's who was involved in publishing. The only thing she'd kept were her illustrations for Freddie the

Flounder. In her rush to return to Hearthstone Manor, she'd left the drawings for that story behind on the desk. She supposed when she wrote to Mr. Booth, the leasing agent, she could ask him to send them to her. She doubted Andrew had stayed at Falmouth Cottage after she left but she would delay the correspondence for another week. By the time her letter informing Mr. Booth that she'd left early arrived, Andrew would most certainly be long gone.

"I think you should nap now," she suggested.

"Must I?" Letty yawned. "Oh, bother. You're always right. I suppose I am tired."

"When you awake, I'll have Burton carry you outside again. I think the fresh air did you good yesterday. We need to take advantage of being outside while we can. The weather is already turning cooler."

Phoebe worked on her story about Freddie and Walter and added a few drawings. She hadn't set any of the tale to paper, only the pictures to accompany it. She outlined it first, thinking of a few new ideas, and then started writing it. When the housekeeper informed her Lady Burton was awake and calling for her, she left and went upstairs.

"Did you have a good rest?" she asked.

"I did," Letty said. "I feel stronger today. And I'm simply starving."

"It's good that your appetite has returned. It's

a bit early for tea but let's have it anyway. Outside."

"Oh, that does sound like a treat."

Phoebe rang for a maid and told the servant to have Cook prepare an early tea that was to be taken outside and then told her to send a footman up in ten minutes to carry Lady Burton downstairs.

As she helped her sister change into a fresh night rail and slip on her dressing gown, Letty complained, "I can't believe I'm still so weak I cannot walk downstairs."

"It takes time to build up your strength. You've been ill. Be patient."

Once they were downstairs in the garden, Letty ate well. The sisters talked about several topics, from their childhood to Letty's romance with Burton.

Finally, her sister said, "I sense something different about you, Phoebe."

"What do you mean?"

"Did something happen while you were in Falmouth?"

"Actually, it did. I met a man."

Letty's eyes lit up. "You did? Oh, tell me about him. I want to hear everything."

Phoebe was reluctant to share about her time with Andrew and said, "He was totally unsuited for me but I came to care for him. Meeting him let me see that I do need to put the past behind me. Though there could never be anything between us, I realized that I want to have a family again, Letty. I'm already looking so forward to my niece or nephew being born and I, too, want another child. Or children."

Her sister's eyes shone with tears. "Oh, Phoebe. I am so glad to hear this. You've been so sad for far too long." She paused. "Do you think to return to London for the upcoming Season? It is the best time to find a new husband, you know."

"I think that's wise. I will put out the word among my friends that I wish to wed again." She took Letty's hand and squeezed it. "I would love for our children to be close in age and enjoy playing together."

"Since my baby will come in January, Burton and I had already planned to return to London for the Season. Although I may not attend a full slate of events, you are most welcome to stay with us. Burton will escort you to whatever invitations you accept."

"I would appreciate that, Letty. Though Borwick left me comfortable and I could afford to lease a place of my own, I would rather stay with family."

"I am glad you have chosen to wed again, Phoebe. I know how Papa practically forced you to wed Borwick." Letty shuddered. "He always seemed so distant."

"He was polite to me but I will be happy to choose my own husband this time."

Phoebe only wished it could be the seductive smuggler who haunted her dreams at night.

CHAPTER SEVENTEEN

ANDREW FELT ADRIFT. His friends had returned to their various estates after staying on for a week. They promised to meet up in London soon, especially if Brock, the Bow Street Runner, had luck in locating Francis. Andrew had tried to bury himself in work but found his concentration waned continually. Every thought brought him back to Phoebe and where she might be.

He decided to make for Falmouth and learn what he could from the leasing agent. That way, when Brock returned—with or without Francis— he would have solid information to share that might help the runner locate Phoebe's whereabouts in London.

Leaving his study, he found his aunt embroidering a pillow in her parlor.

"What is it, Andrew? You look troubled."

He appreciated that she had given up calling

him Windham. Addressing him by his title had put distance between them.

"I must go to Falmouth, Aunt Helen."

"Whatever for? I would think you would never want to see that place again after what happened there." She shuddered.

"More occurred there than I have told you. May I?"

She nodded and he took a seat. "I met someone while I was there."

Understanding lit her eyes. "Who is she? Are things serious between you?"

"Very. She is not of the nobility, though."

Disappointment crossed Aunt Helen's face. "You are a duke, my boy. You have an obligation to—"

"My obligation is to myself, Aunt. To find a woman of worth. One who will make me happy and that I can bring happiness to in return. Mrs. Smith is well-spoken. Intelligent. Caring."

Passionate . . .

Still frowning, she asked, "How did you meet her?"

"She saved my life."

Andrew told his aunt the parts of the story he'd originally left out, making sure to keep to himself the intimacies he and Phoebe had shared.

She shook her head. "This is very unorthodox, Andrew. The fact you stayed at her cottage. I understand that she's a widow but this is unacceptable."

"You would have had her leave me to die on the beach, Aunt?" he asked angrily. "Mrs. Smith took care of me. Nursed me back to health. She asked for nothing in return. I told her I would compensate her and she refused."

Her lips pursed, her displeasure obvious. "Why should she accept it? She hooked a duke on her fishing line and slowly reeled you in."

"That's just it, Aunt Helen. She has no idea that I'm a duke." He chuckled. "She thinks I'm a smuggler of brandy and other illicit goods."

She gasped. "What?"

He told her how Phoebe had the false impression that he was an outlaw, shot by a rival one.

"Despite thinking the worst of me, she still took me in and cared for me. We became close, Aunt Helen. Living together with no others—no family, no servants—you get to know someone quite well. I may not know all the details of her past but I know who she is. The goodness of her character."

"You truly believe she will make for a good duchess?"

"A very good one. She has good heart. A nurturing soul. I must also mention that she is very beautiful."

His aunt thought a moment. "Might you have idealized her, Andrew? After all, she did rescue you."

"I don't think I have, Aunt Helen. I was going to ask her to marry me—Andrew, the smuggler—before she left."

"I don't understand."

Once more, he explained how Phoebe had been called away because her sister was desperately ill.

"Let me understand this. The cottage was leased. She left to go to London. You have no way of locating her."

"That is why I wish to return to Falmouth and meet with the agent who leased the cottage to her. He should have an address for her. Some way for me to contact her." Determination filled him. "I am going to find her, Aunt Helen. I love her."

Her jaw dropped. "You what?"

"You heard me. I love her. I've never loved a woman and I'll never love another one. Phoebe Smith is the only woman for me. I will pursue her to the ends of the earth or die trying."

A radiant smile broke out on her face. "My dear, sweet Andrew. I am so happy for you." She took his hand. "I have longed for you to find happiness. And love." She stood, bringing him to his feet. "Go. Find out what you can about your Mrs. Smith."

He kissed her cheek. "Thank you, Aunt Helen. If Mr. Brock returns, have him stay until I get back and can meet with him. I am hoping to hire him to look for Phoebe in London."

Andrew went directly to the stables and had his horse saddled. He rode straight to Falmouth, arriving in the late afternoon. He didn't want to stop at the Butlers' shop because he didn't want Mrs. Butler gossiping about his reasons for returning. Instead, he stopped at an inn he spotted and called for a tankard of ale. As he sipped on it, he asked the serving wench about Mr. Booth.

"Are you here to lease something, Your Grace?" She shook her head. "If so, it won't be from Mr. Booth."

"Why not?"

"He died two days ago."

"What?"

"It was either his heart or the fire that killed him."

Andrew's heart sank. "Tell me."

She launched into a story about Mr. Booth's weak heart, which everyone knew about since he had trouble walking more than twenty feet at a time.

"They think his heart might have given out and he dropped his cigar. He was always smoking one. If he was helpless or even dead, he couldn't have put out the fire from the cigar. His whole place went up in flames. Not a stick of furniture left."

"I assume you mean his office. Where all his paperwork was kept."

"Yes, he died there. It's a huge mess because he was the agent for all the properties in this area. Tried to get his son to work the business with him but that boy was no good from the start. Last I heard, he'd gone to prison for theft."

A customer called her away and Andrew pushed aside his ale. His one good prospect at finding out Phoebe's whereabouts had literally gone up in smoke. He thought about what to do and decided he had no choice. Leaving a coin for the barmaid, he made his way to Mrs. Butler's shop.

When Andrew entered, she spied him immediately and called out, "Your Grace! It's so nice to see you again so soon. We'd heard that you left Moreland Hall. What a bad business, with your brother and all."

"Half-brother," he muttered.

"Say again?"

When he didn't respond, she said, "What might I do for you?"

"You had mentioned Mr. Booth, the leasing agent to me," he began.

She looked puzzled. "Yes, Your Grace. You said you might have friends who'd want to come and stay near Falmouth."

"Do you know Falmouth Cottage?" he asked.

"I do. That nice Mrs. Smith was renting it but

she hasn't been in for more than a week. Surprises me since she's come two or three times a week since she moved in. A nice lady, Mrs. Smith."

"Do you know how long her lease runs?"

Mrs. Butler thought a moment. "I believe she said for six months though she mentioned she might like to return here next year. She does seem to love the Cornish coast."

"Next year," he said dully. "Do you know where she lives when not at Falmouth Cottage?"

"Now that you mention it, I don't. She was private about things like that. A recent widow, you know."

"Thank you."

He turned and walked out, Mrs. Butler calling after him. Andrew ignored her. If Mrs. Butler didn't know, then no one in Falmouth would know where Phoebe came from or where she'd headed to in London. He would have little to nothing to share with Mr. Brock but hoped the man would still take the case.

If not, Andrew would scour London himself—and then return to Falmouth next year, hoping Phoebe might come back.

Would he have to wait that long to see her?

With a heavy heart, he reclaimed Mercury and rode toward home.

>>>>><<<<<

WHEN ANDREW RETURNED the next day, he
learned that Mr. Brock was a houseguest and
asked that the runner join him in his study.
Within five minutes, Mr. Brock was announced
and Andrew had him take a seat.

"Tell me about Francis."

"I never found him, Your Grace," Brock said.
"I missed him a few times. Gave his description to
those I spoke with along the road and learned
he'd been there but had moved on. I traced him
to the Bristol docks and feel confident he boarded
a ship there."

"Bound for where?"

"America."

Andrew expelled a long breath. It would take
Francis a good while to reach there.

"Hopefully, he'll never be back to bother
you, Your Grace."

"Let's hope so. I do have another matter to
discuss with you. A case I hope you'll take on."

"You are a friend of the Duke of Treadwell.
That is good enough for me. Tell me about it,"
Brock encouraged.

"I wasn't entirely truthful with the magistrate
about everything that happened with my half-
brother."

The runner frowned deeply but kept silent.

"I assure you that everything in my sworn statement regarding Francis' actions was true. What I fibbed about was the fisherman that supposedly rescued me."

He explained about Phoebe finding him and why he lied to protect her reputation.

"I understand, Your Grace. You acted as a gentleman and wanted to keep a widow from harmful gossip. I see nothing wrong in what you did. But how does this woman come into play?"

"I need her found—because I want to wed her as soon as possible."

This statement rattled the runner's detached demeanor. He sat up, his surprise evident. "Go on."

When Andrew exhausted everything he knew about Phoebe and the dead end he'd come to trying to gain information from her leasing agent, the detective stroked his chin thoughtfully.

"As you know, this is very little to go on. Certainly, I will take on your case but I must warn you, Your Grace. Don't expect too much."

"I'm afraid I am expecting a miracle. If you can't conjure one, then my only hope is to return to Falmouth next summer and hope Phoebe does the same."

Brock rose. "I see how much this means to you and I promise to do my level best to find Mrs. Smith."

"How will you even begin?" Andrew asked,

perplexed on how the runner would proceed to look for Phoebe in a city of thousands.

"I'll work on finding her sister. The woman may have lined up a midwife for her birth or be looking to do so since she's to give birth in a little over three months. If I can find this Letty, then it should be easy to find her sister. I'll warn you, though, that this is the proverbial needle in a haystack."

"I understand. I plan to remain at Windowmere for several months. If you find her, send word immediately and I will come at once to London."

Andrew offered his hand and the two men shook. Brock took his leave and Andrew sank into his chair. It was out of his hands for now. He only hoped the Bow Street Runner could find Phoebe.

CHAPTER EIGHTEEN

London—Six months later

PHOEBE AWOKE EARLY. No matter how late she went to bed as she tried to prepare for the upcoming Season's hours, she seemed to always rise when the sun did. She supposed it was from her time in Cornwall. She hadn't wanted to waste a minute of any day when she lived there, especially when she had to do all the menial tasks herself. She'd never realized how hard it was to wash and iron clothes, much less prepare even a simple meal. Her hands told the tale of her time at Falmouth Cottage. Faithfully, she'd slathered lotion on them every night and then slipped cotton gloves over her hands, trying to make them appear more ladylike. Months later, she finally saw some progress though she doubted she'd ever get rid of a couple of the calluses which had formed.

She longed to go back to those days in Cornwall. Walking on the beach. Working on her stories. Most of all, she wished to be back with Andrew. She gave in for a moment and thought of his touch. The feel of his hands running along her curves. His mouth on hers. The heat and passion that had sparked between them. Phoebe had thought time and distance would lessen the desire she felt for him.

It hadn't.

He was unique in every way. A man who had thought of her pleasure rather than his own. No man would ever make her as happy as the smuggler had but she knew it was better to cast aside those thoughts. She'd been lucky to find love briefly and knew lightning wouldn't strike twice. Her best hope was to find a decent man and build a life with him.

She stretched lazily and thought that her most important task this morning would be to go visit Basil in the nursery, first thing after breakfast. It was the best way to start every day. Letty had sailed through the birth and was already recovering her figure. The entire household was taken with Basil, who'd proved to be good-natured and rarely cried. Holding him made Phoebe long for another child of her own. That was why she was in London. Having a baby meant finding a husband.

With Basil less than three months old, Phoebe questioned whether Letty should return with the baby for the Season. Her sister insisted, saying she wanted to be there for Phoebe. First, to ensure Phoebe was actually serious about finding a new husband and not acting half-heartedly. Second, to approve of the match to be made and have Burton act as her representative in the marriage settlements.

She had no illusions of being able to compete with the girls fresh out of the schoolroom who would be making their come-outs. All eyes of the most eligible bachelors would be on them. Her best hope was to gain the attention of an older man. Not one as old as Borwick had been when they'd wed but possibly a man in his thirties. One more settled into life. With as many women who died in childbirth, there had to be several widowers among the *ton* who might be looking for a mama for their children. As long as her husband would agree to also allow her to have a child or two, Phoebe didn't mind mothering his children.

Bored, she rose and rang the bell for Letty's maid to come and help her dress. They shared the servant. It was easy in the mornings because while Phoebe was an early riser, Letty enjoyed sleeping later and then breakfasting in bed. The maid had ample time to prepare them both. It would be much harder in two days when the Season started. They would have to juggle her services. Perhaps she should go ahead and hire a lady's maid of her own and take the girl with her when she left the Burton household. It was something to think about.

As the maid helped dress her, Phoebe worked out a new story in her head. When she'd sent Sir Winston Barnaby her stories and illustrations, she hadn't expected to hear from him for several months and had listed Burton's Oxfordshire address in her correspondence instead of Falmouth Cottage. To her surprise, not long after she'd returned to nurse Letty, Sir Winston had written to her, offering to buy all of what she had sent. Three weeks ago, a collection of her stories had come out. Sir Winston informed her that sales had been brisk and he was eager for more work from her. She devoted her afternoons to writing and drawing. With the Season, though, she would have to work hard to carve out time for her own pursuits since she would attend many events in the afternoon or be making her morning calls then.

Ready for the day, Phoebe went down to breakfast. Burton rose and kissed her cheek.

"How are you today, Phoebe?"

"Quite well. And you?"

He indicated the newspapers next to his plate. "Reading about how we have Bonaparte on the run. It looks as if this infernal war might finally be over soon."

"That is good news."

The viscount took a sip of his coffee. "Are you ready for the Season's start in two nights?"

"I suppose so. Letty and I are going to Madame Toufours' shop this afternoon for the final fittings of the last batch of our gowns from the modiste."

He chuckled. "Then I should be getting a hefty bill fairly soon."

"Don't worry," she assured him. "I am paying for my own gowns from funds Borwick left me."

Burton frowned. "I can pay for those, Phoebe."

"No. I insist. I've been rather reasonable in replenishing my wardrobe. It was quite affordable. I will wear some of the gowns several times. I see no need to be wasteful and wear something only once. It's not as if the bachelors of the *ton* will be making a beeline toward me. They will have their choice of many young and pretty women making their come-outs."

"Speaking of that." Her brother-in-law looked pensive. "I have spoken to a few of the men at my club. About you."

"You have?"

"Yes. I know you've already visited with a few of your old friends since we arrived in town last week and they know you are ready to visit the Marriage Mart again. I took it upon myself to let a select group know you might be interested in entertaining offers of marriage."

"You sly fox," she said. "I must thank you for helping me navigate these waters, especially since I no longer have youth or beauty on my side."

He smiled gently. "You deserve a good man, Phoebe. One who will make you happy. As for your age, I don't believe twenty-seven is so very old. And as for beauty, you will be one of the most stunning women present. You and Letty both have the type of looks that only improve with age, like a fine wine." He patted her hand. "Never fear. Even without help from me, your dance card will fill quickly."

"Thank you for looking out for me, Burton. You are a good brother-in-law and a wonderful husband to my sister."

They finished eating and he left for his study, while Phoebe climbed the stairs to the nursery.

"Ah, good morning, Lady Borwick," the wet nurse greeted. "Master Basil has just finished eating. Care to burp him?"

"Yes, thank you."

She took the cloth hanging over the woman's shoulder and draped it over her own before taking the infant and placing him against it. Patting gently, he let out a huge burp, delighting her. She took a seat in the rocker the woman had vacated and held the baby, softly singing to him. Hopefully, this time next year she would be wed and expecting a child of her own.

DESPAIR FILLED ANDREW as he walked through the streets of London.

Phoebe was nowhere to be found in the city.

Brock had kept on the case for months, interviewing dozens of midwives throughout London since they had no idea what area Letty and her husband lived in. Once January had come and gone and the child should have been born, the runner made the rounds again, trying to locate Letty and, in turn, find Phoebe, as well. No promising leads had been discovered. No sign of Letty, her baby, or Phoebe were to be had.

Knowing Letty had been seriously ill, Andrew had Brock then speak to physicians throughout London. Again, he came up empty, despite the number of men he spoke with.

The detective had questioned Andrew, asking if perhaps he'd gotten things wrong. That maybe Letty lived outside of London, in one of the surrounding areas. Brock had then gone beyond the outskirts of the city, still having no luck. Andrew finally pulled him from the case, fearing that Letty might never have had the baby. That she'd lost it because of her illness.

He'd then covered the same ground Brock

had, going down the list the Bow Street Runner had provided, visiting every midwife and physician on his own, hoping his status as a duke might come in handy and jog someone's memory. It hadn't. No Letty. No baby.

No Phoebe.

For the last week, he'd wandered the streets of London, praying for a glimpse of the woman he loved. The city teemed with people and yet he carried the small hope that he would spy her on a street corner. Finally, in this moment, Andrew admitted to himself how impossible the task had been. That the only hope he had of finding her was to return to Cornwall. He'd already purchased Falmouth Cottage and then left it in the hands of a new leasing agent with orders not to allow anyone but Mrs. Phoebe Smith to rent it. The man had told him without renters that no money was to be had. Andrew merely gave him the ducal death stare and repeated that only Mrs. Smith would be allowed to rent it—and that he was to be immediately contacted when that occurred. When. Not if.

His aunt expected him to participate in the Season. So did his friends. Dancing with any woman but Phoebe was unthinkable. Making small talk with young women looking for husbands was the last thing that appealed to him. No, he wanted his mature beauty, a woman of sterling character and the face of an angel.

It was time to go home. Not just to his London townhouse but back to Windowmere. The gaiety of the Season and its events had nothing to offer him. He would retreat there and wait.

Even if he had to wait a lifetime.

He reached Mayfair, exhausted, and slowed his gait, realizing he was famished. He toyed with the idea of stopping for tea somewhere and then decided to push on toward home. As he moved along the sidewalk, he glanced at the shop windows as he passed. He saw a hat that Phoebe would look smart in. A gown that would have suited her coloring. Then he came to an abrupt halt, lifting a hand and placing it on the display window of a bookshop.

A cover had Freddie the Flounder's picture on it.

He would know that fish anywhere. Of all the stories Phoebe had told him, he liked the one best about the flounder and his friend, a whale. He'd encouraged Phoebe to send off her work to a publishing house. She had—and here was the result.

His heart thundering, Andrew quickly entered the store and found a display of her books in a section for children. He picked up the book and lovingly stroked the cover.

Children's Tales. By P. Smythe.

He flipped through the pages, recognizing the style of her drawings, pausing to read a few passages that sounded so familiar to him. Closing the book, he studied the cover again. It was clever of her to not list her first name on the work. Merely being authored by a woman would have kept most customers from purchasing the book. Changing her middle-class name of Smith to the more upper class-sounding Smythe was also a calculated move on her part that would help the book sell.

"May I help you, Sir? We are about to close up shop."

He turned and saw an eager clerk standing there.

"Yes. I'll take this volume." Reluctantly, he handed the copy to the man and followed him through the store.

As the clerk rang up his purchase, Andrew asked, "How would one go about contacting the author of a book?"

"I would start with the publisher," the clerk said. "Write to the author in care of his publisher. I'm sure they would gladly forward on the correspondence."

"No need to wrap it," he said, paying for the book and claiming it. "Thank you."

Andrew stepped outside and immediately opened Phoebe's book. He saw the publisher was located in London. With it being so late in the day, he would only find the offices closed if he went there now.

But he would be waiting outside first thing in the morning. Nothing would keep him from the information he sought. By God, he was a duke. No one would dare tell him no.

And then he would finally find his love.

CHAPTER NINETEEN

PHOEBE STARED AT the bronze gown that she would don for tonight's ball at the Rivertons' townhouse. Madame Toufours had assured her that the color of the gown complemented the varying shades of gold and brown in her hair. It had been so long since she'd danced. Though she enjoyed doing so, Borwick had loathed dancing. They had only danced twice before he offered for her. Neither time had been enjoyable, with the earl stepping on her toes and dirtying her satin slippers. She had told her friends that she would never dance with him again—and she hadn't. Instead, she'd wed him, thanks to her father's insistence.

Her father was no longer here. Phoebe held the power as to which man she would allow to be her husband. That alone gave her confidence when she was sorely lacking in it. She told herself that dancing was natural and though she hadn't done it for many years, it would come back to her. She regretted not hiring a dancing master to come and refresh her on the dances she'd once learned, as well as help her master new ones that had come out since she'd hung up her dancing slippers.

Tightening the sash on her dressing gown, she left her bedchamber and went down the hall to Letty's suite of rooms.

"Do I look all right?" her sister called out as she entered the room.

Phoebe came to stand before her sister, who rose from the dressing table where the lady's maid was arranging Letty's hair.

"The gown looks lovely on you," she reassured.

Letty grinned. "I believe Burton will like this dress. He certainly likes my new breasts." She sat again so the maid could finish with her hair.

Letty's figure had filled out after Basil's birth. Her once small waist was larger and her breasts had gained a fullness. Phoebe turned away, consumed by a memory of Andrew's mouth on her breast, sucking and nipping and teasing it.

Would it never stop?

She supposed it wouldn't until she found a new man to replace Andrew in her mind. Sadly, she shook her head, knowing no man could be an adequate substitute for the incredibly handsome outlaw. He was an original who had made a lasting impression on her—and her body.

"There, my lady. What do you think?" asked the maid.

Phoebe turned to see how Letty's hair had been arranged. "Oh, you look wonderful, Letty."

Her sister patted her hair, staring into the mirror. "I do favor this style." She stood and looked at her maid. "Go on. Help Lady Borwick to look just as lovely as I do and be quick about it."

"Yes, my lady."

The servant returned to Phoebe's bedchamber and helped her into the layers of clothing. The pair had already decided on the way to arrange Phoebe's hair so it didn't take long to finish.

"You look right pretty, my lady," the maid said.

"Thank you. Let's hope a gentleman or two at tonight's ball agrees with you."

She claimed her reticule and a shawl since the April day had been a cool one and the night was bound to turn cold. Making her way down the stairs, she saw the foyer was empty. Surely, they hadn't left her behind!

Then she heard voices and turned, seeing Letty and Burton coming down the staircase together. They made for a handsome couple.

"Sorry if we're a bit late," Burton apologized. "We had to look in on Basil a last time before we left."

"This is the longest I will have been apart from him," Letty complained.

"He'll be sleeping for most of the time we're gone," the viscount said. "We can stop by the nursery when we get home. He'll probably be up for a feeding around that time and you can hold him for a bit."

The coach ride to Lord and Lady Riverton's residence didn't take long but their carriage became clogged in a mass of other ones, all heading to the same place.

"Feel like walking, my love?" Burton asked. "If not, we may miss half the ball."

"I don't mind," Letty said. "Are you agreeable, Phoebe?"

"I am. Lead the way, Burton."

They walked two blocks and joined the receiving line inside. She had known the Rivertons for many years because they had been friendly with her father.

"Oh, it is so good to see you out and about, Lady Borwick," Lady Riverton exclaimed. "I know it's difficult to be brave and rejoin society again after the tragedy you suffered."

She swallowed down the sadness that thickened her throat. "Thank you for the invitation, Lady Riverton."

The countess eyed her with interest. "I've heard that you might be interested in finding a husband again."

Phoebe smiled politely. "One never knows what a ball will bring."

She left her sister and brother-in-law and joined a few friends. They were all married and all but one had children. The conversation revolved around those children until a newcomer joined them. She vaguely remembered the woman, who'd made her come-out the year after Phoebe had, but she couldn't recall her name.

"Did you hear he's in London?" the woman asked.

"Who?" several ladies asked.

"Why, the duke who returned from the dead, that's who."

She wasn't interested in gossip, especially about an old duke who might have appeared to be dead and wasn't. Gazing about the ballroom, she saw so many young, beautiful women and knew they were her competition. She didn't like to think of them as such but the Marriage Mart could be an unforgiving place.

Then she heard Cornwall mentioned and turned back, now interested. As she listened to the end of the gossip, all she gleaned was that this duke, named Windham, had gone missing for a few weeks while at his Cornish estate. Everyone had thought him kidnapped or even dead until he'd returned, brought home by a fisherman.

"I know there's more to the story," the gossipmonger proclaimed. "Everyone says so. That there's some scandal attached to the disappearance that the family is trying to keep quiet. I plan to learn exactly what it is."

Phoebe realized this must be the duke Mrs. Butler had gossiped so much about. The woman had mentioned how the duke had vanished every time Phoebe had entered the store. At least the man had been found. It would be interesting to see who he was and if he made an appearance at tonight's ball.

A footman handed her a programme and Phoebe attached the silk ribbon to her wrist. Most of the women she stood with began to move away from the dance floor, wishing to sit with the other matrons instead of dancing. Only two remained behind with her. Phoebe closed her eyes and took a deep breath. She hoped some of Burton's friends would invite her to dance. As she opened her eyes, she saw two striking men coming her way.

Maybe one of them would be her future husband.

ANDREW ARRIVED HOME in good spirits, breezing through the door with a smile on his face.

"Where is my aunt, Whitby?" he asked his

butler.

"In her bedchamber, Your Grace. She is preparing for the ball." The servant paused. "You do remember you are to escort her there?"

"Yes, I remember. She is eager to meet up with her friends."

He took the stairs two at a time and went to his rooms, immediately spying Caesar sitting in the middle of his bed. Bagwell looked up expectantly as Andrew entered.

"Your Grace! I'd about given up on you," his valet said.

He placed the book he'd purchased on a table. "I'm all yours, Bagwell. Have at me."

The valet dressed him in evening clothes. Andrew noted how shiny his boots were and complimented Bagwell, who looked pleased.

"I expect you'll be the best dressed man there, Your Grace," Bagwell said with a wink. He finished tying Andrew's cravat and then helped him slip into his evening coat. "Will there be anything else?"

"No. Go enjoy yourself. Take the rest of the night off."

"I planned to wait up—"

"I won't be out late. I have a very important appointment to make tomorrow morning, however, so expect to be summoned early."

"Of course, Your Grace. Good evening."

Bagwell left and Andrew went back to Phoebe's book. He picked it up and sat in the chair next to the table. Holding it was tangible evidence that she did exist. He'd begun to doubt it himself and thought Brock did, too.

Opening it, he glanced once more at the publisher's name on the title page. By this time tomorrow, he would know her address. If she wasn't in London, then he would be on the road, going to her. The first thing he would do when she opened the door is kiss the life out of her. Then he'd ask her to marry him.

Frowning, he remembered that she didn't know he was a duke. Should he leave his ducal coach around the corner from where she lived? Or should he wear meaner clothes? She'd never seen him dressed as a high-ranking peer of Polite Society. He didn't want her perplexed or shocked by his title. He wanted her to say yes to marrying him. Then he could tell her who he was.

Idly, he turned a page in the book and his eyes fell to the dedication.

For Nathan
These stories bring back all the wonderful
memories of our time together. Seeing them in
print helps keep you alive in my heart.

His belly tightened. His mouth grew dry. Nathan must have been her husband. Phoebe had never mentioned his name aloud. He read the words again, nausea filling him. He hadn't thought about her telling her stories to her husband, much less how they would be a reminder of her marriage to the man.

Did he have a chance with her at all? Would he always be competing with the ghost of a man?

Gloom settled over him. His spirits sank. He asked himself if he should even try to find her. If she would be happy to see him—or disappointed? Had she looked upon their time together as a brief affair and her allegiance would always remain with a dead man?

Doubt filled Andrew.

The door flew open and he looked up to see Weston and George charging into his bedchamber.

"Go away," he said as they came near.

"What? You're still moping over Mrs. Smith?" George asked. "Hasn't your runner found her yet?"

"No. He hasn't," Andrew said sullenly. "And neither have I."

"I suppose you'll have to do what you planned and go to Cornwall in a couple of months," Weston said. "I'm sure you'll find her there. For now, you're coming with us."

"Do neither of you understand what it means to be in love?" he shouted.

Immediately, he regretted his words. Both his friends had been in love and their engagements had ended in disaster. It was the reason the two now ran wild and were known as the most scandalous rakes in all Polite Society.

"I'm sorry," he said at once. "Forgive me."

"Love is neither here nor there," George said. "Both Weston and I thought we were in love and found it doesn't exist. For us, anyway," he added quickly.

"We know you are taken with your Mrs. Smith," Weston said. "But she's not here tonight. Since you've had no luck in finding her and probably won't until you return to Cornwall, come with us to the ball tonight. It will cheer you up. Simply everyone will be at the opening event of the Season."

"I don't want to. I can't dance with anyone but Phoebe. All I want to do is go to Windowmere and lick my wounds."

He remained quiet about Phoebe's book being published and the chance he might locate her through her publisher tomorrow. He wasn't at all certain he should try and find her after reading the book's dedication. It would be something he must mull over. Going to a frivolous ball was the last place he wanted to be.

Weston latched on to his arm and pulled him from the chair. "Then if you're headed home, you must spend your last night with us."

"Watching you chase skirts all night long?" he asked drily. "How much fun will that be?"

George took his other arm. "Oh, we won't abandon you entirely. Come along. Your aunt sent us upstairs. You promised to escort her to Lord Riverton's ball. We aim to see you do so." He grinned. "Besides, maybe a pretty girl or two will turn your head and drag you from your depths of despair."

He doubted it but he had promised his aunt that he would take her tonight.

"All right, you win."

"That's the spirit," Weston said.

Andrew followed them downstairs. It was only one night. Surely, he could manage to get through it.

CHAPTER TWENTY

PHOEBE HAD A good idea who the two men were that moved toward her circle simply by the way the others tittered. They had to be the Bad Dukes. She thought she had danced once with the one with tawny hair and green eyes during her own come-out years ago. If so, the Duke of Charm, as he was known in the gossip columns in all the newspapers, had matured into a most handsome man. She didn't think she'd danced with his friend, the equally roguish Duke of Disrepute, who also was very good-looking and self assured, with raven hair and vivid, aquamarine eyes.

She vaguely recalled that both men had become engaged after she'd wed Borwick and given birth to Nathan. Because she was a new mother, she hadn't participated in that Season, the one where both these men had broken off their engagements. Or was it the other way around? It had been too many years to recall the details. She only knew that both men were notorious rakes now, filling the gossip columns with their actions both in and out of bedrooms.

Lifting her chin a notch, she determined these were not the kind of men who would be interested in marriages, dukes or not. They both would probably wed girls a third their age when they were in their sixties and gain heirs that way, having enjoyed decades of debauchery.

The Bad Dukes arrived and both smiled enticingly. They knew the gossiper and Phoebe's friend and greeted them by name. Then the Duke of Charm turned to her.

"I don't believe we've met, my lady," he said smoothly, bowing to her.

"Oh, but we have, Your Grace. You danced with me eight years ago. I was a green girl making my come-out and doubt I made an impression on you or any of your friends."

He took her hand and kissed it. "Forgive me for being a callow youth and not recognizing true beauty then." He smiled enigmatically. "Or perhaps I was merely cowed by your striking looks."

"Your tongue is far more silver than it was in those days," she answered. "I am Lady Borwick, by the way. Dowager Duchess of Borwick."

The Duke of Disrepute stepped up and claimed the hand his friend had just released. He also kissed it. "He is too thunderstruck by your beauty, Lady Borwick. This dunderhead is the Duke of Colebourne. I am the equally thunderstruck Duke of Treadwell."

She curtseyed. "It is a pleasure to make your acquaintances, Your Graces. It is not often I am in the company of two dukes."

"Oh, there are more of us," Treadwell said airily. "Our friend, the Duke of Blackmore, is seeing that his sister, who's making her come-out this Season, is situated. The Duke of Windham, the last in our quartet, is visiting with his aunt and renewing old acquaintances. They'll come along shortly." He smiled. "I'm sure you'll like us better, however."

"Isn't the Duke of Windham the one who was thought dead?" the scandalmonger asked eagerly. "Everyone is curious about where he vanished to."

Treadwell frowned. "It's no business of Polite Society—least of all you, Madam—as to where Windham was."

The insult hung in the air. Bright red spots appeared on the woman's cheeks and she excused herself, hurrying away.

"Excuse me, as well," Phoebe murmured and turned to go.

The Duke of Colebourne had other ideas, though, and followed her. So did his friend, Treadwell. She sensed them on her heels and stopped.

Turning around, she asked, "Is there something I might do for you, Your Graces?"

"Dance with me," both men said.

"I think not," she said succinctly.

The peers looked puzzled. "Why not?" asked Colebourne. "No one ever turns us down."

"Do you know anything about me?"

"No," he admitted. "Only that we danced an age ago and I was foolish and callow enough to let you slip through my fingers."

"And you?" she asked Treadwell, her brows arching.

He smiled charmingly. "I know you are a widow. And that you are beautiful. I would like to spend some time with you. On the dance floor. Or elsewhere." His eyes and tone were suggestive.

"I may be a widow but I'm not the kind of widow you toy with on a regular basis," she told them. "Yes, I lost my husband. And child. Yes, I am once more on the Marriage Mart. I gather that is a place you do not go looking. Do me a favor and don't damage my reputation by speaking to me again. Or asking me to dance." Phoebe smiled sweetly. "I wish you a good evening, Your Graces."

With that, she turned and walked gracefully away. She found Letty, who asked her about the Bad Dukes.

"I saw them talking with you. They *followed* you, Phoebe. They are known for pursuing widows. You must be very careful where those two are concerned."

"I told them I had no interest in them and that I neither wanted to converse nor dance with them."

"You didn't!" Letty was flabbergasted.

"I most certainly did. I aim to claim a husband by Season's end, Letty. I don't want my name coupled with two scoundrels."

"Good for you," Burton said approvingly.

She didn't know he had joined them. "Thank you for siding with me."

He offered her his arm. "Would you care to take a turn around the room with me, Phoebe? Have your programme ready. I believe there are several fellows hoping you will agree to a dance with them."

She let him escort her away and he said, "I'm glad you gave those bounders the boot. You're right in thinking they would do harm to your reputation."

Burton led her to a group of three gentlemen and introduced her. All three eagerly signed her dance card. Her brother-in-law remained by her side as others flocked to them. She liked the caliber of the men who knew Burton and felt certain the rest of her evening would go well.

As she gazed across the room, she spied the

Bad Dukes again, this time with another man who'd joined them. He must be Blackmore or Windham, the other dukes they'd referred to as their friends. She wondered if this was the man who'd gone missing in Cornwall or not.

Then Phoebe grew dizzy. She grasped Burton's arm tightly. He said something to her but she didn't hear it. All her attention was focused on the fourth man who'd joined the three dukes.

It was Andrew.

ANDREW AND AUNT Helen stepped up to the receiving line, which George and Weston blithefully skipped. As the Bad Dukes, a name given to them by the newspapers which they gleefully owned, they didn't waste time on social niceties.

"Receiving lines are boring, my lady," Weston had proclaimed when Aunt Helen admonished them for not greeting their hosts. "George and I haven't gone through one in years."

George took Aunt Helen's hand and kissed it. "It's the line and all that waiting, my lady. Not the people in line. I assure you Treadwell and I always enjoy your company. I can't say the same for Windham here. If you can get him to stop moping about his lost love, then send him our way." He smiled. "It's the first night of the Season and we can't wait to peruse all the new girls making their come-outs."

The pair left and his aunt said, "They both put up a good front but they are hurting as much as you, Andrew. Their terrible manners and outrageous behavior will end once they find the right women to settle down with."

"Good evening, Lady Helen. Windham."

Andrew turned and saw Jon had joined them, accompanied by his sister.

"Hello, Jon. And a special hello to you, Lady Elizabeth. Are you looking forward to your first Season?"

Her blue eyes sparkled. "I've been waiting for this all my life, Your Grace. I cannot wait to dance. My dancing master says I am the best pupil he has ever worked with."

He smiled at her eagerness. "Then once you receive your dance card, I will find you and sign it."

"Oh, would you?" Elizabeth looked at him with adoring eyes. "Jon told me I am not allowed to dance with Colebourne or Treadwell."

"That's right," Jon proclaimed. "They are rogues of the worst kind. I don't want your reputation damaged."

"But it is all right if Windham dances with me?" she asked.

"Windham is fine, other than the gossip about him being dead for a while," her brother said. "He wasn't so don't listen to it. I'll help arrange the rest of your dances this evening."

By now, they had reached their hosts and Andrew and his aunt greeted the Rivertons, chatting briefly and then moving on.

"Shall I help you find your friends?" he asked.

"Would you, dear boy? These affairs seem to grow larger each year. Simply no one misses the opening ball but I wish it wasn't so crowded."

"Come along, Aunt Helen." Andrew took her arm and guided her through the mass of people.

They found her friends and he spent several minutes talking with them. He felt more comfortable with dowagers and matrons than he would young, eligible women who might be eager to claim a duke as a husband. His heart was already taken and other than the one dance with Elizabeth, Andrew didn't plan on partnering with anyone else tonight. He would stay a bit. Perhaps visit the card room. Return to Aunt Helen and hope she would be ready to leave by then. He'd already decided he would go to the publisher's London office tomorrow in order to locate Phoebe's whereabouts. He would rather find her and be second in her heart to a dead man than never see her again and waste his life pining for her.

After fetching ratafia for his aunt and her

companions, Andrew made his way to where Jon and Elizabeth stood. Her color was high and he noted the gaggle of suitors already gathered around her. Even Jon's stern looks aimed at the group didn't seemed to have an impact.

Joining them, he took Elizabeth's hand and kissed it. It would only make her more appealing to these men if they thought a duke was interested in her.

"May I see your programme, Lady Elizabeth?"

"Certainly, Your Grace. I saved the second dance for you. All the others are now gone."

He scribbled his name beside it. "I look forward to dancing with you."

Bowing, he stepped away so she could bask in the attention of the men who were interested in her. Jon moved with him, muttering under his breath.

"You're taking your role of big brother seriously tonight."

"She's like honey, attracting far too many pesky flies," Jon said. "I think I'll tell our butler to reject every other man who shows up to court her tomorrow, else the house will be filled beyond capacity."

"Quit worrying so much. Your sister has a good head on her shoulders. She won't rush into anything. Or be rushed."

"If you say so." Jon paused. "Shall we join the

Wicked Dukes or whatever they're called?"

Andrew had spotted a friend from university whom he hadn't seen in some time. "Go ahead. I'll join you in a moment."

Jon went to meet up with Weston and George as Andrew stopped and chatted for a few minutes. Then he joined the others.

"We were just telling Jon about the beautiful widow who's stolen both our hearts," George said.

"What else is new?" Andrew asked.

"What's new is that she turned us both down," Weston said. "And we are dukes!"

"I thought you specialized in seducing pretty widows," Andrew remarked.

"We do—only this one is having none of us," George said ruefully.

"Which makes us attracted to her all the more," Weston added. "We have a bet now which one of us can get Lady Borwick into his bed first. I'm certain to win."

"Are you serious?" George asked. "*I* am known as the Duke of Charm. I will win her heart long before you."

"Not if she's looking for a husband as she said," Weston said. "She told us not to even speak to her, much less ask her to dance. I suppose she thinks being seen with the likes of us might ruin her chances on the Marriage Mart."

Andrew laughed. "I like this bold widow. I'm

certain neither of you have ever been turned down before. Where is she? Point her out to me. I may have to go and congratulate her on putting your noses out of joint."

Weston glanced about the room. "There she is. With Viscount Burton. I asked and found out he's her brother-in-law. She's wearing the bronze-colored dress. I say, it did bring out all kinds of shades in her hair."

He looked to where Weston gazed and froze. *Phoebe* . . .

Their gazes locked from across the room. His heart sped up, rapidly beating twice its normal rate.

"It's . . . Phoebe," he said, shock reverberating through him.

"What?" George asked, looking at her and squinting. "You're all the way across a ballroom, Andrew. The chit may resemble your Mrs. Smith but I can assure you, she's not. She is Lady Borwick, a widow."

"And she'll be mine," Weston chimed in.

"Sod off!" George told him.

He shook his head, his gaze still on her. "It's her."

As if in a dream, he began weaving his way through the crowd to reach her. Suddenly, the musicians, which had been tuning their instruments, broke out into song. Couples began moving to the dance floor. He watched a man step in front of Phoebe, blocking Andrew's view. The next thing he knew, the fellow led her onto the dance floor.

Watching her move, he had no doubt this was his Phoebe. The graceful line of her neck. The tilt of her head.

Why had she lied to him—and everyone in Falmouth? What was a dowager countess doing living in a cramped cottage, dusting the furniture and scrubbing the floor like an everyday servant?

Guilt filtered through him. He'd also lied to her, as well. He couldn't very well be angry at her for having done the same thing he had. Still, he'd found her.

There would be no stopping him now.

Jon joined him. "Is that truly your Mrs. Smith?"

"Yes," he said quietly. "I don't understand the particulars but I will know as soon as she's finished with this dance."

"No. You may speak to her after the second dance. Or did you forget you'd promised it to my sister?" Jon's eyes darkened. "I'll not have you standing Elizabeth up the first night of her come-out. She would be mortified if a duke ignored her."

"Yes, of course," Andrew said, his eyes still following Phoebe's every step.

One dance. And then he would claim her as his.

CHAPTER TWENTY-ONE

PHOEBE DIDN'T KNOW how she made it through the first dance with her partner. Fortunately, he seemed to be one of those men who had to count in his head to the music and was incapable of carrying on a conversation while he did so. She wouldn't have been able to reply if he had spoken to her.

Andrew was here. At a *ton* ball. He wasn't some smuggler.

He was Mrs. Butler's missing duke.

He had to be, especially since he had joined Charm and Disrepute. They had referred to their friends by name, the Dukes of Blackmore and Windham. It was too great a coincidence for Andrew not to be Windham.

Then why had he lied to her all that time?

She thought back to the first few conversations they had and realized he'd never admitted to her that he was a smuggler. It had been an assumption on her part. The fact that he was shot. The way he was dressed. That they were in Cornwall, which was known for smuggling. Why had he not corrected her all those times when she'd lashed out about his so-called chosen profession? Why keep quiet about the fact that he was one of the highest-ranking peers in the land?

The music ended and her partner smiled at her. "Thank you, Lady Borwick. I am not a keen dancer and have to concentrate fiercely when I'm out on the floor."

"You were very smooth, my lord," she praised, not remembering their dance at all.

"Let me see you back to Burton."

He led her to where her brother-in-law now stood with his wife.

"Might I call upon you tomorrow afternoon, Lady Borwick?" the man asked shyly.

When Phoebe didn't answer, Letty said, "Of course, my lord. We look forward to seeing you." When her partner left, Letty clutched her elbow. "Phoebe? Where are you?"

She quit skimming the ballroom for Andrew and looked at her sister. "He's here."

"Who?"

"The man I told you about," Phoebe said quietly.

"Oh. Well, I hope it won't be awkward for you. You said he was unsuited to you. Was he a bit of a rogue? Or a man who doesn't want children?"

"He's a duke."

Letty's jaw dropped. Before they could continue their conversation, Phoebe's next partner claimed her. It was a lively dance and she had to focus on the dancing and not scouring the room for Andrew.

Until he was suddenly before her.

Somehow, she danced the few measures required and then peeled away from him, eventually returning to her original partner in a daze. The blood thundered in her ears, driving out the strains of the music. When the dance ended, she allowed herself to be swept from the floor and once more found herself back with Letty.

"I saw him," she hissed to her sister.

"I know exactly who he is," Letty replied. "I knew the moment you came across one another in the dance. Oh, Phoebe, tell me."

"Phoebe?"

She stilled, knowing that voice. The way it caressed her name. Willing herself not to burst into tears, she turned and curtseyed.

"Your Grace."

Andrew frowned. "We must talk."

He took a step toward her. She retreated two, bumping into Letty and sensing Burton step forward protectively.

"Your Grace, is there something I can help

you with?" Burton asked smoothly, blocking Andrew from her view.

"There most certainly is. Lady . . . Borwick and I are in sore need of a conversation."

Phoebe heard the haughtiness in his tone. This man sounded nothing like her Andrew.

Burton held his ground. "My sister-in-law has a full programme this evening, Your Grace. Tonight is not a good time for a conversation."

She leaned around and saw Andrew barely contained his fury. "I will see her, Burton," he ground out. "Now."

"And I say that you are about to make a scene, Your Grace. That is the last thing Lady Borwick would want as she reenters society after mourning the death of her husband."

"May I call upon Lady Borwick tomorrow afternoon?"

"We would be happy to receive you. Come at one o'clock," Burton suggested. "Now, smile and walk away, Windham."

Phoebe didn't see if he did as her brother-in-law said because she was hiding behind Burton's large frame again. Letty's fingers had found hers and they squeezed them tightly. After a moment, Burton turned back to them.

"I'm sure you'll tell us all about this, Phoebe. He's gone now. But I hope you realize that I couldn't put a duke off beyond tomorrow."

"No, you were very brave to confront him as

you did, Burton. I appreciate you coming to my rescue."

"I'll want to know how you know him before he arrives tomorrow. I like being prepared."

"Of course."

"Do you wish to leave, Phoebe?" Letty asked.

"No," she said stubbornly. "Why should I? I came to find a husband. I have many gentlemen who wish to dance with me tonight. I am going to thoroughly enjoy myself."

With that, she released Letty's hand and smiled at the gentleman who approached her.

"I believe we have arranged to have the next dance together, Lady Borwick. I am Lord Thompson, in case you'd forgotten. I know your dance card has filled quickly tonight but I hope you'll remember me."

She smiled. "If you are an excellent dancer, that's certainly a way to my heart, my lord."

Phoebe did her best to focus on the men who'd asked her to dance at this first ball. It helped that she spied Andrew leaving the ballroom after their confrontation. He didn't return. By the end of the night, her feet were sore and she was tired in a good kind of way. She thought she'd done a decent job staying in the moment and putting off thinking about Andrew's sudden reappearance in her life.

They returned to the carriage and, once inside, Letty said, "Tell us everything."

She did, explaining how she'd found Andrew washed up on the beach, half-dead from a bullet wound and the surf, and assumed he was a smuggler. How she'd cared for him, nursing him back to health.

"We grew close. I'll admit that I had feelings for him."

"Had?" Burton asked.

She felt the blush heat her cheeks and was glad the carriage was so dim inside.

"I suppose I still have them. But they were for a man I thought was running from the law. A man I believed another smuggler had shot in some dispute. One who seemed to be uncomplicated. Caring. Witty." *Passionate.*

"And now that you've learned he's a duke?" Letty pressed.

"I don't know. I wish I did. I'm confused as to why he hid his identity from me but then again, I did the same. He knew me as Mrs. Smith, a middle-class widow."

"You never told him otherwise?" Letty asked.

"No," she admitted. "I never thought I would see him again. In fact, we didn't even have a chance to say goodbye. He was well enough to leave that morning and went to do something. I have no idea what. Ernest arrived with the news of how ill you were and I quickly packed and left Andrew a note telling him I had gone to nurse you."

"So, not even a kiss goodbye," Letty said softly.

"No. I thought it for the best, parting that way. I'm afraid I would have become too emotional with a conventional goodbye and not been able to hide my feelings for him."

"You'll sort it out tomorrow," Burton declared. "I know a little about Windham. He is a war hero and a good man. I think last Season was the first since his return from the Continent. I don't remember his name being linked to anyone else's."

At least that was good to know. Phoebe would have hated if he had an understanding with someone else when she had given herself to him. Confusion filled her. She knew answers would come tomorrow. Until then, she was in the dark.

⟫⟫⟫⟪⟪⟪

ANDREW'S CARRIAGE PULLED up in front of Viscount Burton's London townhouse.

"I suppose this is it, Caesar," he said to his furry companion.

The tabby blinked at him, his large eyes peering at Andrew questioningly. He nudged the cat down and closed the lid of the basket he sat in. A footman opened the carriage door and Andrew climbed out. At the door, he saw someone delivering a bouquet of flowers. He wondered how many admirers Phoebe had gained last night.

Approaching the door, he waited for the deliveryman to pass and then stepped up. The butler had kept the door open and looked at him expectantly.

"Lady Borwick will be receiving guests at two o'clock, my lord."

So, she had gentlemen callers coming this afternoon.

He didn't bother presenting a card. "It's Your Grace and Lord Burton told me to arrive at one."

"Ah, very good, Your Grace." The butler stepped aside so Andrew could gain entrance. "If you will follow me."

The servant carried the bouquet as he took Andrew up the staircase and to the drawing room. Immediately, he saw half a dozen other arrangements, their perfume filling the air. At first, he wondered if he should have brought Phoebe flowers and then decided what he had for her would please her even more.

At least, he hoped Caesar would be welcomed.

"I will inform Lord Burton that you are here," the butler said as he put down the arrangement and then left the room.

Already, Andrew was irritated. He wasn't

here to see Burton. He needed to see Phoebe. Hold her. Kiss her.

He set the basket down and nervously paced until the viscount arrived. Alone.

"I've come to see Phoebe," he said brusquely.

Burton calmly said, "Sit, Your Grace," and took a chair himself.

Andrew sat.

"Lady Borwick has agreed to see you but she would prefer my wife and I to act as a . . . shall we say . . . buffer. She's afraid you might act rashly."

"What you're telling me is that you're here to prevent me from kissing her," he said flatly.

For a moment, Burton appeared nonplussed. Then he said, "Yes, I suppose that's why she asked us to be present."

Andrew stood. "I'll allow it for now but I'm telling you, Burton, that I plan to wed Phoebe. She is the only woman I want as my wife."

The viscount rose, his attempt to hide his smile failing miserably. "I see. Well, Your Grace, it will be up to Phoebe to make that decision for herself. She was forced into one marriage. My advice is to convince her of your worth and gently persuade her. I do find kissing works with her sister, though." His lips twitched in amusement.

Hope sprang within him. If Phoebe had been forced to wed, would she still be carrying a *tendre* for her dead husband?

"Thank you, Burton." He paused. "If, at any point, you can make up an excuse and give us just a few minutes alone, I would be most appreciative."

"I'll consider it."

The door opened and Phoebe entered, accompanied by a younger woman whom he assumed was the viscountess. They came toward him. Phoebe gave nothing away, her features a mask.

"Good afternoon, Lady Borwick, Lady Burton," he said graciously.

"Good afternoon, Your Grace," they repeated.

An awkward silence followed before the viscountess said, "Please, have a seat, Your Grace."

She sat next to her husband on a settee. Phoebe took a chair. Andrew chose one next to her.

The silence stretched a full two minutes. Phoebe never looked at him while Andrew did nothing but look at her.

Finally, she spoke, her eyes downcast. "I was surprised to see you at a *ton* event last night, Your Grace."

"I was equally surprised to see Mrs. Smith at one, as well."

She stiffened and then turned her head, their gazes finally meeting.

"I am sorry you found out in that way."

Boldly, he claimed her hand, lacing his fingers through hers. "Not half as sorry as I am for you learning who I really was before I had a chance to tell you." He paused, his eyes pleading with her. "We both made a mistake, Phoebe. One I believe we can easily rectify. I would like to explain matters to you in private, however."

She looked at him longingly.

Burton rose, bringing his wife with him. "We need to visit the nursery," he declared.

"We do?" asked Lady Burton, baffled by her husband's sudden comment.

Her husband nodded. "We most certainly do."

With that, the viscount led his wife from the room, leaving them alone. Andrew wanted to breathe a sigh of relief but was afraid even a breath might cause Phoebe to take flight. At least she hadn't pulled away from him. Her fingers rested next to his, their warmth giving him courage.

"Could we move to the settee?" he asked.

She bit her lip. Desire for her rippled through him. Still, he remained unmoving.

"All right," she agreed.

They both stood and he escorted her the brief way there, sitting beside her. Close—but not too close. He kept their fingers entwined.

"The first thing I will say is that I never lied

to you."

She gave him a rueful smile. "I realized that. I thought back to our conversations. I presumed you were a smuggler. You never corrected me."

"You're right. It really was the only falsehood between us. Everything else I said. Everything we talked about. Every moment of our time together was true, Phoebe. What I feel for you is true."

He brought their joined hands up and pressed a fervent kiss against her knuckles. "I love you. I was going to ask you to marry me that last day."

Her eyes widened. Her lips trembled. "You were?"

Andrew nodded. "I had some foolish notion that if you loved Andrew the outlaw and agreed to wed him, you wouldn't mind so much when you learned Andrew was really a duke. I'd only been a duke for a year. I was a second son, destined for the army. My brother was killed in an accident. My father passed away shortly after that, mostly from the shock of learning his heir was dead. There are days when I feel I might never get used to the idea of being the Duke of Windham."

He brushed another kiss upon her fingers. "I still love you, Phoebe. Can you forgive me?"

Doubt flickered in her eyes. "I don't know, Andrew." She swallowed. "Why did you keep your true identity a secret from me?"

"First, let me give you the gift I brought," he

said, reluctantly releasing her hand and retrieving the basket. Placing it in her lap, he said, "Open it."

Phoebe did and Caesar's head popped up. Seeing his mistress, he meowed loudly and worked his way from the basket.

"Oh, Caesar!" she cried, burying her face in the tabby's soft fur, her fingers running through his coat.

When she lifted her head, her eyes brimmed with tears. She said, "I have missed him so much. You took him with you?"

"I did. He was the only thing I had of you. And this." He removed the stocking from his pocket. "I always carry it with me." Andrew replaced it, more unsure about everything.

She settled back, holding the cat in her arms. He knew she wanted the truth. It was time she had it.

"At first, I didn't tell you who I was because I was in shock. I realize that now. Then as I recovered, I wanted to grow stronger. Enough so that I could confront my half-brother."

"I don't understand."

"It was Francis Graham, my half-brother, who shot me."

She shook her head in disbelief. "Your own blood tried to kill you? Whatever for?"

Andrew explained how Francis' mounting debts had led to the confrontation between the two of them. His plan to make Francis stick to his quarterly allowance and learn how to manage his funds better had fallen flat. He spoke of how he'd even put Francis in charge of Monkford, hoping he would learn something about estate management and if he did, his idea to gift Francis with the property to guarantee him a steady income.

"It was all for naught. Francis didn't want to work. He wanted to be the Duke of Windham and fritter away his life with his London cronies, gambling, drinking, and wenching. When I refused to budge, he shot me."

This time, it was Phoebe who took his hand in both of hers. She raised it and tenderly kissed the center of his palm and then brought it to her cheek.

"I cannot imagine the betrayal you felt." She frowned. "But how did you wind up in the water?"

Andrew told her how Francis had kicked him in the chest and driven him over the cliff. That he'd clung to some branch until his half-brother kicked him again, causing him to drop into the sea.

"I was not only physically depleted when you found me, Phoebe. I was emotionally drained. It took days not only for my body to begin to heal but my spirit, as well. You helped in that. I don't know if I would ever have trusted anyone again. You changed that. You changed me."

He cradled her face in his hands. "I knew I needed to confront Francis and see justice served. I didn't want to drag you into the sordid mess, however. I wanted to know we were committed to one another and then I was going to seek him out and hand him over to the magistrate."

"And I left before you could ask me to marry you," she said sadly.

"You did what you had to do. I knew how much your sister meant to you. I'm only sorry we've been separated for so long." He searched her face. "I looked for you, Phoebe. I hired a Bow Street Runner. Both he and I combed London, looking for Letty and hoping it would lead us to you."

Tears cascaded down her cheeks. "I wasn't even in London. I went to Letty in Oxfordshire." Her face crumpled.

"Don't cry, my love." He kissed her tears away. "We are here now. That is all that matters. That is, if you'll have me."

Phoebe's response was to kiss him.

CHAPTER TWENTY-TWO

PHOEBE ACTED WITHOUT thinking. All she knew was that every part of her cried out for this man. Their lips collided and the sparks that had always been between them roared to life.

His thumbs stroked her cheeks, wiping away the tears that fell as they kissed. He kissed her tenderly at first but urgency sprang between them. Soon, his kisses were hard and demanding, branding her as his for always. She opened to him and their tongues tangled as they playfully fought for control.

Andrew's hands glided down her neck, his thumbs massaging it, and then moved to her shoulders. Through her gown, his hands scorched her. Her fingers pushed into his hair, running through it again and again, the familiar thickness and silky texture taking her back to Cornwall and the bed they had shared.

Suddenly, he captured her waist and lifted

her to his lap. Now, her breasts pressed against the hard wall of muscle as her hands clutched his hair, anchoring him to her. His hands skimmed her ribcage and the pads of his thumbs brushed against her nipples, which sprang to life at his touch. He gently kneaded her breasts as he hungrily kissed her.

This was her Andrew. The man she had missed. The one she had ached for.

The one she loved.

Realizing she had never said the words, she broke the kiss, her fingers still tangled in his hair. They both panted, breathless, gazing into one another's eyes.

"I love you," she said. "I love you so very, very much."

He kissed her soundly. "I love you, my darling. It's always been you—even before we ever met."

Phoebe smiled. "I know exactly what you mean." She kissed him gently. "Somehow, fate brought us together. Even if neither of us truly knew who the other one was."

Andrew kissed her soundly. "I've always known who you were. I believe Mrs. Smith is merely a part of my Phoebe." He paused. "Though I would be interested in hearing why you chose to be her. To work so hard."

She stopped playing with his hair. "I do owe you an explanation."

He lowered her head to his shoulder. "You may tell me only if you wish, my love. It doesn't matter a whit to me what came before. We have now. We have our future. If turning back to the past is too painful, I don't need to hear about it."

She toyed with a button on his waistcoat as she said, "I was married before. To Lord Borwick. His surname was Smythe."

"Like your book," he said.

She lifted her head in surprise. "You've seen it?"

Andrew smiled. "Late yesterday. I had almost given up hope of finding you when I passed a bookshop and saw Freddie the Flounder in the window. I'd planned to track you down through your publisher. My goodness, Phoebe, you are a published author!" He kissed her. "I'm so very proud of you. That's a tremendous accomplishment."

Then he went quiet. She gave him a moment and asked, "What are you thinking about?"

"I read your dedication. To your husband."

"What do you mean? I dedicated my book to my son. Not Borwick."

He looked astonished. "Your son?"

She stroked Andrew's cheek. "Yes. Borwick and I had a boy. They were killed in a carriage accident." She didn't want to mention losing her unborn child now. The moment was already so raw. "I wasn't close to my husband but Nathan was my entire world. I used to tell him my stories. I decided writing them down and illustrating them was a way to keep him alive in my heart."

He kissed her tenderly. "I am so sorry for your loss. How old was Nathan?"

"Five." She sighed. "He was all little boy. So full of life and curiosity. He is the one I mourn. Not Borwick."

Andrew took her hand and kissed it. "You went to Falmouth Cottage to grieve."

"I did. More than a year had passed and I wasn't able to put it aside. Then Letty found herself with child and she and Burton were ecstatic. I decided to give them time alone since I'd been living with them. Time to celebrate the life growing within her. I had Burton rent the cottage for me and decided I didn't want anyone to know about Nathan. I wanted to keep him close and, at the same time, reinvent myself. Thus, I became Mrs. Smith, the widowed cousin of a viscount."

She lay her head back on his shoulder. "I needed that time to myself in order to heal. The menial chores were mindless and somehow part of that process. So were the long walks along the beach. And then getting down my stories on paper finally and the pen and ink drawings. They all helped me to grow stronger."

"Then a dashing smuggler came along," he

ALEXA ASTON

teased, kissing her hair.

"Yes, he did. That outlaw brought me to life again. I had already decided before you came that I would return to London and seek another husband. Being a mother was too great a pull. I longed for another child."

"Which is what you were doing last night. Looking for a new husband," he said, an edge in his voice.

"You can't have a baby without a husband," she said lightly, sensing he was upset with her.

"What if you had found yourself with child after we were together?" he asked.

"I didn't think I would. Women talk, you know. I'd heard many of them say how it was almost impossible to conceive a child immediately after your monthly courses. Mine had just finished. I sensed you would soon move on. I wanted to keep a piece of you for myself."

Phoebe raised her head again, gazing deeply into his eyes, the flecks of amber like dancing sparks.

"Coming together with you. Making love with you. It was the most divine thing that ever happened to me, Andrew. I thought I could give myself to you and take it right back, bringing part of you with me. Instead, I left my heart behind in Cornwall. In your hands."

"Yet you were eager to look for a husband last night," he accused.

"I thought I'd never see my sinfully hand-some smuggler again," she admitted. "For all I knew—and feared—the same man who'd tried to kill you would succeed in a second encounter. I knew whomever I wed would never have my heart because it belonged to you, Andrew. I did yearn for another child, though, and wasn't above using a man I wed to get one. I even hoped I would have a boy so that I could call him Andrew."

"Oh, Phoebe." He kissed her deeply. "I want to give you babies. I want you in my bed, now and always. More than anything, I need you as my duchess. You are my very life."

His kiss was spellbinding, taking her away from the past and present, going on for a very long time. Finally, he broke it.

"So, what do you say? Will you marry me?"

"Eventually."

"What?"

"I believe you need to woo me, Your Grace," she said playfully.

"*Woo* you?"

"Yes. We haven't even danced yet. We ha-ven't been properly introduced. In society's eyes, this would be a terrible *faux pas*. I want every-thing about our courtship to be proper. No one should know about our time in Cornwall together. Think of the scandal! You living with me with no acceptable chaperone."

ALEXA ASTON

"You sound like my aunt," he groaned.

"You have an aunt?"

"Aunt Helen. I told her all about us." He grinned. "At first, she thought you were some moneygrubbing woman, after my money and title. That was before I scandalized her by telling her you thought me a common criminal."

Phoebe laughed. "Well, I hope Aunt Helen can keep quiet about our time together."

He gave her a rueful smile. "I may have told my closest friends about it, too."

She gasped. "You told Charm and Disrepute? The Bad Dukes? Oh, Andrew, this is terrible. They will tell everyone."

He brought her hand to his lips and kissed it. "They—and Blackmore, my other friend—will tell no one. Despite their wicked reputations, they are very good, honorable men. Even if the two Bad Dukes wish to bed you." His eyes gleamed.

"Bed me? *Bed* me? I told those fools to stay away from me!"

Andrew laughed. "They took your refusal of them as the ultimate challenge. A beautiful widow who claimed not to have any interest in either one of them. I doubt any female has ever said no to them." He kissed her. "In fact, I had asked them to point out the stunning widow who had done so because I wanted to go congratulate her." He sobered. "That is when I saw it was

272

you."

She wrapped her arms about his neck and kissed him. "No one—especially the Bad Dukes— is going to bed me. The only duke I plan on being with is the Duke of Renown."

"The what?"

Phoebe giggled. "It's your nickname. I heard it last night at the ball. People were talking about how you'd come back from the dead. You are famous, Andrew. I suppose it's what you'll be known as the rest of your life."

He growled and tightened his arms about her. "The Duke of Renown is going to be known for his extreme devotion to his duchess."

"He is?"

"He is. Now, how long does this wooing have to go on before I make you mine, Phoebe Smythe?"

She cocked her head. "I think for the entire Season. Then we can set the wedding for autumn."

"Are you joking? I cannot wait that long to make love to you."

"Half the Season? Is that a compromise?"

"Only if you'll let me into your bed."

"No. You're going to have to wait until we are wed," she declared. "But I'm sure we can enjoy our time together until then."

Andrew shook his head. "You drive a hard bargain, Woman."

As he spoke, his fingers slipped under her gown and stroked her calf. They continued traveling to her knee and up her thigh. When they reached her core, they caressed it. Soon, Phoebe was writhing beneath his touch.

"Who knows?" her new fiancé asked. "I might be able to change your mind."

His fingers caressing her, Phoebe got out, "July. We can . . . announce the engagement in . . . May."

"June," he insisted, pushing a finger inside of her and stroking the tender nub.

Her face flushed with heat. Her orgasm shook her to her core. When she stilled, breathing hard, she shook her head.

"June. *If* you wipe that triumphant grin off your face."

Andrew did his best to look sober. "June first would be lovely."

"Will you always be so stubborn, Your Grace?"

"When it comes to you, Phoebe?" He smiled. "Always."

CHAPTER TWENTY-THREE

Andrew found Whitby and asked the butler, "Is the dining room ready yet? I'd like to look it over."

The butler glanced away, trying to hide his smile. "Yes, Your Grace. The dining room is set to perfection. Both Mrs. Bates and I supervised every piece that went on the table."

"I just want everything right for tonight."

"It will live up to your high standards, Your Grace," Whitby assured him. "Why don't you have Bagwell ready you now?"

"A good idea. Thank you."

He went quickly up the stairs and found his valet pacing.

"There you are, Your Grace. We should get you ready for your dinner party."

The valet fussed over him, first shaving Andrew and trimming his hair slightly. He liked it a bit longer in back because he enjoyed Phoebe twisting her fingers through it but he didn't mention this fact. Bagwell had Andrew's evening wear laid out across the bed and helped him into each piece.

"I'll tie the cravat myself," he said, lifting it from the servant's hand and going to stand before the mirror. He fumbled twice and then said, "Bother. Come do it, Bagwell."

"Yes, Your Grace."

The valet tied it to perfection.

"You shouldn't be anxious, Your Grace. Lady Borwick has already agreed to marry you. She will make for a fine duchess."

"She will." He sighed. "It's just announcing our engagement tonight makes everything so real."

Bagwell said, "You love her, don't you?"

"Of course, I do. I wouldn't bother wedding her otherwise."

"And she loves you?"

His face softened. "Indeed, she does."

"Then as long as the two of you are pleased, who gives a fig what anyone else says?"

Andrew grinned. "You are wise beyond your years, Bagwell."

"I'd like to think you and Mr. Whitby have rubbed off on me, Your Grace."

He leaned over to stroke Caesar and then

remembered the cat was with Phoebe. He'd gotten used to the furball sleeping on his bed. With Phoebe's return, both she and Caesar would once again become his bedmates. He couldn't wait for that day.

She hadn't budged regarding their wedding date. She had made him keep to their bargain. For the past month, Andrew had seemingly competed with other gentlemen of the *ton*, vying for her hand. She would only allow him to dance with her twice in one evening. He had to put up with keeping company with her at times along with her various admirers. Gradually, though, she had allowed him to take her driving in the park. They rode together in Rotten Row. He'd escorted her to garden parties and routs. Musicales. The theatre. Slowly, he'd seen his competition melt away.

They'd agreed that tonight they would announce their engagement to Polite Society. Jon was hosting a ball for Elizabeth's come-out and had graciously said Andrew could share his good news there. Jon was the only one of his friends who knew this, except for Sebastian. He'd written at length to the Marquess of Marbury, who still served alongside Wellington. They had recently fought in the Battle of Toulouse. Not knowing when Sebastian might come home, Andrew had posted a letter to his friend just this morning, informing him of his upcoming vows with the

Dowager Countess of Borwick and sharing with his close friend some of their backstory.

As for the rest, they would learn at dinner tonight of his plans. George and Weston already teased him unmercifully regarding his relationship with Phoebe, especially about whether or not he had beat them to the punch and taken her to bed. Andrew was enough of a gentleman to keep from them that it had already happened months ago in Cornwall. His hope was once tonight's announcement had been made that she would allow him back into her bed. They planned to wed in a month. If a baby came after only eight months of wedded bliss, who was to say the child wasn't a tad early?

Andrew went downstairs and found his aunt already in the drawing room. She had taken to Phoebe instantly, which endeared Phoebe to him even more. Aunt Helen had always been as a mother to him and to see the two women getting along so splendidly made him very happy.

"Good evening, Aunt Helen," he said, making his way to her and brushing a kiss upon her cheek.

"Do I look all right?" she asked, smoothing her gown.

"Why, yes." It puzzled him why she would ask this because she never had before.

"I want to look my best tonight at Blackmore's ball because I know I will be receiving many felicitations regarding your betrothal."

Startled, he asked, "Who told you?"

She chuckled. "My dear boy, *you* did. Your behavior has been nothing short of anxiety-laden. Why, I haven't the foggiest notion. Phoebe is a darling girl. You will make each other most happy. She even has asked that I remain at Windowmere with you."

"Where else would you go? It's your home."

"Things change when couples marry," she said sagely. "I will certainly remain in London while you go to Windowmere on your honeymoon. I will return, though, once the Season ends. Phoebe has made it quite clear that I'm expected to continue residing there."

He liked that his fiancée thought so lovingly of his aunt and had reassured her how welcome her presence would always be.

"I think you will make wonderful-looking babies," she declared.

"Aunt Helen!"

"You will."

Whitby announced Phoebe and her family's arrival then. He met her and kissed her cheek, inhaling that lovely lavender scent that always clung to her. Then he greeted the viscount and viscountess.

"How is Basil doing?"

"Oh, very well, Your Grace," Letty told him. "He seems to grow every time I visit the nursery."

Phoebe had taken Andrew to meet Basil. She had resembled the Madonna as she held the baby in her arms, cooing to him softly. It helped him understand how, by losing her own boy, she needed to fulfill herself by having another child. If it were up to him, they would have half a dozen sons and daughters.

Whitby entered again. "The Dukes of Treadwell and Colebourne," he announced.

Weston and George breezed into the room, both looking debonair, Weston dark as a devil and George his counterpart, a blond angel. They greeted the others and he couldn't help but feel a pang of jealousy as George lingered over Phoebe's hand and Weston drew her aside and sat beside her. His friends knew how much in love he was but still constantly needled him.

"Shall we have a drink before dinner?" he asked, nodding to Whitby, who poured glasses of wine for all present.

Fifteen minutes later, they adjourned to the dining room. Both Phoebe and Letty remarked upon the beautiful centerpiece of flowers and how elegant the table looked. He waved off a footman and seated Phoebe himself, directly to his right. After everyone had taken a place, he nodded to Whitby. Within moments, a footman entered with a tray of champagne flutes, which he quickly distributed to those gathered around the table.

Rising, Andrew said, "Those of you here are very important to me. Because of that, I wanted to share our good news with you before we speak of it in public."

He took Phoebe's hand in his. Gazing into her eyes, he said, "Phoebe and I are going to be married in a month's time."

A beautiful blush tinged her cheeks. He held his glass high in his other hand and said, "To my beautiful bride."

The others echoed his words and Burton added a hearty, "Hear, hear."

Andrew seated himself but kept his fingers wrapped around Phoebe's.

"Will you two quit being so distracted with one another?" Weston asked. "We need to talk of important things. Such as my standing up with you."

"No, I should be the one who stands up with him," George said. "That will put me closer to Phoebe at the altar. In case she changes her mind and decides to run away with me." He winked at her.

"Neither of you will stand with me," Andrew proclaimed. "I knew you'd argue about it so I've already planned for Jon to do so. Unless by some miracle Sebastian returns from war. Then he will be allowed to be a part of things."

Aunt Helen added, "You two will sit on

either side of me, separated so that you'll behave yourselves. I want this wedding going off without incident."

Everyone laughed and true congratulations were then given. Andrew signaled Whitby and the first course came out.

When dinner ended, the ladies went to freshen up and, soon after, they went outside to the two waiting carriages in order to make their way to the Blackmore townhouse.

"Remember, not a word of this to anyone," Andrew warned his friends. "I won't have you spoiling Elizabeth's ball. We'll make our announcement after dinner."

"We've already forgotten your pedestrian news about marriage," George assured him. "Both Weston and I are focusing on far more important things."

"What is her name?" he countered and everyone laughed.

"Let's ride with the Bad Dukes," Letty said. "I think they're ever so much fun."

"As long as you sit close to me," Burton said, slipping an arm about his wife's waist.

The four entered Burton's coach and Andrew handed up his aunt and Phoebe into his. They held hands the entire way, Aunt Helen smiling approvingly at them.

Inside the Blackmore townhouse, they were greeted by Jon and his sister. Andrew thought

Lady Elizabeth quite pretty and hoped she would make a good match this Season. He even wondered if Jon might make his own announcement on behalf of her tonight.

"Have you met anyone you particularly like?" he asked when he and Phoebe reached Elizabeth.

"I've met several good men. If you're asking me if I'm ready to settle down with any of them, Your Grace, then I must tell you no. I'm enjoying the Season far too much to think about marriage."

"Good for you," Phoebe said. "Dance every dance you can. Go to every event you're invited to. Make new friends but keep the old."

"That is lovely advice, my lady," Elizabeth said. She looked from Phoebe back to Andrew. "Might you be settling down anytime soon?"

"You'll have to wait and see," Andrew said mysteriously and led Phoebe away before her pinkened cheeks gave them away.

A footman handed her a programme and Andrew said, "Allow me," attaching it to her wrist. Then lifting it, he perused it thoughtfully. "Hmm. I think I will take this waltz. And the supper dance, of course. We're to sit with Jon and Elizabeth."

He scribbled his name twice and she slipped the card from his fingers. "That's enough for you, Your Grace."

"Only two?" He waggled his eyebrows at her.

"But I should get at least one more after supper. With my fiancée."

"Once the announcement has been made, I believe we should leave." She bit her lip. "I was hoping you might want to come back to Burton's with me."

His pulse quickened. "And?"

She leaned close. "And do whatever you like with me." Phoebe straightened again, mischief dancing in her azure eyes.

Andrew took her hand and brought it to his lips for a kiss. "Is there any way I can convince you to make our announcement now?"

She swatted him with her fan. "Go away, Windham. I will see you later."

He retreated reluctantly, making for the card room. It was difficult for him to see her dance with other men. He'd discovered a jealous streak a league wide grew within him regarding Phoebe. He joined a table and claimed a drink, trying not to think about returning to her bed tonight, else he'd lose every bet he placed.

Making his way back to the ballroom an hour later, he saw she danced with Jon. Though in the past, Jon's reputation was tinged by his association with the Bad Dukes, his friend had walked the straight and narrow this Season for his sister's sake. If anyone had to be dancing with Phoebe, it might as well be his old friend. He was still disinclined to allow her to dance with Weston and George but she had convinced him she was perfectly safe with them. Weston claimed her from Jon as the dance ended and Andrew kept his eyes on them for the next several minutes. He loved his friend. He just wasn't sure he could entirely trust him, at least where Phoebe was concerned.

By now, it was time for their waltz. He led her onto the dance floor and they moved to the music as one. Perhaps he did hold her a bit too close but she let him get away with it.

"I'll be back for you at suppertime," he promised.

Andrew partnered with Elizabeth after that, finding her dancing had continued to improve throughout the Season.

"Do gentlemen still line your drawing room?" he asked.

"On a daily basis," she replied snappily. "I don't understand why any girl chooses to wed after only one Season. You men have a much better plan, coming back multiple times until you select a wife." She glanced over his shoulder. "If you haven't decided yet, you ought to. Lady Borwick is lovely and you look absolutely perfect together."

"Are you trying to play matchmaker, Lady Elizabeth?" he teased.

She shrugged. "If you wed, perhaps Jon and the Bad Dukes will see how happy you are and they, too, will consider finding their own wives."

"I will see you at supper," he said, returning her to her overly protective brother.

He danced again with Phoebe and then led her into the supper room, joining Jon and Elizabeth. Burton and Lady Burton were already there, along with Aunt Helen and his disreputable friends. Three other gentlemen seated themselves, all in Elizabeth's vicinity, and the trio seemed to hang on her every word.

He fetched plates from the buffet for Phoebe and himself but she merely picked at her food.

"I can't help it," she said when he asked her why she had no appetite. "I am a bit nervous," she admitted.

Andrew took her hand under the table and gave it a squeeze. "Surely, marrying again doesn't make you apprehensive."

"No. My mind is made up. You are the only man I would consider wedding. I fooled myself into thinking I could come to London and marry someone else."

"Then there is no need to be anxious. I will worship you every minute of every day. Until we have a daughter, of course. Then I will find it necessary to spend some of my time adoring her."

"What if we have a son?"

"The boy and I will be at your mercy, Your Grace."

Phoebe laughed. "I'm not a duchess yet."

"You will be soon."

"Do you really want a daughter?" she asked. "Most men care little for them. They prefer all of their children to be sons."

"Until I met you, my love, I might have been of the same opinion. Now, I want to fill our household with girls as sweet and caring and wonderful as their mother. Not only will that make me happy but think of all the fortunate men who will someday wed them."

She laughed. "You've doomed me then. I'll probably have nothing but sons."

"Then you have an army at your feet, Phoebe Smythe. All worshipping you and your goodness."

"Are you ready for the announcement?" Jon asked.

Andrew turned and nodded. "Whenever you wish."

His friend stood and cleared his throat. He took a spoon and tapped it gently against his glass. The room gradually quietened. All eyes focused on the Duke of Blackmore.

"I want to thank you for coming out tonight and attending the ball in honor of my sister, Lady Elizabeth. I think she sprang from the womb eager to make her come-out."

The crowd chuckled and Elizabeth blew her brother a kiss.

"I also have some news to share with you tonight. My good friend, the Duke of Windham, has asked Lady Borwick to be his duchess. Shall we raise a glass to them?"

Jon turned and faced Andrew and Phoebe, his glass held high. "You are an extraordinary pair and I am delighted to call you both friend. Together, though, you are truly special. Here's to many years of wedded bliss. To Windham and Lady Borwick."

"To Windham and Lady Borwick," the room called out.

Andrew beamed at Phoebe. This woman had made him a new man. Without regard to convention, he leaned over and gave her a spontaneous kiss. He broke it quickly as several men cheered.

"I love you, Mrs. Smith," he said quietly.

Love shone in her eyes. "I love you, my dangerous smuggler."

"Let's go home," he suggested.

Phoebe's radiant smile filled him with joy. "Let's do exactly that."

CHAPTER TWENTY-FOUR

ANDREW NEVER WOULD have believed he could ever be giddy but that's exactly how he felt as Bagwell dressed him this morning.

Today was his wedding day. Soon, Phoebe would become his duchess. Love for his beautiful, caring angel filled his heart.

The valet stepped back and admired his handiwork. "You look most handsome, Your Grace. Who'd have thought this day would have come, back when all we knew was blood and guts and piss-poor food?"

He placed a hand on the servant's shoulder. "You are right. I, for one, am glad our war days are behind us, Bagwell."

"You can say that again, Your Grace. I hope you and Lady Borwick enjoy a long and happy life together."

"Thank you."

Andrew left his rooms and hurried down-stairs, his step light. He saw Aunt Helen already standing in the foyer.

"I hope I didn't keep you waiting." He kissed her cheek.

"You kept me waiting long enough for you to wed. I wish you could have found Phoebe years ago. That girl is lovely."

He liked that the two had grown even closer since the engagement had been announced.

"Shall we?" He offered her his arm as Whitby let them out, wishing him well.

Two carriages stood outside his townhouse and Jon, Weston, and George waited beside them.

Jon stepped up. "Would you care to ride with me and my sister to St. George's, Lady Helen?"

"That would be nice, Your Grace. Only if these two promise me they'll follow directly behind us with no stops in-between."

George took her hand and kissed it. "We wouldn't dream of it, my lady. And Treadwell and I are looking forward to being seated next to the most beautiful woman attending the wedding."

She frowned. "You should have said most lovely, Colebourne. At my advanced age, it would have been more appropriate flattery." She glanced at Weston. "Anything from you?"

"No, my lady," he replied. "You quite terrify me into silence."

"Good. Come along, Blackmore."

Jon helped her into his carriage and winked at them before climbing in himself.

"She is a jewel," George said. "You are lucky to have her."

The three men got into Weston's carriage and made their way toward St. George's.

"What is this?" Andrew asked. "A last plea for me to remain a bachelor?"

"Oh, no, we quite want you to wed today," George said. "You are far too handsome and wealthy. And you're a duke. You turn too many heads. Weston and I don't need the competition from you."

"I will say that you better make your wife happy, though," Weston added. "You know George and I specialize in unhappy wives."

"Phoebe is more than satisfied," Andrew confirmed.

"A-ha!" Weston said. "I told you, George. They've been at it. Our friend here has looked far too smug the last few weeks."

He let them continue to tease him without protest, keeping silent.

Then George said, "We are happy for you, Andrew. That's what we wanted to say. You've always been the model for what a gentleman should be. To see you now, so content with

Phoebe, it does a soul good."

"She is my life. I would die for her," he said fiercely, knowing he would.

"Let's hope it doesn't come to that," Weston said lightly.

They reached St. George's and entered. His companions went to join Aunt Helen and Lady Elizabeth, while Andrew went to the room off the side, one designated for grooms to wait in before the ceremony began. He thought of how George and Weston had once waited inside this very room and how terrible it had turned out for both of them. He hoped Aunt Helen was right and that these two loveable rogues would one day find the right women to turn their lives around.

"Everything is set," Jon assured him. He patted his pocket. "I have the ring. I've spoken to the clergyman. All we do is wait for the masses to descend."

Most weddings occurred after the Season. With this one in June, at its height, Andrew knew the chapel would be filled with hundreds of guests. Phoebe had agreed to a grand wedding at St. George's in exchange for the wedding breakfast to be an intimate affair. It would be hosted by the Burtons. Andrew had grown fond of the pair.

He and Jon sat and reminisced about their university days until the clergyman performing the ceremony arrived and told them it was time. Following him, they went into the chapel, which was packed to the gills. He saw Letty already stood at the altar and nodded to her.

Then he turned his gaze down the long aisle to the closed doors. His heart sped up as they opened and Phoebe entered on her brother-in-law's arm. He watched her come to him, joy on her face. She arrived at the altar and the sweet smile she bestowed upon him made him the happiest man in all of England. He took her gloved hand in his. The rest of the world faded from view. There was only the two of them.

They spoke their vows and he heard the words that they were now man and wife. Andrew kissed her, hoping the promise in his kiss spoke as loudly as the words he had pledged to her. He broke the kiss and they beamed at one another.

"Shall we, Your Grace?" he asked, tucking her hand through his arm.

They quickly went and signed their registry and then reentered the chapel. They marched down the aisle to thunderous applause, gazing at one another the entire time. When they came through the double doors into the sunshine of the June day, Robbie Jones stood by the carriage, grinning from ear to ear. Andrew remembered how the driver had been so kind to him that day Andrew returned to England after so many years abroad and how faithful a servant he'd been ever since.

"Good morning, Your Graces," Robbie said, signaling the footman to open the door. "May I be the first to congratulate you on your marriage."

"Thank you, Robbie," Andrew said.

"Straight to Viscount Burton's?" he asked.

"It's a beautiful day," he said to Phoebe. "Why don't we drive through Hyde Park on our way there?"

She nodded and he helped her into the carriage. Once he sat beside her, she asked, "Are we taking a detour because you want to see the park in its glory—or do you plan to thoroughly kiss me, Your Grace?"

He slipped an arm around her. "Why, I hadn't thought of that at all, Your Grace. I find it a delightful idea, however. I hope you will be full of them for the next fifty years or so."

With that, Andrew enfolded her in his arms and pressed a kiss against her lips.

PHOEBE AWOKE, COCOONED by a warm man. Not just any man.

Her husband . . .

They had been wed for a month now. What had to be the most wonderful month of her life.

After their wedding, they'd gone to honeymoon in Surrey. It was only four hours outside London and one of many properties owned by the Duke of Windham. It was smaller than most of his estates and they had spent many hours walking, talking, and making love.

Afterward, their idyllic time continued when Andrew took her west to Devon and Windowmere, the country seat of his family. They had ridden together every day. He had wanted her to see every inch of the property and meet his tenants. She'd been pleased at how many of them pulled her aside and told her what a good landlord Andrew was. How diligent he was about addressing their problems and how involved he was regarding the estate. Phoebe already knew many of their names and looked forward to spending a majority of their time at Windowmere.

Andrew had insisted on holding a country ball. Though most of his neighbors were still in London for the Season, several of the locals came out from the nearby village. She met the doctor and mayor, a solicitor and veterinarian, and all of the shopkeepers. Not only had local residents been invited to the ball but her husband had also issued invitations to all of his tenants and everyone who worked at Windowmere, from the blacksmith to the bottler. She'd never experienced such an event and thoroughly enjoyed herself, dancing with grooms and footmen and even their butler. Her favorite partner had been Robbie, their coachman, who had more energy and enthusiasm than ten men combined and twirled her about so many times that she grew dizzy.

It was a happy life she was settling into. Andrew wanted her to make her own mark on Windowmere and had told her he wanted their rooms refurbished so that they reflected her style. She'd spent the past few days meeting with tradesmen and today would be the start of the renovations. New carpet would be laid and fresh paint would go on the walls. She'd chosen draperies and a few new pieces of furniture. Because of the work that would go on, they would need to move to another chamber for a week or more.

Andrew's breathing changed and she knew he was awake. Now would come the favorite part of her day.

Warm lips caressed her nape. "Good morning, Your Grace," Andrew said huskily, his fingers splayed against her bare belly. She'd given up wearing night rails entirely.

"And a good morning to you, Your Grace," Phoebe replied.

He turned her so they faced one another. "How did I ever manage to wake up without you in my bed?"

"It's our bed, Your Grace," she said saucily.

"You have a smart mouth on you, Duchess."

"Do I?"

He kissed her, a long, lingering kiss. His hands began to wander and, soon, he had her panting, begging for him to enter her. When he did, Phoebe soared as high as the seagulls she loved.

Afterward, she lay in his arms, her ear against where his heart beat. Slowly, it returned to normal as her fingers smoothed the hair on his chest. What they did together in no way resembled what she and Borwick had done when they coupled. She was glad of that. She hadn't wanted her previous marriage to haunt this one.

"We should rise," she told him. "They're going to begin work on our rooms today. We'll need to move elsewhere."

"I've given that some thought."

"You've thought about curtains?" she teased.

"We'll go to a new place I've recently bought," he informed her.

"Oh? Where is this estate? Why did you purchase it?"

Andrew kissed her. "I think it will be a surprise." He rose and took her hand, pulling her from the bed and into his arms. "I hope you'll think it's a wise investment."

She shrugged. "I don't know anything about those things. I'm sure I'll like it just fine."

He released her and retrieved her dressing gown, helping her into it.

"Go get ready. We'll leave immediately."

Phoebe wondered what the rush was but returned to her room. She didn't have to ring for her maid because the servant was already there with a breakfast tray.

"His Grace wanted you to eat a quick meal," she informed her mistress.

Her curiosity grew. They always breakfasted together in a small, sunny room downstairs. She also noticed traveling clothes spread out across her bed.

"Do you know where we are going?" she asked.

"I haven't a clue, Your Grace. His Grace said to pack a trunk for you with simple clothes and have you downstairs early this morning."

She supposed they wouldn't do any entertaining at this new property since nothing fancy was being packed for her. Obviously, Andrew hadn't met anyone in the area yet. She wondered where they were going and how long it would take before they arrived. Uncovering the dish that covered her breakfast plate, Phoebe ate quickly as her maid bustled about the room, slipping items into a trunk. Once Phoebe finished, she washed and dressed and went downstairs.

Her husband exited his study, a small case in his hand.

"What do you have?"

"It's the chessboard and pieces. I thought we could play some."

She'd never played the game before marrying Andrew. He'd begun to teach her about it once they'd come to Windowmere. Though she had a long way to go before she mastered chess, she was starting to understand the subtleties that went into strategizing. It surprised her, though, that the new residence wouldn't have a board. Unless Andrew meant they were going to play in the carriage. She didn't think that wise with all the bumps along the road that might disturb the pieces on the board.

He took her elbow and escorted her outside. She saw a footman loading her trunk onto the carriage. It surprised her that only one vehicle stood waiting.

"Where is the other carriage?" she inquired. "For the servants."

"We're not taking any with us."

"No Bagwell? He will be upset to be left behind," she teased.

His eyes darkened. "Why do I need Bagwell when you've become so skilled at undressing me?" he asked, his voice husky.

A frisson of pleasure shot through her.

"Come, Your Grace. Your carriage awaits."

Andrew helped her into the vehicle and joined her. He placed the case with the chessboard on the seat opposite them. His arm went about her shoulder and he pulled her to him. He smelled wonderful, the spice of his cologne wafting from his warm skin.

The coach began to move and she snuggled close. "Do we have far to go?" she asked.

"We'll get there today. That's all you need to know," he said mysteriously.

They stopped to change horses and again to dine at an inn. Phoebe napped after that, curled up in her husband's lap. She was having the most marvelous dream when he nudged her awake. As she opened her eyes, the immediate scent of salt in the air greeted her. The door opened and Andrew got out, helping her. She glanced about and was dumbfounded.

They were at Falmouth Cottage.

"*This* is the property you bought?"

His smiled warmed her to her soul. "Yes. I thought it could be our special place. Where only the two of us come, every now and then, to escape the rest of the world."

Phoebe threw herself at him, kissing him enthusiastically.

"I love it," she proclaimed. "I love you."

Robbie carried in both their trunks, as well as several baskets.

"I had Cook pack some supplies for us so we don't have to go into Falmouth right away," he told her. Then to Robbie, he said, "Wait at

Moreland Hall for us. Come back in a week."

"Very good, Your Grace." The driver grinned cheekily at them and then returned to his seat.

They watched him pull away and then looked at one another.

"Now, the real honeymoon begins," her husband said.

CHAPTER TWENTY-FIVE

PHOEBE TURNED IN a circle, taking in the place that had meant so much to her.

"Thank you," she said. "I can't believe you thought to buy it."

Andrew came behind her and slipped his arms around her. She leaned into him and closed her eyes, thinking miracles do occur.

"After I chased Francis back to Windowmere and he fled, I came back here. I had high hopes of finding you via your leasing agent. Unfortunately, he perished in a fire and all the documents regarding his rental agreements were destroyed."

She placed her hands atop his. "I'm so sorry that Mr. Booth passed and that we were lost to each other all those months."

He chuckled, his breath warm against her ear. "I was so desperate that I even went to see Mrs. Butler."

"You didn't!"

"I most certainly did. She fainted when I told her who I was."

Phoebe laughed. "The dead duke come back to life. I'm sure that gave her something to gossip about with her customers for weeks."

He leaned his chin against her shoulder. "When she came to, thanks to smelling salts I found, I pumped her for information. I was subtle but all she knew is that you hadn't come in for over a week and that there was a possibility of you returning the following summer."

Phoebe reached up and stroked his face. "I did tell her that. It's so peaceful here and I'd learned to be content. I found who I was as a person during my time here."

She turned so she could face him. "I had hopes that my new husband could be persuaded to bring me here after we wed."

Andrew kissed her. "Thankfully, he did. I bought Falmouth Cottage and told the new leasing agent it was only to be let if Mrs. Smith were to be the occupant. He thought me foolish, turning down paying tenants."

"As if the Duke of Windham needed the extra income."

His gaze held hers. "The Duke of Windham desperately needed his Mrs. Smith."

She cradled his cheek. "Mrs. Smith urgently needed her smuggler. Or duke. Whatever name he chooses to go by."

Andrew kissed her again, so tenderly she thought she might dissolve into tears. Then he broke the kiss and swept her into his arms.

"I never carried you over any threshold after we wed. I think it appropriate this be the one. This is where we found our happiness. I hope we'll return to Falmouth Cottage for years to come. Just the two of us."

"If you told me you wanted for us to live here, I'd be content with that decision."

As they entered the cottage, he said, "No, this will always be our special hideaway. We'll come here to escape the world every now and then." Easing her to her feet, he added, "With the number of children we plan to make, a two-room cottage isn't feasible for raising a large family."

Tears filled her eyes. "You really do want a lot of children?"

"As many as we can have. I want Windowmere to be filled with the sound of children's laughter."

"It's not always laughter," she warned. "There are tears and shouts. Babies cry an awful lot."

He nuzzled her neck. "They'll be our babies, though. I suppose that's easier to tolerate when they're your own and screaming at the top of their lungs."

He glanced around. "I had my housekeeper at Moreland Hall send maids to clean the place once a week. I wrote her and had her stock the larder for us. That, along with the items we brought from Windowmere should be sufficient. We'll only go into Falmouth if you wish to."

"I'm sure it would delight Mrs. Butler if we did drop by. She might even faint again when she discovers plain Mrs. Smith caught herself a duke."

"Actually, I just remembered something. I told her the next time I was at Moreland Hall, I would have her and Mr. Butler for tea."

"Then perhaps when Robbie comes to pick us up, we can return to Moreland Hall and have tea with them before we go home to Windowmere." She paused. "For now, I'd like to walk on the beach with my duke."

"An excellent idea, Your Grace."

They left the cottage and made their way down the familiar path to the beach. She remembered finding him half-dead on the shore and how long it had taken her to get him back to the cottage, worried the entire time that he might die on her. Andrew climbed up the rocks and reached out a hand, helping her over them.

"Sit here. I'll remove your shoes and stockings."

Memories flooded her as she recalled him doing the same thing months ago. That was the day they'd returned to the cottage and made love for the first time. As he bent, Phoebe ran her fingers through his hair, still amazed this man was all hers.

He looked up, a gleam in his eyes. "If you keep doing that, Your Grace, you'll not get in your walk."

"Why is that?" she asked coyly.

His hands caressed her thigh as he loosened the ribbon and pulled her stocking down her leg and over her foot.

"Because I will throw you over my shoulder like some caveman and return to our cottage and toss you upon our bed."

She bit her lip, fighting a smile. "Is that all you would do, Your Grace?"

"Don't tempt me, you little minx," he warned, laughing. "As it is, this may be the shortest stroll along the shore you've ever taken."

Andrew stripped her other stocking away and sat beside her. His hand captured hers, lacing their fingers together. He raised it and kissed it several times.

"Allow me," Phoebe said, pushing herself to her feet. "You could easily get your work boots off before. This time, wearing those Hessians, you'll need my help."

She tugged and managed to remove both, though it wasn't easy. While she set them aside, he pulled off his own stockings and wriggled his toes in the sand.

Leaping to his feet, he grabbed her hand. "Come on!" he said and they ran down to where the waves washed in and out along the shore.

"Look! Two gulls," she exclaimed.

They watched the birds at play. Andrew slipped his arm around her waist and she leaned into his warmth. The seagulls finally flew off and they turned away.

After a quarter-mile, he said, "Let's see if it's still here." He started leading her away from the water.

"What are we looking for?" she asked, curiosity filling her.

"You'll see. I placed it far enough up so it wouldn't wash away. I don't think many people frequent this stretch of beach."

Phoebe spied a grouping of shells and found that's the direction her husband pulled her. As they came closer, she saw the shells were in the shape of a heart. Inside the heart more shells had been placed. She read the message and tears sprang to her eyes.

"*Will you marry me?*" she said aloud. "This is why you came down to the beach that last day."

Andrew nodded. He slipped his arms about her waist. "It took much longer than I thought to find enough shells to spell out my question. I'd realized that I loved you and that's why I wanted the words surrounded by a heart."

"Oh, Andrew." Her mouth trembled. "I broke your heart that day by leaving without a goodbye."

She reached up and cradled his face in her palms. "I don't know how to make it up to you."

"No one is keeping score, Phoebe. What happened, happened. What matters now is it's in our past. Our separation only proved to me how much I truly love you."

"I loved you even before we parted," she said softly. "I will love you until the end of time."

She pulled him toward her, his lips touching hers. The kiss went on for some time. When they finally parted, breathless, he said, "You've seen my handiwork and had your stroll. I say since it's getting late and the sun is setting that we return so I can ravish you repeatedly."

"You think to ravish me, Your Grace? What if I plan to do that to you?"

Andrew beamed. "You may try, Your Grace. I think I will enjoy your efforts." He took her hand in his. "Time to go."

They returned and claimed their possessions and then hurried toward the cottage.

"At least we'll have the bed to ourselves," he noted. "No having to watch for hissing cats whose sleep has been disturbed by our romping about."

"You would make Caesar sleep in a basket?"

"Do you think I could make Caesar do anything he didn't want to do?" he teased.

"I have ordered us a larger bed as part of refurnishing our rooms at Windowmere. There'll be plenty of room for husband, wife, and cat," Phoebe said.

They reached the cottage and left their stockings and shoes by the door. Andrew lit a candle and led her into the bedchamber. Slowly, they undressed one another until they stood unclothed.

He pushed his hands into her hair. "I tell you that you are beautiful all the time. I hope the frequency in which I say it doesn't take away from the meaning, my love. You are not only physically beautiful but your true beauty lies within you. You are the kindest soul I will ever meet, Phoebe. You are my angel of mercy."

He kissed her, slow and sweet. Her skin heated as her blood warmed. Her heart raced as the familiar excitement filled her.

Leading her to the bed, he went to the other side and helped her turn back the bedclothes.

"Sit down," she said, moving to her trunk, where she removed one of her silk stockings and returned to the bed.

"What are you up to?" he asked, his hands capturing her waist as he sat.

She brought the silk to his eyes and placed it against them. Leaning into him, she tied it behind his head, her breasts brushing against his mouth. His tongue flicked out and touched her nipple. Phoebe stepped away.

"Lie back on the pillow," she instructed.

Andrew did as asked.

"Pillow your hands beneath your head. They must remain there."

"Aren't you the bossy one?" he teased.

She got onto the bed and straddled him.

"Hmm. I like this."

"Remember, keep your hands where they are."

"Yes, Your Grace," he said, his voice low and rough, causing her to smile.

Phoebe then proceeded to kiss her husband in every spot imaginable. Her lips brushed against muscle, seeing it flex. She licked and kissed her way all over his body, from the pulse pounding in his neck down his flat belly. Across his biceps. She nipped his calves and grazed her teeth against his knees.

Then she moved to his cock, which was standing straight out, thick and strong. Though she'd never done this before, she kissed its tip and then licked it. Andrew groaned and she looked up.

"Hands," she warned, seeing them start to come out from behind his head. "I'm the one in charge and doing all of the touching, Your Grace."

Returning to his member, she worked along it, using her hands and mouth and tongue. It didn't take long for her husband to groan and move, calling her name. She'd never felt her feminine power more than in that moment, knowing she could make him tremble with desire for her.

Suddenly, he moved swiftly, grabbing her by the waist and pulling her into the air before impaling her on his shaft. A sweet rush of satisfaction filled her.

"Ride me, darling," he gasped. "Hurry."

She began undulating against him, moving up and away and then coming toward him, his cock buried deep within her. His hands held fast to her waist as she began increasing her speed.

"Yes. Yes. God, yes," he cried out and spilled his seed into her as she collapsed atop him.

Andrew's arms came about her, holding her to him. She smelled the warm musk of him mixed with his cologne. His skin was slick with perspiration. They remained joined together as their breathing returned to normal.

"My senses were heightened being blindfolded," he said.

Phoebe glanced up and saw her silk stocking still flat against his eyes. She pulled up on it and removed it from his head, tossing it aside. She kissed his hard, muscled chest and rested her cheek against it again.

"I think I'm going to enjoy our visits to Falmouth Cottage, Your Grace," she said.

He laughed and reached for her silk stocking, placing it around her eyes and tying it behind her head.

"Your turn," he said.

CHAPTER TWENTY-SIX

PHOEBE WALKED WITH Andrew into Falmouth. They hadn't needed any supplies since his housekeeper from Moreland Hall had stocked the larder and their own cook at Windowmere had sent along food, as well. It was their last day, though, and they'd decided to go into town and purchase some of the raisin scones that Andrew had been so fond of. First, though, they would visit the Butlers at their store and invite them to tea.

"Do you think Mrs. Butler will faint again when she sees you?" she teased.

"No. She knows I'm back from the dead. What she may faint at, however, is learning that sweet Mrs. Smith wed the Duke of Renown. Or perhaps being invited to tea with the Duke and Duchess of Windham might cause her to grow weak in the knees. Either way, I'm familiar with where the smelling salts are located."

She squeezed his arm, leaning into him as they walked. She'd found that she needed to touch him constantly, as if to make sure he was real.

And her.

They arrived and entered the Butlers' shop. Mr. Butler was on his knees, stocking items on a bottom shelf. He rose to greet them. His wife was at the counter with a customer and immediately abandoned her conversation, rushing over.

"Good day, Mr. Butler, Mrs. Butler," said Andrew pleasantly.

"A good day to you, Your Grace," Mrs. Butler replied as her husband echoed the greeting. She glanced to Phoebe. "And Mrs. Smith. How nice to see you, as well." She turned back to Andrew and smiled.

"I've stopped by for two reasons, Mrs. Butler. First, I'd like to introduce you to my wife, the Duchess of Windham."

Mrs. Butler's jaw dropped. "She . . . Mrs. Smith . . . is . . . oh, my goodness." She looked apologetically at Phoebe. "I am so sorry, Your Grace. I . . . it's wonderful news. I mean . . . to think *you* . . . and His Grace . . ." Her voice trailed off.

Phoebe took pity on the woman being flummoxed and smiled. "I met His Grace in London after I left Falmouth Cottage. We both learned we were familiar with the area and talked about how much we enjoyed the rugged beauty of Cornwall. One thing led to another and we decided to wed."

"Well, congratulations to you, Your Grace," Mr. Butler said, beaming at her. "To the both of you."

"We've also come to ask you to tea," Andrew continued. "I had told your wife the next time I was at Moreland Hall that I would do so."

Mrs. Butler swayed unsteadily on her feet. Her husband latched on to her elbow. "Oh, my. I don't know what to say," she said breathlessly.

"Say yes, Mrs. Butler," Andrew smoothly suggested. "Both you and your husband have been especially kind to the two of us. I know Mr. Butler used his wagon to take supplies to my wife at Falmouth Cottage when she rented it last summer."

"Didn't mind a bit," the proprietor said. "Mrs. Smith was a good customer. No one's been at Falmouth Cottage since she left."

"It's a bit mysterious," Mrs. Butler said.

"I bought the cottage," Andrew revealed. "My wife fell in love with it. It's my wedding present to her."

Phoebe smiled up at him. "Yes, I have lovely memories of the cottage."

She had to keep from adding *both then and now*. This last week living there with Andrew had been the happiest time of her life. The fact that they could come to it any time brought a sense of peace to her.

"About tea?" Andrew prodded. "The day after tomorrow if you can make it. I'll send my carriage for you around three."

Mrs. Butler was speechless. Phoebe did think the woman was about to faint. Mr. Butler tightened his grip on his wife and replied, "We would be happy to come to tea, Your Grace. Thank you for your kind invitation."

"Very good. We'll see you the day after tomorrow then," Andrew said and nodded, leading Phoebe from the store.

"You almost had to grab the smelling salts," she said. "I think Mrs. Butler getting to ride in a ducal carriage might be the high point of her life."

"She seemed a little surprised that I married Mrs. Smith."

"Mrs. Smith would have been surprised to find herself married to a duke."

"And the Dowager Countess of Borwick?"

"Well, she was most happy to be courted by a handsome duke. Every now and then, though, she misses her smuggler."

Andrew laughed. "I feel that smuggler beds you as much as I do."

They went to the bakery and bought half a dozen raisin scones. Her husband ate two of them as they strolled back to Falmouth Cottage and they each had one with a cup of tea after they returned.

"You know what scones make me hungry for?" he asked, his eyes alive with the amber flecks. "You."

Phoebe found herself scooped up and placed upon their bed. He leaned down and licked the corner of her mouth.

"Mmm. The last bit of the scone. I wonder what the rest of you will taste like?"

"You'll have to find out, Your Grace."

THEY TOOK A last early morning stroll along the beach. Andrew patiently watched Phoebe continue to pick up seashells and supposed she wanted to take home a collection to remind her of their time in Cornwall.

"Robbie will be here soon to take us back to Moreland Hall," he reminded her.

"I almost have enough," she said and bent to pick up a few more.

"Should we head back?" he asked.

"In a moment."

He watched her step away from the water and realized they'd reached the point where his handiwork still remained. Phoebe knelt in the sand and began placing the seashells she'd collected along the sand. He went and stood behind her as she set the final one down and stood.

Yes, my love.

Andrew slipped his arm around her. "You did already say yes to my offer in London."

She smiled. "I wanted a record of it here, though. I wonder how long the heart and its message will stay?"

"Very few people come along this stretch," he noted. "Perhaps until we return next time."

"If it's gone, I want you to recreate it again. Every time we come to this spot, I want to see this tangible evidence of our love."

He chuckled. "The next thing I know, you'll want it replicated in our garden at Windowmere."

"That's a lovely idea," she declared. "Perhaps the gardener could spell it out in flowers. Or shrubbery."

He kissed her. "Whatever you wish. Come along. We need to get back."

They returned to Falmouth Cottage and saw Robbie already waited in the clearing.

"Good morning, Your Graces," the driver called out to them.

"Good morning, Robbie. Have you been here long?"

"No, Your Grace. Just a few minutes. Can I collect your trunks?"

"Yes, they're already packed," Phoebe said.

"They're in the bedchamber."

"Back in a jiffy," Robbie said.

They followed him inside and Phoebe walked around, checking to make sure they left nothing behind. She paused in front of a drawing of Freddie the Flounder. Andrew had it and two other sketches she'd left behind framed and hung on the wall. Phoebe touched the glass with her fingertips, a smile on her lips.

"I think we have everything," she told him as Robbie carried the second trunk to the carriage.

"Then we'll lock up the place until the next time we visit."

"Will that be every summer?" she asked hopefully.

"Certainly, we'll come then. If we feel the need to escape at other times, Falmouth Cottage will always be waiting for us."

She pulled his head down until their lips met and gave him a sweet kiss.

"I'm so glad to know this was my wedding present," she told him. "The best present any bride has ever received."

Andrew escorted her to the carriage and, soon, they were headed in the direction of Moreland Hall.

"What do you want to do with the rest of the day?" he asked.

"Naturally, I'll want to see the house. I'd also enjoy riding the property and seeing the land, as well. This will be the third estate of yours I've seen since we've been wed."

"Four. Of course, I'm counting Falmouth Cottage. I do want you to see all the others but we've got time for that. I visited all of them once I gained the title but I was on the road quite a bit. I'd rather us settle into Windowmere more and only take the occasional visit to one of them."

They arrived and he saw his butler awaited them.

"Good morning, Martin. This is my duchess."

"It is a pleasure to meet you, Your Grace," the butler said as Robbie lowered their trunks to the ground and he and a footman entered the house with them.

"I'm glad to be able to see another property of my husband's," Phoebe said.

"We may be smaller than some of His Grace's residences but I believe you will find Moreland Hall more than adequate."

"I think we'll take a light luncheon in the small dining room, Martin. For now, we're going to explore the house together and then ride the estate once we've dined."

"I'll see to luncheon, Your Grace," Martin said.

Andrew took Phoebe through the house. She noticed a chessboard set up for play in the library. They'd left behind the board and pieces he'd brought so they'd always have a set at the cottage. They had played every day and he was proud of how quickly she'd caught on to the game. Before long, she would beat him regularly.

They ate and then went to the stables. Once horses had been saddled for them, he took her around the entire perimeter and then to the cliffs. For a moment, a sense of dread passed through him as they tied their horses to the same tree he'd used on the afternoon his half-brother shot him. He forced all thoughts of that event away and they walked to the edge of the cliff.

"Oh, the view here is spectacular!" Phoebe exclaimed.

She took a step forward and he yanked her back, his heart racing.

"Are you afraid of heights?" she asked and then frowned. Then he saw understanding dawn in her eyes. "Oh, Andrew. This is the spot where he shot you, isn't it?"

He nodded. "I saw you too close to where I tumbled over. For a moment, I had that same sensation of falling again."

She took his hand and led him a few steps further away from the edge. "We should leave. I don't want these awful memories surfacing for you."

"I'm all right. I have you with me," he said, slipping his arms about her and bringing her close.

His mouth sought hers and their kiss went on

for some minutes. Finally, he lifted his head.

"I think we should christen our visit to Moreland Hall with a visit to our bedchamber now," he said, his voice low and rough.

Phoebe smiled. "I do believe that is my favorite part of visiting one of our houses. Making new memories with you."

"Hopefully, making a baby along the way," he added and kissed her again, hard and swift.

Instead of enjoying the kiss, he felt her tense. Breaking the kiss, he asked, "What is wrong, love?"

Tears misted her eyes. Her mouth trembled. Andrew framed her face in his hands.

"You can tell me anything. You know that."

Phoebe swallowed. "I so want a baby with you. But . . . I am afraid."

"Why? Is it because you lost Nathan and fear giving your heart to another child?"

"I lost more than Nathan," she told him, tears cascading down her cheeks. "I was with child when I learned of Nathan's death. The shock . . . it caused me to lose the babe." She bit her lip. "I worry that it could happen again. I have heard talk that once a woman miscarries, it is more likely to happen again."

His heart absorbed her ache, knowing how alone she must have felt in losing both her beloved boy and a child yet to be.

"I am here with you, Phoebe. Always. You

have my love. My support. My strength. Together, we will deal with whatever the future brings."

Andrew kissed her tenderly and enfolded her in his arms, hoping he might allay her fears and bring her some small measure of comfort.

She looked up at him. "Thank you. You always know the right thing to say."

They returned to their horses and he handed her into the saddle. He walked around to mount his own horse and heard a gasp and thud. Quickly pulling his foot from the stirrup, Andrew wheeled and saw Phoebe on the ground, a man in rags next to her. The man jerked her to her feet and pulled her against him, an arm banded about her waist. His hair was long, greasy and unkempt. His thick beard was flecked with leaves and twigs, as if he'd slept in the forest. An eerie light shone in his eyes.

The stranger lifted his free arm, pointing a pistol at Andrew. Recognition seared him.

It was Francis.

CHAPTER TWENTY-SEVEN

"DON'T HURT HER," Andrew warned, seeing the shock and fear in Phoebe's eyes.

"Like your hurt me?" his half-brother asked.

"She hasn't done anything to you. I'm the one you want." Andrew took a step forward.

"Stay back!" shouted Francis, retreating a few feet with Phoebe in tow.

She clawed at his forearm, trying to free herself, to no avail.

"Calm down, Francis," Andrew said soothingly. "We can work this out."

"I thought I had," Francis said, "When I shot and killed you. You are like a bad penny, Windham. Turning up where you shouldn't have. Why couldn't you have died? I shot you. I tossed you into the sea. You had to be the golden boy, though. Untouched by war and the same by me."

Francis cocked the gun. "And now you'll die again."

Phoebe shouted, "No!" as she squirmed, trying to push Francis from her.

He swung the gun around and pushed it into her temple. She stilled immediately. Andrew's heart pounded violently in his chest, his mouth dry, as he hoarsely called, "Don't, Francis. She is innocent in this."

"Not such an innocent," he murmured. "I saw how she kissed you. Like a whore would. I would know. I've had my share. Of course, you cut me off from that, Windham. You stole my life from me."

Andrew wanted to protest that it was Francis who had made the mistakes but he didn't dare anger the man, not when he held a gun to Phoebe's head.

"I went to London, you know," Francis said. "I couldn't face going to America. I jumped from the ship at the last moment. I'm an Englishman. I didn't want you chasing me from my homeland." He spat on the ground. "London held nothing for me, though. Even my good friend, Parks, wanted nothing to do with me. You must have scared him spineless, Windham, for Parks to abandon me like that."

"Francis, let Phoebe go," Andrew pleaded.

His eyes gleamed with madness. "Maybe I will make her my duchess." He leaned close and licked Phoebe's cheek, the gun still held to her head.

Phoebe shuddered but kept silent. Then she looked at Andrew and mouthed, "I love you."

He wanted to reach out. Touch her. Assure her all would be well. With Francis teetering on the edge of sanity, though, he didn't dare.

"You can't be the Duke of Windham," he said gently. "There's a warrant out for your arrest, Francis. I was made to give a sworn statement. The magistrate knows you attempted to murder me. He has proof you killed another man and pretended he was me so that you could claim the dukedom."

Francis made a guttural noise deep in his throat, tightening his grip on Phoebe. "Then if I'm to swing from the gibbet, it won't matter if I kill again."

"Me, Francis," Andrew implored. "Shoot me." As he spoke, he saw tears well in his wife's eyes.

"No. Me," Phoebe said, her voice calm and surprisingly strong. "You can easily pull the trigger now, Francis. Let Andrew live."

He clucked his tongue. "Both of you, so self-sacrificing. I wish I could kill you both. Let me think."

"There's nothing to think about," Andrew

said, shakily, his heart racing as he caught sight of Robbie Jones silently creeping toward Francis.

The coachman had appeared from nowhere. If Andrew could keep Francis talking, it would give Robbie time to reach Phoebe.

"Let's talk about this, instead, Francis," he continued, making certain his gaze connected with Francis so as not to give his half-brother any reason to turn.

"I am *done* talking!" Francis shouted. "I am done listening to you. You have taken everything from me. I want to take everything from you. Everything."

Andrew's gut tightened hearing those words, knowing how volatile Francis was and that he might fire the pistol at any moment.

His half-brother smiled. "I want you to suffer as I have. I want you driven to drink. Mired in the depths of unhappiness for the rest of your life. It seems losing this pretty little wife of yours is the answer."

As Francis cocked the pistol, Robbie crashed into him from behind, jerking Francis' wrist away. Francis' shot, meant for Phoebe, fired into the air instead as the threesome tumbled to the ground.

His hold broken on her, Phoebe scrambled away as Andrew launched himself at Francis. With glee, he slammed his fist into his half-brother's face.

Francis cried out, bringing his hands up to block Andrew's next punch. He diverted it, punching Francis in the throat instead. It knocked the wind from the madman and Francis fought for air. Andrew stood and Francis rolled to his side, wheezing. Without any regret, Andrew kicked their attacker in the head. Francis didn't move.

"Watch him," he told Robbie.

"Andrew!" Phoebe cried, running to him and throwing her arms about him.

He enfolded her, stroking her back, kissing her hair. "Are you all right?" he asked, gently taking her chin in hand and lifting her face.

"No," she said angrily. "You were begging him to kill you."

"I didn't want him to shoot you."

Fire lit her eyes. "And I didn't want to live without you," she said, defiance lacing her voice.

His thumb stroked her jaw. "Then the next time a madman is holding you hostage, you suggest I allow him to shoot you?" he said lightly.

"Oh, Andrew." She clutched his waistcoat and forced his mouth to hers.

They kissed one another greedily, knowing how a split second might have changed the courses of their lives.

He broke the kiss. "We have someone to thank and I need to see to Francis."

She shuddered and clung to him. "I wish you

could kill him. I know I sound like a savage but he almost killed you. Or me."

"He will die for his crimes," Andrew assured her.

Gently easing away his wife, he turned and saw Robbie had already bound Francis' hands behind him. How his one-handed driver had managed the task, Andrew hadn't a clue. Gratitude, though, filled him as he strode to his driver.

"What in God's name brought you here?"

"A soldier's gut instinct, Your Grace. I sensed something was off today. So I grabbed a horse and followed you."

"Just like my gut instinct in hiring you to begin with."

Both men grinned at each other shamelessly and Andrew said, "We make a fine team, Robbie."

"That we do, Your Grace."

He looked down and saw that Francis was beginning to stir. His nose sat crooked from the blow Andrew had landed the first time. Blood stained his grimy clothes. Andrew understood exactly what Phoebe meant. He wished he could shoot his half-brother and toss him into the sea but he kept his head. With Robbie's help, they brought Francis to his feet, both keeping a tight grasp on Francis' elbows.

"Get the pistol, Phoebe," he called. "Be careful."

She went to it, looking at it with distaste as she lifted it with two fingers and then brought it to him. He slipped it into his coat pocket.

"I will make sure he doesn't escape. Robbie, retrieve your horse and see Her Grace safely back to Moreland Hall. Then ride for the magistrate and tell him Francis Graham has returned—but not what you witnessed. I don't want anyone overhearing your conversation and gossiping about it. Have Sir William bring several men with him to Moreland Hall. Once he is here and my half-brother is in his custody, Sir William will need to take your statement regarding today's events."

"Yes, Your Grace," his driver said.

"I will have Martin send several footmen back to you," Phoebe told him.

"I'll start heading in your direction so I'll meet them along the way."

"You'll meet *us* along the way," she said with determination. "I will bring them back."

Andrew smiled at his fearless wife. "Then I will be watching for you, my love."

Phoebe went to her horse, allowing Robbie to give her a boost into the saddle before he swung up onto his own horse.

"I love you," she told Andrew. "Even if you are pigheaded and far too handsome for your own good."

With that, she nudged her horse and she and Robbie took off at a gallop for Moreland Hall.

"Come along, Francis," Andrew said, taking the reins of his horse in one hand and leading his half-brother with the other.

"You think I want to rot in prison while awaiting trial?" Francis asked. "And then hang as the public jeers at me?" He shook his head. "You always were a fool."

Francis tore himself away and ran.

Toward the cliff's edge.

Andrew gave chase but Francis had a sole purpose in mind. A quick death. He reached the precipice and flung himself over without hesitation. By the time Andrew arrived seconds later, he saw Francis crash into the sea, the waves swallowing him whole. If he survived the fall, drowning was almost a certainty since his wrists were securely bound behind him.

He continued watching for several minutes and never saw Francis surface. Returning to his horse, Andrew mounted and rode back to Moreland Hall. By the time he arrived, he saw Phoebe moving from the stables toward the house. She gasped when she saw him. He rode to her and dismounted.

"Where is Francis?" she asked.

"He broke away and flung himself over the cliff."

"Is he dead?"

"Most likely. Wait here."

He took his horse to the stables and gave his reins to a groom and then joined Phoebe again.

"I think our idea of christening Moreland Hall will have to wait until Sir William has come and gone."

They entered the house and he called for tea. He told Martin that Sir William was expected and to have him and the tea brought to the library. He lifted Phoebe in his arms and carried her there, sitting in a large chair with her curled upon his lap, her head resting against his shoulder. She trembled for a few minutes and then seemed to calm as he stroked her back and murmured softly to her.

Martin wheeled in the teacart himself and silently poured both of them a cup, doctoring them with a heavy dose of milk and sugar before retreating without a word.

Andrew reached for the nearest cup. "Phoebe, the tea is here."

She raised her head and he held it to her lips.

"I can hold it, Andrew. Really, I'm fine now. I was just upset and crazed at the notion of you being shot before my eyes. I'm much better now."

She started to rise and he restrained her. "Stay. I like you here."

Grinning, she said, "I like it here, too."

Taking the cup from him, she sipped at the

hot tea and he did the same.

Within an hour, they'd finished their tea and sat talking quietly when Martin entered the room.

"Sir William Rankin has arrived, Your Grace."

"Show him in."

Phoebe suggested, "Let's move to the settee. It's one thing for our servants to see me in your lap. Quite another for the local magistrate."

"As you wish."

By the time the butler showed Sir William in, they sat side-by-side on the settee, looking perfectly normal.

Andrew rose and Phoebe did the same. "Sir William," he greeted.

The magistrate came toward them. "Your Graces. Congratulations on your marriage. I heard the news from Mrs. Butler."

He chuckled. "I'm sure the entire community of Falmouth has heard from Mrs. Butler."

"I also know she is coming to tea at Moreland Hall. In the Windham carriage, no less."

"Did she mention Mr. Butler is to accompany her?"

"I assumed he would," Sir William said, also chuckling.

"Won't you have a seat, Sir William?" Phoebe asked, indicating a chair.

"Thank you, Your Grace."

They situated themselves and the magistrate said, "I was told by your coachman that my presence was needed regarding Graham."

"Yes. He returned to Cornwall and confronted my wife and me this afternoon while we were out riding."

Phoebe's hand sought his and he laced his fingers with hers as he told Sir William what had occurred, noting Robbie's role in Francis' capture and that the coachman could attest to what had unfolded.

"I thought restraining him was the safest way to return him to Moreland Hall," Andrew concluded, explaining how Francis had broken free and hurled himself over the cliff. "I only wished I could have acted quickly enough to prevent him from leaping to a certain death."

"You did nothing wrong, Your Grace," Sir William reassured him. "The man knew he faced the gallows and took a coward's way out. I will send the men I brought with me to the beach to look for him at once. Hopefully, the body will wash up soon and we can close this case. I brought along three men with me."

The magistrate rose and Andrew did likewise, offering his hand. "Thank you for coming so quickly."

"Will you be at Moreland Hall long?"

"No. After tomorrow's tea with the Butlers, we plan to return home to Windowmere the following day."

"I will send word to you, wherever you are," the magistrate promised.

After he left, Andrew sat. He placed his arm about his wife's shoulders and drew her to him. Her familiar lavender scent and warmth comforted him. They sat without speaking for several minutes. He gave thanks that they were able to do so. That neither of them had been hurt or killed by his insane half-brother. He also prayed that Francis was truly dead and would never trouble them again. Hiring Robbie Jones had saved the former military man from his unhappy life but Robbie had returned the favor a hundredfold by stepping in and saving Andrew and Phoebe from a madman.

The next afternoon, the Butlers arrived for tea, looking awestruck by their surroundings.

"Would you care to look around the house?" Phoebe asked Mrs. Butler. "We can delay having tea sent for half an hour."

The woman's eyes lit up. "You would do that?"

"Certainly. Come along, Mrs. Butler. I'd be happy to show you Moreland Hall. Would you care to go as well, Mr. Butler?"

"If it's no trouble, Your Grace," he said eagerly.

Andrew joined them and they showed the couple every floor and each room. Compliments flowed from Mrs. Butler. He supposed she'd never been inside a house so grand.

They returned to the drawing room and tea arrived moments later. Phoebe poured out and they spent three-quarters of an hour in conversation and eating sandwiches and small tea cakes.

"I am so glad you could join us today," Phoebe said.

Martin appeared. "Your Grace, Sir William Rankin has arrived."

"Show him in," Andrew said, knowing they must have discovered Francis' body. He looked at Phoebe, who bit back a smile, knowing their guests would have a front row seat to what the magistrate would share.

"I hope you don't mind Sir William interrupting our tea," he said. "I believe he has important news for us."

"Not at all," Mrs. Butler said, curiosity eating away at her.

When Sir William arrived, they greeted him and asked him to join them. Phoebe rang for another cup and gave him tea.

The magistrate glanced at the Butlers and back to Andrew. "I suppose you know why I came, Your Grace."

"I have a good idea, Sir William. Speak freely."

After a moment's hesitation, he did. "The body of Francis Graham was discovered a few

hours ago. I had it brought back here. I understand if you wish to refuse it, however."

He thought a moment. "No, Francis should
be buried at Windowmere. It's where his mother
and father lie. He should be at his final resting
place near them."

"That is very generous of you, Your Grace,"
Sir William said.

"I'm just happy to see this matter finally
closed," he said.

Sir William rose. "I will take my leave then."

Mr. Butler also stood. "Would you mind if
we rode back with you, Sir William? That way,
His Grace's carriage doesn't have to go to
Falmouth and back."

Andrew saw Mrs. Butler was outraged at her
husband's suggestion and said, "I'm sure Sir
William has things to do regarding this case, Mr.
Butler. I would prefer you and Mrs. Butler return
in the ducal carriage."

"Oh, thank you, Your Grace," Mrs. Butler
said quickly, her relief obvious. She also stood.
"Tea was lovely, Your Grace," she said to
Phoebe. "Perhaps we can do this again the next
time you are in Cornwall."

He was proud of the gracious smile his wife
gave the gossipy woman. "We'll certainly
consider it, Mrs. Butler. It was lovely seeing you."

Martin showed their guests out. Andrew
waited for the door to close before he burst out

into laughter and pulled Phoebe to him.

"It seems as if you have a new best friend in Cornwall," he teased.

"I'm afraid you will always be my best friend," she replied.

He kissed her. "I'm happy Mrs. Butler will not replace me in your affections."

Phoebe's smile was radiant. "You will always be my one true love, Andrew."

EPILOGUE

Windowmere—April 1815

PHOEBE GROANED AS another birth pain racked her body. Her maid wiped a cool cloth against her forehead again.

"You're doing fine, Your Grace," the servant encouraged.

"She's right," the midwife agreed.

The pain lingered longer than before and she couldn't stop the scream that erupted from her. Suddenly, a need to push overwhelmed her. She vaguely recalled having the same feeling when she'd given birth to Nathan.

The midwife nodded. "You want to push, don't you?"

"Yes," she said through gritted teeth. "Yes."

"Let me check again."

Lifting the sheet, the midwife disappeared from view for a moment. When she lowered the sheet, Phoebe saw the woman smile.

"It's time, Your Grace. Bear down as hard as you can and push with all your might."

Phoebe did so repeatedly. Her strength began ebbing.

"I'm so tired," she said, her voice sounding as if it came from a distance. From some other person.

"You're almost there, Your Grace," the midwife encouraged. "Just once more. Twice at the most."

She scrunched her face and bore down with all her might, a guttural, animal noise coming from her. It did the trick, though, as she felt the baby leave her body.

"Is everything all right?" she asked worriedly.

A wail began. The most beautiful noise she had ever heard.

"You have a boy, Your Grace," the midwife told her, handing the baby to the maid. "Get him cleaned up," she instructed. "I will attend Her Grace and collect the afterbirth."

Phoebe lay against the pillows, exhausted, as the process continued. Relief swept through her, knowing she had given birth again. Another boy. This one could never replace Nathan in her heart but she was so eager to be a mother again. To Andrew's son. Their boy together.

Another maid appeared and helped her from the night rail she wore, bathing Phoebe's limbs and then helping her to stand while fresh sheets were placed upon her bed. The maid slipped another night rail over her head and helped her into her dressing gown before easing her back onto the bed.

Then her maid appeared with the swaddled bundle and she saw the sweet, tiny face that she already loved so very much. The maid placed the baby into Phoebe's arms.

"Bring His Grace," she said, wanting Andrew to share in the joy of their new son.

Within moments, her handsome husband bounded into her bedchamber, causing her to think he must have been waiting just outside the door.

He rushed to the bed and then halted. She saw the hesitation on his face.

"Could you give us a few moments of privacy?" she called out.

Quickly, everyone vacated the room, leaving them alone.

Andrew perched on the bed and glanced down.

"It's a boy," she told him. "We have a son."

Reverently, he kissed her brow and then did the same to the babe.

"He is utterly beautiful."

She heard the wonder in her husband's voice. "I totally agree. Would you like to hold him?"

"May I?" he asked hesitantly.

"I am hoping you will hold him frequently," she said, passing the bundle to him. "He will need his papa to rock him and tell him stories."

Andrew gazed at the child, shaking his head. "There are no words to capture my feelings." He kissed the boy again. "I already love him so much. I feel as if love is bursting from me."

Phoebe smiled. "And he hasn't even done anything yet."

The baby opened his eyes and sighed sleepily.

Andrew chuckled. "If I feel like this now, what it will be like when he smiles? Or says his first word?"

She placed her hand on his arm. "The love inside will magnify tenfold," she said. "I guarantee it."

His gaze met hers. "We will tell him of Nathan," he said with determination. "Our son needs to know he had a brother."

Tears welled in her eyes. "That is very sweet of you."

"It's important that he know." Andrew smiled. "Perhaps you can write new tales for this little one."

"I have already been thinking of some," she said. "What would you like to call him? We've never discussed it."

When Phoebe had finally told him of the child she had lost on the day Nathan and Borwick were killed in the carriage accident, Andrew had

341

held her close, weeping with her for the double loss she had suffered. It had seemed then that something unspoken passed between them and they deliberately chose not to discuss a name until they saw their child in the flesh.

"Are you partial to any male name?" he asked.

"What about Robert?" she asked. "If not for Robbie, none of this would even be possible."

He tried it out. "Robert. Robert Graham." Andrew broke out in a grin. "I like it. He could even be Robby—with a y—until he is older. Then Rob or Robert. Whichever he prefers." He bent and kissed his son. "Hello, Robby. What do you think of the world?"

The baby looked up, taking in his father's face. The poignant moment moved Phoebe to tears.

"He'll be the first of many, I hope," Andrew said. "And he'll hopefully have friends close to his age to play with."

She knew he referred to George, who'd wed less than six months ago, and was eager to start his own family. They had also received a letter yesterday from Weston, who wrote to them that he was about to wed a widow who had a daughter named Claire. Weston was mad for the little girl and also shared that he couldn't wait for more children to come. It seemed the two Bad Dukes had been tamed by good women.

Suddenly, Robby let out a piercing wail, startling them both.

Laughing, Phoebe said, "I told you that babies could be rather loud."

Andrew handed the boy back to her. "I will look to you to help guide me. I know you raised Nathan for the most part and I will bow to your experience." He smoothed the baby's hair. "I do plan to play an active role as a father, however."

"I would expect nothing less from you. As long as you don't teach Robby about smuggling," she teased.

He burst out laughing, causing the baby to cease his crying and stare at his father.

"No smuggling. Only snuggling," he told her, climbing into the bed beside her and slipping his arm about her shoulders.

They were a family now. One which would grow and thrive. Phoebe gazed up at her perfect husband.

"I love you, Duke."

"I love you even more, my wonderful, marvelous duchess."

His tender kiss was perhaps the sweetest she'd ever known. Contentment filled her. She had her husband. Her son.

And a life of love to come.

About the Author

Award-winning and internationally bestselling author Alexa Aston's historical romances use history as a backdrop to place her characters in extraordinary circumstances, where their intense desire for one another grows into the treasured gift of love.

She is the author of Regency and Medieval romance, including: Dukes of Distinction; Soldiers & Soulmates; The St. Clairs; The King's Cousins; and The Knights of Honor.

A native Texan, Alexa lives with her husband in a Dallas suburb, where she eats her fair share of dark chocolate and plots out stories while she walks every morning. She enjoys a good Netflix binge; travel; seafood; and can't get enough of *Survivor* or *The Crown*.